BADGE IN THE DUST

Dan Mitchell moved down the street's center. A new group of cowhands swung around the corner. These men stood in their stirrups and howled at the dark sky and dust boiled around them and their scorched faces looked upon him, streaked with arrogance.

They saw the star pinned on his vest. Other riders, traveling through River Bend, had carried the news of the town and of its marshal down the trail. Now they meant to make him give ground, but he held the buckskin to the center of the street.

"Put away your guns with the first barkeep you meet," Mitchell called. "Otherwise the town's yours."

A rider grazed him in passing, and then the cowhand wheeled his horse, his hand moving toward his holstered .44.

"Hold on there, Marshal," the hand said, deviltry making its points in his eyes. "Just how much of this street you got to have?"

ERNEST HAYCOX
IS THE KING OF THE WEST!

Over twenty-five million copies of Ernest Haycox's rip-roaring western adventures have been sold worldwide! For the very finest in straight-shooting western excitement, look for the Pinnacle brand!

ERNEST HAYCOX

TRAIL TOWN

PINNACLE BOOKS
WINDSOR PUBLISHING CORP.

PINNACLE BOOKS

are published by

Windsor Publishing Corp.
475 Park Avenue South
New York, NY 10016

First Pinnacle Books printing: December, 1989

Printed in the United States of America

Chapter One: This Is River Bend

Wearing the star, Dan Mitchell was a man whose tenure on living expired and was renewed from hour to hour, and since certainty was a thing he could never have in the major run of his life he prized it greatly and made the small details of his day into a patten that seldom varied.

Exactly at seven he came to Webber's House for breakfast, occupying the table in the far corner, facing the door. Invariably he left River Bend at eight on his gray road horse, making the ten miles to his hide-out ranch in the Aspen Hills by half past nine, there to idle away an hour with his morning cigar.

He had this one fine hour of natural ease before swinging to the saddle again. On the return trip he customarily paused at the break of the hill road to view the blue and yellow and gray plain below him as it ran into the far curve of the earth. Spanish River, leaving the Aspen Hills, made its sweeping bend over the prairie and fell into a canyon for its five-hundred-mile journey to the Missouri. River Bend's crosshatch pattern of irregular streets and houses lay in the bight of this curve. Its chimneys spiraled smoke into the clear morning light and its windowpanes set up bright flashes of sunlight. South of the river was the dust and dun scatter of cattle herds driven up from Texas to this town which was the shipping-point at the end of a thousand-mile trail.

Standing on this high ledge, Mitchell looked out upon the town in which for twelve hours each day his life ran its hard and narrow and never certain way. For this one brief interval he was free of its treacheries. For this little while he escaped the pressure of its dark alleys and lightless windows, its suspicions and lusts and violences; and during this time he relaxed and breathed the morning's winy air and was his own man.

At twelve he entered Race Street, put up his road horse and took noon meal at Webber's House. Thereafter he lay back in Fred Henkle's barber chair for a shave while the idleness in him gradually gave way to a fine-hard edge, and at one o'clock precisely, the second cigar of the day freshly burning between his teeth, he crossed Willow and entered the jail office beneath the courthouse.

Ad Morfitt, the night marshal who covered the slack-tide period from midnight until noon, had come in from his final tour of the town. Ad Morfitt was a gray, competent man turned taciturn from observing the sins of the world during the drab hours of his shift. He murmured, "Hello," and hung up his belt and gun on a peg. He stood in the room's center and looked out upon the bright street, sleepy but reluctant to go home. Middle-aged and married, he had little pleasant to expect from the contentious Mrs. Morfitt waiting his return.

Mitchell said, "Anything new?"

"Couple drunks in the cooler. Was a shootin' scrape about two this mornin' but nobody hit nothin'. And a free-for-all in Straight-Edge Lizzie's. She had the boys laid out by the time I got there. Nothin' much."

Mitchell said, "Fine fresh day."

Ad Morfitt gave Mitchell an older man's critical eye. Mitchell was twenty-eight, half an inch over six feet, and weighed a hundred and ninety pounds. He had the weight

6

and build for his job; he could buck his way through a saloon crowd to come out with his man and had often done it. In a rough-and-tumble fight he was as tough as a marshal had to be if he wanted to survive the punishment of those wild and salty riders who rode up the trail with Texas cattle. Nor was there a streak of concealed fear in him, for Morfitt had long watched for it and had not found it. Mitchell's hair was the shade of dressed harness leather and brushed down at his ears in frontiersman style. He had full long lips and a heavy nose and rock-gray eyes and big bones and the strong juices of a young man's vitality bubbled in him. He could play the quiet game or the quick one, and though there was a broad streak of kindness in him he could be, as Morfitt well knew, cruel in a tight place.

Morfitt said, "All mornin's are fine to you. Wait till you get my age."

When Mitchell smiled one deep line broke out from the corner of each eye. He put on his gun belt. "Lot of fight left in you yet, Ad."

"Nothin' ever happens to a night marshal. Them hours are quiet. I been at it sixteen years and I'll live a long time. You're the target, not me. You're the big fellow on a buckskin horse—you're the law of the town. I seen a lot of marshals come and go. Loud ones and soft ones. Good ones and some that was no better than outlaws. Not many are livin'. They either died in a hurry or somethin' else happened. You know what that was?"

"You say it."

"Pressure. Walkin' down the street it pushed on their shoulders. One day it opened a hole and the sand started pourin' out these fellows. Either they just broke and ran or else they lost judgment and got sucked into a play they shouldn't of, and died right there. You been here a year. You're feelin' it, too. That's why you get out of town in the mornin'. Let me tell you somethin'. When you walk down these alleys at night and you keep wantin' to turn around and see what's behind, then it is time to quit." He had meanwhile built himself a smoke and now took a swipe at it with his tongue, sealed it, and lighted it. "It'll be active around here after supper. Couple more big outfits came up the trail today."

He started for the doorway and paused in front of an incoming man so tall that he had to duck his peaked hat beneath the doorframe, a great florid Texan with massive jaws and a golden goatee and eyes of marbled agate.

This man pointed a finger at Mitchell. "You the marshal here? I'm Cap Ryker, Anchor outfit, Texas. Just brought a herd up the trail. Payin' off my boys here so's they can take a fling at the honeypots. Been sixty days on trail, so they're dry. Might be a little noise and hell but it is all in fun."

"The town," said Mitchell, "is open."

Cap Ryker's natural voice seemed to be a shout. "What I came to tell you was I want no funny stuff. These boys are entitled to a run for their money. Anybody try to put 'em through the wringer or slug 'em in a back alley and I'll get these Texas outfits together and clean this place from hell to breakfast. You understand?"

Mitchell's answer remained soft. "Just two things. Your boys stay below the deadline on Willow Street and they check their guns. Beyond that the sky's the limit. If they don't want to get trapped in an alley tell 'em to stay out of the alleys."

Cap Ryker shouted again, "No funny stuff," and ducked out of the room. He paused on the walk and he let go a shrill whoop whose echoes broke through noon's quiet, and stamped away. Ad Morfitt shrugged his shoulders and passed to the street, finding no element of surprise in one more Texan blowing off steam.

Mitchell moved back to the big cell behind the office

and unlocked the door on a pair of cowhands, sallow and scratched and hard-used by the night.

He said, "Go on."

"How about our money?" one of them asked.

"Where'd you leave it last?"

The puncher spoke to his companion in a dreary voice: "Where was we last, Fog?"

They departed, leaving behind the stale incense of whisky and cigars. It was a quarter of two by Mitchell's watch when he wound it. He lifted his gun to have a look at the loads; he gave the cylinder one brief whirl and replaced the gun. Leaving the office, he faced the length of Race Street with the sun in his eyes. Behind him, too, lay Willow Street, the deadline between respectability and the town's lusty evil. Four blocks onward, at the foot of this street and adjacent to the stockyards, stood The Drovers' Hotel. Between Mitchell and The Drovers' lay twelve saloons, The Dream dance hall, Naab's shooting-gallery, three stables, and the scatter of general stores catering to the trail cowboy's trade. Except for three narrow cross streets these places stood shoulder to shoulder. South of Race and parallel to it ran Bismarck Alley with its cheaper saloons, its rooming-houses, and its mansions of amusement from which late at night pianos issued their bawdy invitations.

Ford Green, the county's prosecuting attorney, stepped from the main door of the courthouse and gave the sun a wry glance. He paused to look both ways on the street and his eyes touched Mitchell and issued no warmth. He said, "Hello," and moved down Race, his passage ruffling the dust of old enmity. He had long legs and a thick upper body which made him appear top-heavy, and one hank of black hair stood on his uncovered head like a disturbed crow's wing. Mitchell jiggled the cigar between his teeth and set out on his first round of the day, following the exact route he had established one year before when new

9

at the job.

Behind him on Willow there was some display of activity but here on Race Street, the playground of the trail rider when night came, lay the drugged and uneasy quiet of a quarter sleeping off its excesses. Roustabouts swept out the trash of the previous night, and as he passed one saloon doorway after another he moved through the bitter-reeking gusts of burned tobacco and spilled whisky and the dead air wherein many men had left their earthy odors.

He passed the Arcade, the Bullshead, and diagonally crossed Briar Street to come to Charles Fair's saloon. This, The Pride, occupied a half block and was the largest place of its kind between Texas and Montana, its row of double doors flashing their inlay of green and red glass against the rising light.

Charley Fair moved from the place's emptiness and came into the sunshine, his eyes squeezed against unaccustomed brightness. He had a round head bulked on a short, tremendous neck; he was built in the shape of a barrel, immovable and powerful, and he invariably carried one hand—from which three fingers were missing—jammed beneath the band of his trousers. In this town Charley Fair spoke for the gambling element and therefore in this town Charley Fair was half the law.

He said, "Three new trail outfits camped across the river. Be lively here tonight."

"Expect so," assented Mitchell.

Adjoining The Pride was The Dream dance hall. Now he crossed Ute Street, skirted Jack McGeen's saloon, Spreckel's Cowboy Store, Naab's shooting-gallery and Solomon's Notion Emporium. The last block, beyond Sage, contained saloons solidly and brought up against The Drover's, which was favored by the trail cattle owners and by the sports of River Bend who, because of the invisible deadline on Willow, were denied the

10

comforts of Webber's House. East of The Drovers' were the stockpens to hold Texas beef and the loading-spur of the railroad.

He circled The Drovers' and entered Bismarck Alley which paralleled Race as it moved back toward Willow. Its cheap saloons were closed; the green shades of its houses were tight drawn against the day. One lone woman stood in this alley, warming herself in a patch of sun and as he came up she turned a white sleepy face to him and smiled.

"Morning, Dan."

"Morning, Rita."

At intervals on the alley small back lots lay crowded with empty boxes and junk and the litter of careless living. The rear compound of Brinton's stable also faced the alley. Going forward, he watched these places for whatever change might be in them, and he scanned all the windows of the surrounding houses; for in this alley at night he had once been shot at, and would be again, and now he measured it for warning of that second time.

The alley came into Willow, which was a long T cross stroke at the top of Race. On Willow were the town's substantial stores and shops, shoulder to shoulder without break all down to the yellow depot shack on the north edge of town. Willow was the barrier against which at night the wild tide of Race Street broke and fell away. Willow was the parapet behind which in the west quarter of River Bend, on Antelope Street, the general and respectable citizens lived.

He had made his first swing, so exactly patterned in his regular routine that when he stepped into Brinton's stable to saddle his buckskin the whistle of the three-o'clock train sounded over the prairie, as it did on all other days. In front of the stable, now mounted, he paused to look along Willow. A freighter, six horses and heavy wagon stood in front of Dug Neil's wholesale

11

warehouse, ready for a long haul over the prairie to War Bonnet, eighty miles west. The county's sheriff, Bravo Trimble, sauntered forward to meet Ford Green in front of Ed Balder's big general store. A moment later Ed Balder came out and these three made a casual group, accidentally formed.

Perhaps accidentally. This was River Bend, wherein the pressures and schemings of men moved beneath the surface. In the narrows of Bismarck Alley Mitchell had watched those upper windows from which one night a bullet might come; now he looked upon those three gathered men with the same awareness of possible danger. He knew the wants of each. Singly they could not hurt him but if, in the shifting balances and changing secret liaisons of this town, they joined their wants together they could destroy him. He stored the scene in his head and turned from Willow to Antelope. Looking behind, he saw a single puncher come slowly up Race, early drunk.

Antelope Street lay behind the shelter of Willow's business buildings. Here stood the houses of the merchants and of the cattlemen who came out of the Aspen Hills to winter in town, each house centered in its brown and lifeless lawn. The day was warm, the sun half down the sky. The Eastern train had arrived at the depot, its engine's bell sharp-ringing through the heated quiet. Coming to the depot, Mitchell reined in to watch the passengers arrive at this last milepost on the prairie— townsmen returning from distant Omaha, commercial travelers and settlers who, drawn by the magic of free land, were here to find homesteads. Bill Mellen, the town's real-estate agent, spotted this last group with an unerring eye and soon had them collected. Bill Mellen was an enthusiastic talker. Mitchell noticed how these people hung to his words, their faces growing light and pleased.

As he watched them a streak of motion appeared at the extreme edge of his vision and he swung about to see Sherry Gault step from Balder's store and advance toward Fogel's meat market, and now the lone cowpuncher who had been weaving up Race crossed the invisible deadline in Willow's deep sheet of silver dust and reached the sidewalk. He walked with his head down, seeing nothing until he came dead against Sherry Gault. He stopped, straightened, and gave her a long stare.

Mitchell swung his horse and moved toward that scene. Sherry Gault was saying something to the cowpuncher, for Mitchell saw her lips stir. Then the puncher reached out to touch her. Mitchell dropped from his horse, at the same time noting that Ford Green now came from Henkle's barbershop at a half run. Mitchell closed in on the puncher. He caught the man at the coat collar and swung him, arm's length, in a wide circle; he braced his feet as he turned and flung the cowpuncher hard against the wall of the butcher shop. The puncher's head slammed the wall and he whirled and struck out with his hands, catching Mitchell in the face and belly. Mitchell came against him, shoving him back to the wall with his shoulder.

Ford Green rushed in. He got beside Mitchell and he landed a blow on the puncher's unprotected face, crying, "I'll show you what happens to a damned drunk bum—"

Mitchell turned and put the flat of his arm against Ford Green's chest, the force of the blow knocking the prosecuting attorney off his feet into the dust of the street. The puncher, meanwhile free, cut into Mitchell wildly with his fists. Mitchell lifted a shoulder and used the flat of his hand full on the puncher's face, batting the puncher's head against the wall until the man's eyes began to dull up. After that he stepped away. Wind drew in and out of him, deep and even while he waited; he showed no anger and he showed no excitement.

13

Ford Green stood at the edge of the sidewalk. "What'd you do that for?" he said. "I was giving you a hand."

The puncher, once drunk, now was sober.

Mitchell said, "What's your outfit?"

"Anchor."

Ford Green said, "Throw him in jail!"

Mitchell kept his glance on the puncher. "You got yourself in a little trouble. That's too bad. Pull out of town—and don't come again."

"Throw him in jail," repeated Ford Green.

The puncher laid a rebel glance on Ford Green. He drew one hand across his face and saw blood on it and anger turned his eyes pale. He was a lad toughened by the trail, hungry and lawless and proud, and his pride had been affronted.

"Damn right I'll go," he breathed. "But, by God, I'll get my crowd and we'll be back tonight!"

Mitchell said, "Don't make that mistake, friend. No harm's done so far. Might be next trip."

"We'll see—we'll see!" cried the puncher and rushed across Willow into Race, so angered that he could not walk straight.

Ed Balder had watched this from his store and the people from the train stood by with Bill Mellen. This audience had observed Mitchell knock Ford Green into the dust and now Ford Green stood close at hand, humiliation shaking him out of his dry caution. "If you're a marshal why don't you do a proper job of it? What are you for?"

"To keep the fools from the respectable, and the respectable from the fools," murmured Mitchell. "Ford, never interfere with me when I'm handling a man."

"If a woman can't be safe on this street—" said Ford.

"On this street," said Mitchell, "she's safe," and turned to Sherry Gault. "Nothing happened to her."

She had not spoken, this tall daughter of Mike Gault

14

who ran his ranch twenty miles away in the Aspens. She had shown no surprise, no excitement. She stood calmly back from the scene, a girl wise in the ways of the land and its men and quite accustomed to its violence. She wore a riding-skirt and a green jacket and a small round hat on dark hair. She met his glance in a full way—self-assured and with her temper willfully set against him. Her lips were red and expressive and full at the centers.

"Why did you rough him up?"

"An example for the rest of the boys."

"Then why did you let him go?"

He still had part of his cigar. He made a point of lighting it before he spoke. He found some humor in the situation and that humor slid into the angles of his brown face; it was a humor that held some acid and some iron.

"The fault was not entirely his."

Ford Green said, "What's that?"

"Why wasn't it?" asked Sherry Gault, probing into Mitchell's mind with her steady interest. This girl, he remembered, wore Ford Green's ring and this was a puzzle he could not unravel, knowing Green's dry and calculating spirit. Green was a man who wanted something from the world and proposed to get it. This girl, for all the reserve she put against the world, had fire and striking aliveness.

He said, "The boy came across the street with his head down. Then he looked up and saw something in front of him. He knew he was drunk and didn't believe what he saw. So he put out his arm and touched you."

She had a strong mind and she was resisting him, silently and stubbornly. Out of some strange reason she wanted no interference from him, she wanted no part of him to intrude upon her. Her eyes were hazel and deep and they held his glance, and curiosity at last made her say:

"What did he think he was seeing?"

15

"What does a thirsty man want?"

She dropped her eyes, meaning to break the effect of his words. He knew she did it deliberately, her will unable to endure interference. He pulled on the cigar; he watched the exhaled smoke spiral into the air; he saw her head lift.

Her words held short, faint scorn. "What was it, then?"

"Beauty."

She looked aside quickly at Ford Green and her voice was light and hurried. "Walk to the hotel with me, Ford." She started to turn away, and he knew what was in her mind. She had been trapped into this talk and now regretted it. Humor showed in him again and she noticed it and stopped at once, her head rising. "Well, did he see it, or didn't he?"

"I forgot to ask him," was Mitchell's dry answer.

Storm moved darkly over her face. She said, "Come on, Ford," and went down the street. Mitchell stepped to the buckskin and mounted. This was near four-thirty and the sun, dropping below the parapet of the store buildings on Willow, began to throw longer shadows down Race. The cowpuncher from the Anchor outfit at this moment left The Pride saloon, made a quick jump to his horse, and left River Bend with a long yell. Will Gatewood, the Wells-Fargo agent, came from his office.

"He'll cause you trouble, Dan."

"Expect so," agreed Mitchell. As he turned into Race for another tour of the town he saw Sherry Gault pause at the entrance to Webber's House. She was speaking to Ford Green but suddenly she ceased speaking and her face turned and he received the full strike of her eyes. He held her complete attention and during that moment he saw her as the cowpuncher had seen her, the shape and dream of beauty, the image of a still flame burning in the night, perfect and pure-centered with white heat. Afterward he swung down Race.

She said to Ford Green, "You hate him, don't you?"

"Just say he stands in my way."

She was impatient with his roundabout words. "If he stands in your way then you hate him. Don't be afraid of the word. It is an honest word."

"Afraid?" he said, and was affronted. The dryness grew more pronounced on his face. "You don't know me, Sherry. Riding back to the ranch tonight?"

She said, "Yes." She stepped away from him, with Race Street before her.

All along those walks men began to move in preparation for the coming night. A floorman stepped from The Pride and opened the swinging doors, pair by pair, latching them to the outer wall. Big Annie, broad and buxom in her high-colored silks, appeared from Bismarck Alley and entered Spreckel's Cowboy Store. Half a dozen riders appeared in town and filed through the Arcade's door. The piano player in The Dream dance hall idly warmed his fingers with little pieces of tunes. George Hazelhurst, a gambler in The Pride, strolled up from The Drover's, neat in his black suit and stiff white shirt.

Will Gatewood's wife came out of Antelope into Willow and strolled forward with her parasol gaily raked. She was a small and dark girl with a pair of eyes quickly inquiring into the sights and sounds of this town—ready for instant laughter. Love of color showed itself in her clothes, which were brighter than those worn by other women on Antelope, and as she walked along she seemed to have about her an eagerness to please and be pleased. She smiled across the dust at her husband and waited for his sober face to break and when this man only nodded with a kind of preoccupied courtesy her smile turned wistful. In another moment he swung back into his office.

Hazelhurst moved up to Fred Henkle's barbershop and paused there to light a cigar. Idling along the opposite walk, Will Gatewood's wife looked at him with steady interest, observing the length of his hands and the fastidiousness of his dress. His face was rather pale and his reputation was wholly a gambler's reputation, yet he carried himself very straight and he looked out on the world with a pair of black, lost eyes which mirrored a steel pride. He was a polished and courteous and soft-voiced man holding himself deliberately aloof from his fellowmen. He had finished lighting his cigar and his glance came about so that he saw Irma Gatewood. The street was between them, the deadline was between them, the whole world of social pattern was between them. Both of them knew it, yet Irma Gatewood held his glance and for a moment they were completely engrossed in each other. It was Hazelhurst who knew his place and at last slowly dropped his head.

All this Sherry Gault observed, particularly the way in which the gambler turned and moved into Henkle's. Looking then at Irma Gatewood, Sherry noticed strong interest liven the girl's prettiness. In River Bend Will Gatewood's wife was a lonely soul, loving a gaiety seldom found here and hungry for an ardent and tempestuous kind of affection her husband was far too sedate to show. At this moment Mitchell was riding toward the end of Willow, high and solid in the sun.

Sherry, unaccountably changing her mind, said to Green, "No, I'm staying over tonight."

Chapter Two: Heart of Night

Mitchell came in from his six-o'clock swing of the town and went directly to Webber's House for supper, sitting alone at the accustomed table in the corner, his back to the wall. Sherry Gault later entered with Ford Green and in a little while Ed and Josephine Balder joined them. The windows were open to let in the first small breeze and the sun dropped and a girl circled the room to light the kerosene bracket lamps and then the glass and silverware in the room were shining and through this bright glow he saw Sherry Gault's face turn to ivory and old rose. The Gaults had a set of rooms in the hotel for use whenever they came to town; and she had changed into a dress of black and gold. Her shoulders were erect, rounding into deep breasts, and her lips struck a strong line of color across the oval of her face, and against her all other women were pale and unfilled.

This was the second time during the day he had seen Ford Green with Ed Balder, so that he now knew the first meeting had been no accident. Behind the bony freckled mask of Ford Green deep ambitions lay, pinching the corners of his lips and making his talk softly calculating. He was a close-mouthed man who moved cautiously and painstakingly from afar to gain his purposes. Those purposes, whatever they were, made him draw toward Ed Balder. Balder, who ran his big general store on Willow, was a power in this town because he spoke for the merchants. Balder was the other half of the law in River Bend.

Mitchell lighted his third cigar of the day and moved idly through the dining-room. Ed Balder looked up and said, "Hello, Dan." Josephine Balder ignored him, and Ford Green nodded without speaking. These various reactions he noted with eyes accustomed to the reading of people's motives for what they might mean to his own life and safety. Sherry Gault's glance lifted and her attention reached him and remained a long moment, reluctantly interested. The light of the room made its pattern of shadows along her cheeks and the hazel surfaces of her eyes glowed. He passed on to the street and crossed to Brinton's stable.

Dick Lestrade, who was twelve years old, stood in the arch of Brinton's and tried to look as though pure accident brought him here. Mitchell stopped. He put his glance along the street, not directly at Dick, and he spoke as a man would speak to another man. "Been a hot day."

"Sure," said Dick Lestrade, from the bottom of his throat. "Mighty warm." He wore long trousers and a thin cotton shirt and his hair was black-damp, whereby Mitchell knew he had been swimming under the Spanish River bridge. He had the burned blackness of boyhood running free and he had boyhood's lank shape. Each day, somewhere along this street, Dick Lestrade made it a point to stand where he might see Mitchell or Bravo Trimble or Haley Evarts, who drove the War Bonnet stage.

"Kind of like to jump in the river on a day like this," said Mitchell.

"I been," said young Dick. "I hit bottom today. Twelve feet under."

20

"Why, now," observed Mitchell, "that's pretty deep diving."

Dick Lestrade's voice sank deeper in his chest. The men of this town, particularly the men he silently admired, were all brief with their words and so far he was brief. "Not hard, when you get the hang of it."

"Sure," said Mitchell and moved into the stable. He saddled the buckskin and came out. He said, still man-to-man, "Another night. Guess I better get about my business."

Dick Lestrade's youthful imagination at last broke through, so that he was no longer a man. He said in a small, quick voice: "Think there'll be trouble tonight?"

"Looks like just another night, Dick," observed Mitchell, and rode to the head of Race.

Night's soft and warm and earth-stained blackness lay across the land. Except for Webber's House, the stores and shops on Willow Street had closed and all those buildings made a black bulwark, but on Race a thousand lights broke in fractured splinters and fan-shaped gushes from the windows and doors of saloon and dance hall, from Naab's shooting-gallery and Spreckel's Cowboy Store and Solomon's Emporium, from every aperture wherein man spread his wares for the gratification of the Texas cowhand made lusty and hungry and wild by the long ride up the trail. These lights formed a yellow glow in the heart of River Bend and music spilled out and barkers stood at the doorways of The Pride, sing-songing: "This is your house, friend! Best whisky on the trail—the squarest games! Give it a try—give it a try!"

Horsemen swept up Race and wheeled at the hitch racks. They came singly or in solid groups and their shrill crying sailed out along the housetops, dying back somewhere in Antelope's quiet. At this hour River Bend surrendered its respectability and its solid citizens withdrew before the violent night trade upon which, though it fed them, they discreetly closed their eyes.

He moved down the street's center. A new group of cowhands swung around the corner of The Drover's and charged on. These men stood in their stirrups and howled at the dark sky and dust boiled around them and their scorched faces looked upon him, streaked with vital arrogance. Rushing forward, they meant to make him give ground but he held the buckskin to the center of the street. One cowhand yelled his warning. Then dead before him that solid wave split and milled and a rider grazed him in passing, and somebody said, "How much of this street you got to have?"

They saw the star pinned on his vest. Other riders, traveling through River Bend, had carried the news of the town and of its marshal down the trail and now these men ringed around him and watched him with a speculative interest, deviltry making its thin points in their eyes.

Mitchell said, "Put away your guns with the first barkeep you meet. Otherwise the town's yours." He rode on. A woman slipped from an alley into Race and moved with the tide of men, her back to Mitchell. She touched a man's elbow and laughed at him and then her face turned and she saw Mitchell and she wheeled, running back toward the alley. Mitchell thrust the buckskin into the alley, blocking her way. He looked down.

"You know the rule, Florida. No walking on Race. Go on back to your house and stay inside. Last warning."

"What'll you do?" she said in a hard, defiant voice.

"Next time you'll leave town."

He gave ground to let her vanish and swung down Race again. All the doors of The Pride stood open, the crowd growing dense inside. He heard the roulette man call, "Odd and black. Get your bets down." The music in The Dream tumbled into the street and a woman's high, unnatural laugh rasped above the music and the boots of the dancing cowhands shook The Dream with a solid stamping. Over on the edge of town one shot halloed through the night and the buckskin, long experienced, picked up its ears and moved faster. Turning the corner of The Drover's Hotel, he saw the round disk of a campfire on the vacant ground next to Bismarck Alley. He went toward it.

There was a big wagon and four horses unhitched and standing on picket. Beneath the wagon four children lay asleep in an improvised bed; a man and woman stood by the fire. The man came about at Mitchell's approach, thick and short and reserved.

"Passing through?" asked Mitchell.

"Stayin' here," said the man, "if we can find the land. We're from Minnesota. That," he said, and waved a hand at the steady boil-up of noise on Race Street, "that happen every night?"

"All summer long. You've camped in the wrong place. These trail hands will be riding past here around midnight, drunk and full of trouble. You should be over on the quiet side of town."

"I've got a gun."

Mitchell said at once, "Don't attempt to use it. I'll be coming around the corner of that hotel every hour, or I'll be up that street. Call me if you need help."

"My name's Wallin," said the homesteader. "Which part of this country's best for farmin'?"

"See Bill Mellen in the morning. What's the heavy load in the wagon?"

Wallin took time to kick the fire together with the point of a boot. "Seed wheat. Winter wheat. Think it will grow in this country?"

"Maybe," said Mitchell. "Good luck." He swung back to Bismarck Alley. Impelled by an afterthought, he turned in the saddle. "Don't settle too close to a cattle outfit."

23

"Free land—Government land, ain't it?" asked Wallin.

"Yes, if you can make it stick," answered Mitchell and went on.

He threaded Bismarck Alley, passing the narrow fronts of the town's cheap saloons at the lower end of the alley. Farther along houses stood with drawn shades showing green stains of light. He passed a vacant lot and skirted Big Annie's, which was a lodging-place for the girls of The Dream dance hall, and came by Brinton's into Willow. Crossing Willow, he turned into Antelope and moved by the big houses set back in their dry lawns. This was the town, the high and the low of it as seen from the deck of a buckskin horse. Riding through it day after day, he saw it completely and came to know its people, their intrigues and their hungers and the odd patterns moving through their heads to stir their hearts. He had his bird's eye view of River Bend, knowing more of the town than a man ought to know and locking it away in a secret place. This job made a man lonely.

It was eight o'clock when he turned by the depot and paced down Railroad Avenue along the black areas of corral and warehouse and the row of small dwellings north of the town's heart. The big passenger engine, waiting its morning run, stood on the siding with its steam faintly simmering and its line of cars dark-shadowed. A man threshed through the boards and loose wire in the Wells-Fargo compound, cursing slowly, and then turned still. Mitchell listened to that a moment and went on. After a year's practice, a peace officer got to know which sounds were dangerous to him and which were not. It was a sense that grew stronger and stronger until, as Art Morfitt had said, it broke through a marshal's nerves and began to haunt him.

He passed the mouth of Lost Horse Street, from which two months before a man had taken a futile shot at him. He made a wider circle of town and came again to the head of Race. The big bell in the tower boomed out curfew in a round, sullen tone; and hard on its last smoldering echo a shot broke through The Pride. Mitchell said to the buckskin, "Go after it," and moved down the street toward the saloon. Men ran out of other saloons and crossed to The Pride. A second shot broke. Both of those echoes were lighter than the report of a .44 and by that sound he knew it would be one of Charley Fair's gamblers in trouble.

The three big rooms on the front second-floor corner of Webber's House were the year-around quarters of the Gaults when in town; and here Sherry and Ford Green went after dinner. She had not seen Ford for the best part of a month and yet there wasn't much to be said. Neither of these people did a great deal of talking. Ford Green had a dry caution with words and Sherry Gault inevitably expressed everything she felt in the quickest, briefest way. Having known each other for a good many years, their engagement had simply grown into a fact, without great courtship or drama. One day Ford Green had said, "You know me pretty well, Sherry. Will I do?" And she had said, "All right, Ford."

One thing he had in great measure, an infinite patience. Lacking it, she admired it in him. Physically, she was a restless girl. While he sat idle in a chair, content with the run of things in his mind, she ranged the room, touching objects about it, coming back to stand before him, moving on to the window. She was at the window when the two shots broke from The Pride. What arrested her attention was the unhurried manner of Dan Mitchell as he moved down Race toward the saloon and the broadside shape he made against the light.

"Somebody ought to tell him," she said, "that he makes too plain a target on that horse."

25

The sound of the shooting had not brought Ford Green from his chair but he knew she would be speaking of Mitchell. "Man on horseback," he said, "that's his own idea."

She watched Mitchell round in at The Pride and step from the horse. Other men rushed at the saloon and street dust grew thick, so that Mitchell's shape was half hidden. He moved at the crowded doorway and suddenly his arms flung men aside, rough and quick, and he vanished inside. She put both hands on the window's sill, struck by his directness in action, her mind fully on him.

"No man," she said, "can rule a town like this very long without making enemies. He knows that. It is like going into a cage of lions. One day he'll be killed, as Curly Ed Gray was before him. Does he know that, Ford?"

"He rules the town," said Ford Green, dry and softly positive. "But he doesn't run it."

"What's the difference? Except for him there wouldn't be a safe hour in River Bend."

"There's a difference," said Ford Green. Now he was interested and bent forward in the chair, using his hands to shape his thoughts. "This town splits in the middle. The gamblers and saloonmen and honky-tonk people on one side, Charley Fair speaking for them. The merchants along Willow Street on the other side, with Ed Balder doing their talking. Those two men run the town. Charley Fair wants no more law than he's got to take. Ed Balder wants law and order, but not the strict kind that will scare the trail cowhands and their money away. There's the law Friend Mitchell is to enforce. He walks a tight rope—not too much, not too little. If he let the toughs have their way the town would die of its own excesses. If he clamped down the lid on the toughs all the trail trade would go somewhere else and the town would be just a little bunch of empty buildings ready for the wind to blow away."

26

"But it is Mitchell who makes your nice theories work. Do you see Fair or Balder or even yourself out there handling that crowd?"

She was a blunt girl even to those whom she liked or loved. Ford Green gave her a strange glance and his freckled, dry cheeks took on a small color. She had touched him somewhere on a vital point of pride. Recognizing that, she wondered about it.

"But," he said in quiet contradiction, "he understands what he's to do. Just four people around here do understand—Balder and Fair and Mitchell and me. Balder and Fair watch him every minute. If Mitchell were to swing too far either way he'd be knocked out, either by Balder or by Fair. You see?" This was the kind of complicated analysis he loved most of all, satisfying the thoughtful part of his nature. "Then there's the homesteaders, with Bill Mellen. But they're just a few. They don't count."

She came back to an earlier guess. "You hate Mitchell. You really do."

"He stands in my way."

"Why, Ford?"

He looked at her with a strangely diffident expression. He seemed to debate with himself. Self-revelation came hard with him after the lifelong habit of secretiveness. When he spoke it was in the driest, softest way. "I want to represent this state in the Senate."

"Why, if that is really what you want, go ahead and fight for it. Men have to fight for something. They can't stand still."

"This is a small town clear out on the empty side of the state," Ford Green said. "All the political power lies in the eastern half. But I know people. I know how to catch their eyes. I'm prosecuting attorney in the toughest town, the most sinful town west of the Missouri. I smash the crooks and the gamblers, I drive out the toughs and I clean up the town and I ride east with that reputation. That's how it's done. People love a crusader riding out of the west. It is sure medicine in this state. It always works."

She spoke with a note of wonder. "But you said that if this town were cleaned up it would blow away."

"But that's how I'll get my job. What difference does one dirty, dusty little crossroads make to a man if he's fighting his way up? Towns come and go. A man has got only one life and a lot of things to do. Maybe he leaves some breakage behind him. What of it?"

She studied him with a centered attention, as though she were seeing him in a new light. "You're really a cold devil, Ford. How did I ever come to like you?"

"Is it nothing better than liking, Sherry?"

She said quickly, "Let's not be sentimental." Afterward she wondered why she had so swiftly moved away from sentiment and for a little while she let herself think of the feeling she had for Ford Green. Nothing much had ever been said about love. He had not bothered to sweep her off her feet. He had been only Ford Green, characteristically dry and cautious in his proposal. "It is odd," she murmured, more to herself than to him.

"What's odd?"

"I have always had some very fixed ideas about a man and a woman in love. I wonder—" But again she evaded her thoughts. One very realistic corner of her mind held its doubts for a moment, and its barbed and insistent demand that she come back and face the question directly, as she liked to face all things. It was very strange that she deliberately closed out that part of her head.

"To close this town tight I'll have to maneuver around Mitchell," Green said. "Time will come for that."

She didn't wholly like his casual way of saying it. "He's a big target, Ford. He's easy to shoot at. Fight him as hard as you please, if that is what you want. But do it as he does

28

it. Don't shoot from a dark alley." She gave him a searching glance. "But that isn't the whole reason for your hating him."

He showed a small flush of color again. "You've got sharp eyes."

"What's the real reason?"

His answer came out with reluctance. "I never could like a man who throws away his strength and laughs at the world and doesn't give a damn for anything. A man who's got things in him I'd give my right arm to have—and throws them away. I'm honest about it, Sherry. I have to work hard for what I want. He wants nothing and everything comes easy for him." Then he added one impulsive phrase: "I don't like the way he looks at you."

"Ah," said Sherry and turned to the window. Her lips changed, she drew a long breath. "I can take care of myself, Ford." She held her glance on the doorways of The Pride.

Men blocked The Pride's nearest doorway. The buckskin, following the sound of trouble like a trained hunting dog, swung abreast the door and stopped. Mitchell got down, walking against the back edge of the crowd. He said, "Give way," but his talk wasn't heard. Everybody faced the doorway, looking into The Pride's packed hall. In there a long silence lay until one man's voice gritted through it, full of outrage. "A tinhorn sport!"

Mitchell moved to the back edge of the crowd. He thrust both hands before him, parting the nearest men. He moved between them and felt their resistance. Suddenly he stiffened his legs and bucked into this mass and tore it loose with a ramming impact of his elbows. Men swung around at him and somebody said, "What the hell—" and tried to reach at him through the jam. Mitchell got to the doorway. There was a cowhand blocking it; he caught the man by the coat collar and flung him back and passed into The Pride.

The Pride's brackets and chandeliers built up a strong silver flare against the great back-bar mirror. The crowd, caught flat-footed by trouble, stood in separate groups, at the bar, at the tables, along the walls; and all men faced the center of the room where the gambler Hazelhurst stood beside a capsized poker table with his small pistol half lifted.

Mitchell cut a way through the crowd with his shoulders, hearing the stamp of his own boots in the dead-locked quiet. A trail cowhand lay face down and dead on the floor, one hand clinging to a gun and the other gripping two playing-cards, so revealing the full story of what had happened. The huge Texan, Cap Ryker, stood over the dead man, his face turned scarlet. Charles Fair had moved behind Hazelhurst to cover the gambler's rear. Hazelhurst, cool and deadly calm, stared at the crowd with a pride that would never break. At the moment his pale face hated them all and despised them all.

Seeing Mitchell, Ryker began to yell at him. "That's an Anchor man dead there—that's one of my men! I told you I'd bust up this damned town if anything happened, and by God, I will!"

Charley Fair's smooth voice followed. "Don't get excited, friend. Your boy made a rough remark about the dealer and went for the gun first."

"The deal was crooked!" shouted Cap Ryker.

Charley Fair said patiently, "Careful about that. Never was a crooked game played in this house."

"That man," yelled Cap Ryker and swung his arm toward George Hazelhurst, "won't see another sunrise in this world!"

"Cool off," urged Charley Fair. "You're squawkin' like a short sport." His glance moved over to Mitchell and remained there, waiting for Mitchell to speak, to act.

30

The saloonman, Mitchell knew, was accustomed to tight squeezes and could handle himself in any situation, but this moment was bad and would grow worse.

Cap Ryker said, "We'll take care of Anchor and we'll do what Billy Blades tried to do. Gambler, you're dead as hell right now, and you'll be deader!"

Men swayed under the compulsion of Cap Ryker's voice; they came up beside him and behind him. This was another heart of night on Race Street and this was another one of those savage silences beneath which wildness burned like fire. The faces of these men grew long and thin light touched off pale, strange flares in their eyes. In the stillness Mitchell heard the rustling rasp of death and he felt the pulse of trouble, all this so old and familiar to him that he could close his eyes and know at what precise instant fury would break.

There was always one man whose single word or single motion unloosened the wild strength of a mob. In this instance it would be Cap Ryker. Cap Ryker turned half around, looking at all the Texas trail hands waiting, and he filled his chest and opened his mouth and said, "All right—" and said no more. Mitchell's voice struck in:

"That's enough from you."

Ryker slashed his great hand downward. "Marshal, I'm going to show you—"

"Stand fast," said Mitchell, "or you'll be the next man in boot hill."

A crowd was a harp on whose strings a man played a tune, but it depended on which man played the tune, he or Cap Ryker. He saw a greater floridness spread across the Texan's massive cheeks, he watched the big body freeze. The crowd was waiting, but this break was not enough. The crowd was still dangerous. So he said to Hazelhurst, "Walk out with me. Walk out ahead of me. I'll lock you up."

Charley Fair opened his mouth to speak, and closed it.

George Hazelhurst gave Mitchell an affronted stare; he had wrapped himself in a shroud of bitter-proud fatalism and it took a moment for the words to get through. Presently he turned and stepped ahead of Mitchell. At that moment Mitchell's glance, sweeping the crowd, saw in the background the little redheaded Anchor man he had earlier warned out of town.

Between the center of the room and the door was the solid mass of the crowd. Its pressure stopped George Hazelhurst dead. He looked around at Mitchell and said in a tone which ran ringing through the stillness, "I won't wrestle with these dogs, Mitchell. I'll stand here. There's four loads left in this gun."

It was like pitch thrown on flame; he saw brightness flash higher in all those waiting eyes before him and he knew he had to arrest that fire before it broke through. Knowing it, he swung around, speaking to the red-headed Anchor cowhand in the back end of the room. "I warned you to stay out of town, son. When I get this chore done I'm comin' back after you." Turning, he gave George Hazelhurst a boost forward with his hand.

He had shifted the crowd's thinking from this present moment to what would happen in the future; and through this little hole of indecision he shoved George Hazelhurst. The nearest man stepped aside, making a track in the crowd. Mitchell put both broad hands on Hazelhurst's back, ramming the gambler onward. Hazelhurst struck these slow-yielding Texans and looked back at Mitchell with distaste, and then grew angry and plunged at the door, using his elbows.

Charley Fair's round, easing talk made a play for attention. "Where's the music—where's the music? Hit the bar, boys. It's on the house."

Men moved from the doorway, letting Hazelhurst and Mitchell go by. Music poured into the silence. Out on the walk, Mitchell caught Hazelhurst's arm and guided him across Briar Street toward the jail office.

Hazelhurst grumbled, "Never mind—never mind. We're out of trouble."

"No," said Mitchell, "you're not. I'll lock you up until the town's empty."

Hazelhurst moved into the jail office and stopped while Mitchell unlocked the jail door. He scowled at Mitchell's pointing finger. Thin and pale as he was, a fastidious self-respect burned in him. "The man called me a crook," he rumbled. Mitchell pushed him into the jail cell and locked it.

"Dan," complained Hazelhurst, "I don't like this." Then a grudging admiration came out of him. "You're smart as hell. You handled that bunch. Don't let 'em pull you into The Pride again tonight. Stay out on the street."

Mitchell stared at him. "You heard me talk to the redhead, didn't you?"

"Just a play to change their attention, wasn't it?"

"It was a promise," said Mitchell. The night had made him rough, it had stretched his nerves. There was always a time when trouble broke, that the caution in this man went completely away so that he became as reckless and as rash as the wild ones marching up the Texas trail. He said, "You damned card players make a hell of a show about your pride. I've got mine, too, George."

"Ah," murmured Hazelhurst, "I'm sorry." But he added, "It is different, Dan. A man like me has nothing but pride. It is just a front, like a white shirt. Take that away and I'm just George Hazelhurst, no damned good." He held the silence a moment, later to add morosely, "It would be the best kind of an end for a fellow like me—one touch of dignity in a useless life. But not for you, Dan. You've got too much. Don't let your pride kill you, which it will certainly do."

33

Mitchell turned into the street again, moving back to The Pride. A new group of horsemen came around the corner of The Drovers' and charged up Race, their dust thickening the yellow lamplight, and other men came out of the adjoining saloons and stood along the walls of Race to watch the scene whose warning had somehow gotten through town with the swiftness of an electrical charge.

Chapter Three: Sherry

The near doorway of The Pride was empty, the onlooking Texans having moved back along the street and along the saloon wall. As Mitchell reached the doorway he cast one glance behind him and his eyes lifted and he saw Sherry Gault framed in her window on the second floor of Webber's House. Every thought in him had become fixed on the chore ahead but now one sweep of feeling took him away from this night so that the shape of her body, full and rounded and still, caused all his imagination and all his desires until there was no other thing which greatly mattered. He had known her for a year, had seen her frequently, had now and then spoken to her; but this night it was as though, long looking at the cold and distant brightness of a star, he saw that star blaze and fall and fill the sky.

In the deeper shadows he heard a familiar voice call, "Wait—wait," and that sound brought him all the way back to Race Street. Turning, he found Tom Leathers in the middle dust of the street, watching this scene with a practiced eye; for Tom Leathers, long his close friend and once his riding companion in younger days, was a man who had seen sin in its many forms and knew the shape of it from memory. Leathers was laughing as though this night amused him, but even in his laughter was the small metal strike of temper rising to the occasion.

"Wait for what?" asked Mitchell.

"Why," said Leathers, letting his smile grow, "I just wanted to ask you if I could get drunk."

To the Texans massed along The Pride's outer wall he was only a lone man, moved by no serious purpose. Mitchell knew him better. Tom Leathers had warned him to use a little caution and now, as he smiled and spoke, Tom Leathers looked at the Texans on the street with his bright, guileless smile and searched them for trouble.

"I guess," said Mitchell, "you know the way to do it."

"Why," called Leathers, enjoying himself, "I have looked on the flowers of nature and I have listened to the little brook and I have smelled me the smell of summer in the hills and I am a virtuous man on the edge of embracing the wicked temptations of this here Babylon."

"You're full of hot air, which is worse than whisky," Mitchell told him and turned to The Pride's door. He stood in the outflashed beam of light, facing The Pride's long barroom. The piano music went on, without much melody, and Charley Fair stood at the bar with a few of his horsemen around him, vainly waiting for the crowd to march up for the offered free drink. The Texas trail hands made a wall across the room and they faced the doorway and they were waiting. The redhead puncher stood behind that wall.

He turned from the doorway and walked to Briar. Behind him, Tom Leathers's voice issued its mild reflection: "I will just get a temporary smell." Swinging into Briar, Mitchell looked back and saw that Leathers now strolled idly toward The Pride as though nothing mattered. Mitchell walked swiftly down the Briar Street side of The Pride and came to the saloon's rear door, which was closed; he opened it, coming into Charley Fair's back office and laid a hand on the inner door's knob, turning it and pulling the door wide. When he stepped through it he was behind the crowd and he was close by the redhead puncher.

"All right," he said. "Come with me."

The redhead wheeled, half lifting a hand, and the nearest men pivoted and somebody yelled, "Anchor!" The piano stopped and Cap Ryker's voice rolled out its massive thunder: "Knock him down—knock him down!" Cap Ryker was near the bar. Charley Fair reached out a hand to restrain him but the huge Texan came through the crowd, tearing a broad pathway and roaring as he rushed. He had not checked his gun with the barkeep and now, ten feet from Mitchell, he reached for it. Mitchell knocked the redhead aside. He jumped at Cap Ryker and brought the barrel of his own gun overhand and cracked it across Cap Ryker's temple. Cap Ryker fell like a mountain landslide, the sound of his collapse running back throughout the great hall.

The redhead cried, "Somebody get a gun! Shoot this proud—!" All these Texans were moving in on Mitchell; they swayed in a slow mass, not yet fully gathered for a run. The redhead started a second yell.

Mitchell reached back and caught the redhead at the shirt collar, pulling him in. He slid the crook of his arm around the redhead's neck and bent the redhead backward, slowly cutting off the man's cry, slowly strangling hm, slowly twisting his spine. He dropped the redhead, hearing that man's great gasp. He said, "You boys have had your fun. Now the town's closed for the night. Kill your lights, Charley, and shut up the bar."

Charley Fair said, "Wait—"

"Turn out those lights," said Mitchell. He watched the crowd, he felt its hatred as a scorching heat. But he had stopped trouble dead, he had tied this crowd up. Having done so, now he had to get it in motion again, toward the doors. Charley Fair's housemen moved around the walls, turning down the lights until half darkness came.

Mitchell said, "Sorry, Red. You bucked the tiger on the wrong night." He watched the redhead pull himself from the floor, but from the edge of his vision he noticed the slow shift of the men in front of him. Some of the Anchor outfit came up to take care of Cap Ryker who lay senseless still, and a hole appeared in the crowd. Mitchell moved into it and walked out across the room and into the street.

Leathers murmured softly, "That's luck," and continued to watch the saloon with his steady eye.

Trouble had telegraphed itself all through the town. Men remained along both sides of Race, listening and watching. The music in The Dream had quit and the women there clustered around the corner of Ute Street, the sequins of their dresses glittering in the light. The buckskin stood in its tracks, its ears lifting when Mitchell moved from The Pride. Mitchell stepped into the saddle and waited.

Light died from The Pride's windows and men moved out. He watched them drift along the walk and scatter toward their racked ponies. He watched them swing up. But they stood fast, waiting for another break and eager for it, and somebody called in a steady, hard voice, "Anchor, come here."

Cap Ryker rolled out of The Pride with two men giving him a hand. He stopped on the street to pull himself together and he saw Mitchell above him on the buckskin. He looked long at the marshal, never speaking, and moved on. All the outfits were collected and the riot and revel had gone completely from Race Street, leaving it dismal. Cap Ryker climbed to his saddle and took up his reins. He swung half around, facing Mitchell, and his voice began to roar.

"Now I'll tell you something, friend! This is what I say and I swear on my mother's memory! I am going back down the trail. I am going to spread the name of this dirty, crooked, miserable, cheating hellhole, and I am going to spread your name. And I will be back before the month is out. Before the month is out this town will be dead—and so will you! Anchor—come on!"

The outfit whirled away. One by one, other outfits and other groups trotted down Race, turned the corner of The Drovers', and were gone. Presently Race was empty and the music had entirely faded and the lights went out one by one. Charley Fair came from his place and looked up at Mitchell.

"This time, Mitchell, you went too far."

"Figure out a better way."

"You buffaloed the wrong man. He's no cowhand to be kicked around. You did a lot of damage."

"Figure out a better way," repeated Mitchell, and rode up the street to the jail office. Ad Morfitt stood in the doorway.

"You're early," said Mitchell.

"Midnight," grumbled Morfitt. "Sounded like there was some fun going on."

"Another night." Mitchell went into the jail office and walked over to unlock the cell.

Hazelhurst came out complaining. "Damned vile smell in there."

"The smell of sin," said Mitchell.

Morfitt turned in the doorway. "Man's only got so much luck in the bank. Your account is gettin' small, Dan."

Hazelhurst said, "The odds are wrong."

Mitchell hung up his gun. "Your town, Ad," he said, and moved toward the doorway. The twelve-hour pull, with all its action, had tired him. He didn't know it, but his nerves were wire-tight. He looked back at Hazelhurst, smiling. "You know a better game, George?" he asked, and moved into the street.

From her window, Sherry Gault had closely watched everything occurring on the street, and had guessed at the scene inside Charley Fair's saloon. Mitchell alone had broken up the crowd, alone had emptied the town. Perhaps Balder and Fair laid down the rules but to her logical mind it was Mitchell who made the game work. This man had power and power was a thing she greatly admired. It was one thing to be farseeing and scheming and tirelessly shrewd, as was Ford Green; it was another thing to sit on a horse in the middle of Race Street and look out on a mass of men, gambling with every passing moment, and at last breaking those men to a stronger will. Reluctantly, Sherry Gault gave Dan Mitchell credit for his strength. And then as he wheeled from Race Street into Briar her admiration changed to scornful anger. One moment great in her eyes, he now became common and unadmirable. For she knew, as the whole town knew, that when his night's tour was done he turned toward Big Annie's. Methodical in all things, he was methodical in this.

"You fool," Shery Gault said aloud, "you cheap fool." And standing quite still, she was astonished that he had the power to make her angry.

Mitchell took the buckskin to Brinton's stable and returned to pass down Race. Ad Morfitt at this moment moved along the lower end of the street, a stolid, unimaginative night watchman setting forth upon his weary rounds. In the space of a quarter hour River Bend had made the full swing from sound and fury to an impoverished stillness through which Ad Morfitt's boots beat up dismal echoes. Here and there saloonmen stood before their establishments to catch the night air and the gamblers strolled down to The Drovers' for a late game themselves. Mitchell entered Briar, reached Bismarck

40

Alley, and let himself into Big Annie's house without knocking. Tom Leathers had preceded him and now sat in the ornate parlor, idly tinkering with a little jug that gave out music when lifted. This parlor reflected Big Annie's tastes—its red-rose-spattered rug, its ebony Chinese chairs, and its mirrors all gilt and cupid-strewn—and it had been bought from the ample revenues of The Dream dance hall, which Big Annie owned.

Somewhere in the back of the house Big Annie's raw Irish voice called: "I'll be in."

Deep in a chair, Tom Leathers relaxed and beamed like a brother. "You sure ran that string right down to the frayed end."

"One more night," said Mitchell and let all his muscles go idle.

"This is sure one giddy palace," observed Leathers. "One jump from sagebrush to the foot of Chinese emperors." He was pleased with the fancy. He was a healthy man with a fair, smooth face and a shrewd eye. His seeming youngness and his complete attitude of "I don't give a damn" were an excellent mask for a tough, quick-witted fighter. The gleam of affability and sound good humor in his brown eyes was real, but he had a bottom beyond that, made of rock.

"You're a stranger in town," said Mitchell.

"Got tired of being pure and uncontaminated. Thought I'd steep myself in sin for a couple of days." He grinned whitely at Mitchell. "You look thin. Sorrows and cares of the world have got you down. Burdens on your shoulders. What's a free man doing in harness when he don't have to be?"

"Don't know," Mitchell said. With this man in older days he had ridden the desert and searched the hills. The memory of that freedom and irresponsibility came to him now as a strong, raw wind. He had not known until this moment of contrast how completely Race Street im-

41

prisoned him. After a twelve-hour tour he felt dry, like an apple run through the mill. He spoke softly, begrudging Leathers's freedom: "You damned saddle bum."

"Last night," drawled Leathers, knowing this would sting, "I spread my blanket on Cabin Creek. I hooked a trout for supper and built me a fire and rolled in the blankets. I heard a big bullfrog honk. There was a bear a-gruntin' in the thicket. And I got to thinkin' of a fellow I rode with once. But he turned proud and went to town and took to packin' a star and now there's a crease down the middle of his eyes from waiting for somebody to dry-gulch him. The man's a fool. Life's mighty sweet when you take it as she comes."

"Sand in your boots," said Mitchell. "Holes in your socks. You've got dyspepsia from your own cooking. If life's so damned sweet why come to town? Don't sit there and lie to me."

"I sleep well," pointed out Leathers, "and I don't have to watch any alleys when I ride by."

They bickered amiably until Big Annie came in with a jug of hot water, a bowl of sugar, and a whisky bottle. She put these things on a table and mixed a toddy for both men and one for herself. She took a chair and reached down and removed her shoes and greatly sighed. As she sipped her drink she kept her eyes on Mitchell. The study of man was Big Annie's trade, from which she had grown rich and powerful in this town, knowing as much of its politics as any man. Liking Dan, she had on occasion dropped stray pieces of information which had served him well. Now she said:

"Charley Fair won't love you for what happened tonight. Neither will the storekeepers. You'll hear from Ed Balder. The Texans will hate you more—and so you have pleased nobody."

"Just like him," said Leathers. "Nothin' small about

the things he does. Whole hog. Large and fancy and complete."

Big Annie, being twenty years older than Mitchell, spoke to him as a son. "A peace officer never has any real friends. He's always in the middle. Now if you were a politician you'd join up outright with one side or the other and be safe, as long as your side was safe. But no, you play it alone. You ought to get out."

"Sure," chimed in Leathers, "He has got to share the burdens of the universe."

Mitchell grinned at these good friends, slowly relaxing and losing the tension of the day. It was for this reason he came to Big Annie's at the end of his long tour. This woman asked no favors. Here he might sit and drink his toddy and smoke his night cigar and feel no need of vigilance. Riding the streets of River Bend from noon to midnight, a man grew cold and aloof, he became an animal on the prowl with every muscle drawn and every nerve strained. He grew to look upon people with suspicion until all faith in human nature went away. So now he sat in this big chair and nursed back his faith and his sense of humor and his ease.

She said, "You're in the middle. This town is two sides, Balder's side and Charley Fair's side. It's like two bulls in the same pasture. You're the man keeping them apart. But someday they'll meet, head down, and you'll be caught between the horns."

"That's right," he said, still smiling at her. "This is a good drink, Annie."

"Ah," she said, "you're proud. You think you can ride between the factions. So has many another man. Sooner or later one side will get too strong, and then the fight will come and you will be caught in it and you'll be alone, neither side helping you."

"This town is mine," he told her, "until some man

comes along who can bring on the fight."

"He'll come, Dan."

"Why," said Mitchell, "he's here now but he's not ready."

"Who's that?"

"Ford Green."

Big Annie thought about it, wrinkling her homely face. "Maybe. I don't trust quiet men. But how will he do it, and what does he want?"

"Don't know yet," said Mitchell.

The girls from The Dream, done with work, came into the house and moved up the stairs in their short, bright dresses. Having smiled steadily during the night, they were weary of smiling now; having danced through four solid hours with the wild and clumsy Texans, they had no present interest in men and glanced incuriously at Mitchell and Leathers and went on up to their quarters.

Leathers, always cheerful and self-possessed, suffered an odd change. He sat low in the chair, growing grave. He watched these girls and he watched the door and presently when a last girl came in and paused before them, Leathers sighed quietly to himself and dropped his eyes to the toddy glass.

Mitchell said, "Better have a toddy, Rita."

She was slim, with black hair pulled back from a round, pale and lost face. She said, "No," in a disinterested voice.

Mitchell said, "You want to walk out in the sun and put on some color."

"Why?" she asked. She watched Mitchell, as though she really wanted to know if he had an answer for that. She had not looked at Leathers, but in a little while, with a rather deliberate effort, she turned her attention to him and said, "Hello."

Without his smile, Leathers had a sharp pair of eyes, and it seemed to Mitchell, who observed this scene with

44

his interest hidden, that Rita was afraid of Leathers and made herself look at him out of effort. Mitchell had noticed this before and had also noticed that Leathers's laughter and easy humor always dried up before her.

"Guess you'd be tired," said Leathers, just making talk.

"Oh," she said indifferently, "I suppose," and turned away from them. She walked up the stairs slowly, her hand pulling on the banister. Leathers stared at that stairway after she had gone. He had forgotten his drink.

Mitchell got up. "What's troubling her, Annie?"

Big Annie, a talkative woman when she chose to be, could also be reserved; and it was a point of pride with her that she took care of her girls and neither talked about them nor permitted talk about them. So she only said, "Didn't notice she was."

Mitchell drawled, "Good night," and left Big Annie's, Leathers trailing behind. Down Briar, Leathers stopped and murmured, "See you later," and faded away. Warmed by the toddy, Mitchell came to Race and aimed for Webber's. The night was soft and warm and the town silent and as he strolled forward he saw Sherry Gault's room lights die. He moved up the stairway to his own room and went to bed and for a little while his mind played over every scene of the day, selecting those things which had a meaning and putting them in a back part of his head; and then he remembered Sherry Gault as she had been silhouetted against the light of her window earlier in the evening and one fresh, strong wave of imagination tumbled his other thoughts away. And so he fell asleep.

Leathers returned to Bismarck and stopped at the back end of The Pride. He built a cigarette and lighted it, the match a startling burst in the alley's dark. He heard Ad Morfitt plugging up the alley and he spoke in a casual voice, so as not to take Ad by surprise: "Evenin', Ad."

Morfitt said, "Don't you ever sleep?" and went on.

Leathers settled against The Pride's wall and looked up at the second floor of Big Annie's, and had his own long, wondering thoughts.

At seven-thirty in the morning, crossing from Webber's to the stable, Mitchell met Ad Morfitt at the mouth of Bismarck Alley. Morfitt gave him a sleepy look and continued on, but in a moment he swung back. "Jett Younger came in with four of his crowd about three o'clock this mornin'. Still here—at Thacker's Lodging House. Rode up in a hell of a hurry."

Mitchell went on to the stable. He saddled the gray road horse, turned through Willow and Antelope and struck out across the flats toward the Aspen Hills. Not more than a mile ahead of him another rider raked up a steady dust, traveling at a lope. The gray had the morning bit in his mouth and went on at a first great run, eating up the interval, and presently the rider ahead looked around and drew in. Coming abreast, Mitchell lifted his hat to Sherry Gault.

The early air had brought strong color to her cheeks. She sat quite straight on the sidesaddle and her glance forced its reserve steadily against him. She said in a neutral voice, "Since we are going the same way we might as well ride together."

"That's the reason I let the gray have its head."

Always she had for him that mixture of interest and revulsion, as though she were drawn by certain qualities she saw and yet could not wholly believe them. He turned beside her and for half a mile they rode on in silence. Sun struck the surface of Spanish Fork's water in bright, slanting flashes and changed the color of the creases in the nearing Aspen Hills. They came upon the footslopes of the hills, rising with the loops of the dirt road.

She said, "Do you know just what your job is in that town?"

"Yes."

"Do you really know?" She spoke in a slightly different tone, less friendly. "Your job was described to me last night by a man who called you a chore boy for Ed Balder and Charley Fair." She was never less than blunt to him, her talk consistently warmed or chilled by an emotion toward him that he could not define.

"Probably right," he agreed.

"If I were a man I would rather be called a scoundrel or a thief. Anything but that."

"Maybe," he said. He was easy in the saddle, the sunlight reaching beneath his hat and painting its stain on the dark tan of his jaw. He had his own rough temper and when he looked directly at her she saw an expression that brought up her full guard. But he had nothing to offer and so she spoke again.

"You run through a good deal of danger on that street at night. What holds you to a job in which you are not your own master? If you must fight for something, why not for something of your own?"

"Pride," he said. "The same kind you have."

"And it permits you to spend time in Big Annie's?"

He had never had a woman speak so plainly to him and for a moment he was embarrassed and showed it. The words had come out of Sherry Gault in a kind of thoughtless haste and when he turned he noticed her color deepen; she had rather shocked herself. "Big Annie," he said, "is one of my best friends. I go there because she likes my company and I like hers. She asks for nothing and her place is safe."

"Safe?" said Sherry Gault.

"Maybe the wrong word. Should have said a refuge. A refuge from Race Street and the Charley Fairs and Ed Balders of the town."

47

They were on the Aspen grade, climbing slowly around its turns. Near the summit she turned on him again. "Why did you want to overtake me?"

"Last night," he said, "I saw you standing in the window."

He added nothing to it. At the top of the grade, at the turnoff to his own ranch, he pulled in and removed his hat. But Sherry Gault said, "What else?"

"Every man sees his own kind of beauty." He smiled, and ceased to smile. The guard was up in her eyes again and she looked at him with an expression she had shown him so many times before, full of dislike and some scorn and yet with an interest she could not suppress. Then he dryly added, "Tough on me, but you are the kind of beauty I see nowhere else. No other woman possesses it for me."

From the moment he had first met this girl he had guessed her depth. No woman could show the world so much pride without having somewhere the power of great emotions. In her eyes and lips lay flexible capacities carefully controlled—as though she feared to reveal herself. Now he had a view of the undertow of her spirit. Startled by his direct words, she forged her reserve and looked upon him with the full-open eyes of a woman momentarily and completely engrossed.

"From you," she said in a wondering tone.

"From the man who rides in dust and deals in the grime of other people. From the man who may be Ed Balder's chore boy or Charley Fair's crook."

She threw her question at him: "Are you either of those things?"

"I ride the town twelve hours a day. Nobody knows what I am and nobody will know until the town breaks up."

"Will it break up?"

"Nothing stays half one thing and half another. It

48

will break."

"And where will you stand then?"

He said, "We were talking of what a hungry man sees in a woman, Sherry."

She dropped her eyes and her lips moved and pressed together. When she again looked at him she was once more hiding behind reserve. "Don't say that to me again."

"I probably will."

She had on riding gloves. Suddenly she removed the glove from her left hand and held it out, showing the engagement ring on her finger. This was her answer, but he shook his head. "That makes no difference to me."

"In some things," she told him, very carefully choosing her words, "I admire you. Last night, watching you on Race Street, I thought you were a great man—until you turned into Bismarck. For a little while you were all that a man should be. But this job has left its scars on you. Some of the deception and brutality and looseness you see all day has gotten into you. When you speak to me as you do now it is as though you laid the barrel of your gun over my head." She was on the edge of real anger. "Go tell Ford Green what you have said to me."

"I will," he answered. "I will, today."

She gave him a half-startled glance. The anger dissolved. "No, don't do it. You have enemies enough."

"It won't be adding another. He's my enemy now."

"How did you know that?"

"The man's ambitious. What does he want?"

"I'll let him tell you that, in his own good time." She straightened in the saddle. "I like ambitious men. I like men who go after the things they want. I don't like men who are content to ride through their days without effort."

His body threw a shadow across her. Sometimes, as at

49

present, he seemed taller and heavier than she supposed him to be. His face had its heavy, solid bones covered by a skin deeply tanned and without a wrinkle. When he smiled—and he was smiling now—he seemed very young and in his eyes was his approval of her and a clear, bold expression of want.

She said, rather hurriedly, "Don't ride with me again, please. It might lead Ford to think the wrong things."

Now he was pleased and let out a great, long laugh. He dipped his hat to her, watching resentment cover her cheeks. She was really angry. He said, "I'll ride with you again some other day," and took the trail toward his ranch.

Chapter Four: Seeds of Treachery

Jett Younger came from Thacker's Lodging House around nine o'clock and took his breakfast from the previous night's leavings on The Pride's free-lunch counter, buying a whisky for a chaser. He might have had a decent meal from any of the three eating houses in town, but in this man there was a streak of closeness. He was a strange-shaped individual, big of leg and hip and gradually tapering to small shoulders. The sun had scorched him rather than blackened him, so that the surface of his cheeks and the tip of his nose were a fire-red; and to this bright blaze of color his eyes were like blue marbles, close-set, beneath pale brows.

Charley Fair came from his back office, saw Younger, and turned into his office again. Younger followed, closing the door behind. Observing that instance of caution, Charley Fair asked, "What's the trouble?"

"No trouble," said Younger. "You got another cigar, Charley?"

He took the cigar and wasted some time lighting it. Charley Fair stood against a wall, knowing Younger too well to rush him. Presently Younger spoke up in a kind of idle, roundabout fashion: "We came in about three this mornin' and put up. I sort of hankered for a bed with springs on it. We started from the foot of the Aspens, down by Little Bear Creek, and made it here in two hours and five minutes. That's good ridin'.''

"All right—all right," Charley Fair grumbled.

"Last afternoon we happened to come across a trail herd and told the fellow we wanted to cut it to see if they was any strays bearin' our brand. Well, we weeded out about twenty and I thought the trail boss was goin' to be smart enough not to squawk about it, but the damned fool trailed us into the hills." Jett Younger blew a good deal of smoke from the cigar, quietly adding, "We had quite a scrap and we killed one of those fellows. It was the Crazy L outfit, so their brand read. They'll be in here today makin' a stink about it. I reckon Bravo Trimble will have to put on a chase just to make it look right. Tell him we'll get out of his way so he won't bump into us."

Charley Fair said, "What did you do with the twenty beeves?"

"Way back in the hills. Thought I'd work over the brands a little and sell 'em to you next week."

"Not this tme. Take them over to Chuck Milner at War Bonnet."

"He don't pay much. Why don't you buy 'em?"

"There was some trouble here last night. Now you get into a scrape. No use making it worse. And don't come clattering in to see me the morning after a deal like that. It looks bad."

"Why sure," admitted Jett Younger with some surprise, "but who's goin' to kick, outside of the trail boss, which don't matter?"

"Might matter if we get all these outfits sore. You better do your stealing farther down the trail. You're too close to town, which gives the town a worse reputation. Have to think of those things or these trail outfits will pass us by."

"You're the doctor," said Jett Younger. At the office

doorway he repeated, "You see Bravo Trimble," and moved across the saloon.

Charley Fair followed as far as the walk. Putting himself beside one of The Pride's doorways, he watched Younger lead his four men out of River Bend at a run. Ad Morfitt came down Race, weariness knotting his face muscles; he went by Charley Fair with a nod, crossed Ute, and turned from sight. Jack Poe swept out his saddle shop on Willow, and women strolled along Willow's walk, their dresses very fresh and colorful in the sunlight. The War Bonnet stage waited by Webber's House, ready to go, and a commercial traveler hurried from Webber's and took his place on the high seat beside Haley Evarts, the driver. Young Dick Lestrade stood near the stage and looked up at Haley Evarts and when Evarts grinned at him young Dick drew a deep breath and moved away.

Bravo Trimble turned into Race, idling under the deep shade of the overhanging board galleries. Bravo took his job as sheriff the easy way, wishing neither to disturb anybody nor to be disturbed. He had passed his able years and faced the world with a faint anxiety and met people always with a mixture of affability and concern. He looked behind him and he looked before him and when he reached the saloonman he said, "Hello, Charley," and paused. "Nothing new?"

"A little trouble down the trail last night," offered Fair.

"I noticed Younger came to town," said Bravo Trimble and began to show apprehension. "What'd he do?"

"I suppose there'll be a trail boss in to see you today. If you happen to make a hunt for Jett he'll stay out of your way."

"Damn him," said Bravo Trimble, "why don't he leave the country?" He went on down the street, murmuring to himself. Charley Fair tried another match to his cigar and

53

eased himself gently against the wall of The Pride, bulky and thick-shouldered and attentive to the day and its scenes. A little later three horsemen moved around The Drovers' into Race and went up to the courthouse, going inside. Presently Ford Green came out alone and walked to Ed Balder's store. Within the turn of a minute Balder returned to the courthouse with Ford Green and somewhat later Bravo Trimble appeared and entered the courthouse. This was at eleven. At twelve, as regular as a clock, Dan Mitchell returned to River Bend, put up his horse and went to Webber's for noon meal. On this man Charley Fair laid the whole weight of attention, studying him with a greater care than he troubled about to study any other man.

Mitchell reached the jail office at one o'clock. He was smiling and he kicked his palm against Ad Morfitt's shoulder. "Now all you've got to do for twelve hours is sleep."

"The hell you say," grumbled Morfitt. "What makes you so fine-feathered? Goin' to be hot and goin' to be trouble. Never is a day in this town that ain't full of trouble. Trail boss came in a while back. Seems like Younger cut this fellow's herd on the old yarn about there bein' some Younger beef that got strayed into the herd. Younger lifts twenty head, which is a plain steal as the trail boss knows, and marches 'em away. But the trail boss is tough and goes after Younger and there's a fight and a man's killed."

"Outside of town—outside of my job."

Morfitt hung up his belt and gun. He moved to the door and stood uncertainly there, half asleep yet reluctant to go home. "Maybe not. Everything comes back to this town. You'll get saddled with it. Which will be one more chunk of meat for the tiger." He turned on Mitchell. "I'm going to quit this job before fall comes. If you're smart you'll do the same thing."

54

"Why?"

"When the lid blows off where's your hole card? You ain't got one. For the sake of keepin' this town straight, keeping one side off the other's neck, you're the fellow that cuts the ground right from under your own feet. There's another way, of course."

"What's that?"

"Tie up with Fair or tie up with Balder. Then you'll have friends."

"No," said Mitchell. "I'll play it alone."

Morfitt sliced a finger across his neck. He said, "So long," and left the jail office.

Mitchell moved to the street and walked down Race, the old stale smells drifting against him as he passed the open doorways of the saloons. Chappie Brink, the town drunk, sat against the wall of the Arcade, soaking sunlight into his shriveled, punished body. Near him, also in the wall of the Arcade, the blackened punctures of three bullets showed, where Dill Gatchell had been killed in his fight with Mike Potter six months before. The scars of trouble were all over this town, seen and unseen. Mitchell turned the corner of The Drovers' and discovered the Wallin family hitched up and ready to leave their campsite under the guidance of Bill Mellen.

Mitchell said, "Where you taking them, Bill?"

"On the flats beyond Beat's Crossing."

"A good place," agreed Mitchell. Wallin's four flax-headed children sat high on the wagon load and looked down on Mitchell with a shy, unsmiling interest. "Noise bother you last night?" Mitchell asked.

"No," said Wallin, "but it is a sinful town. Makes me sad to see it. If I had the power," and he closed a powerful hand and moved it through the air, "I'd sweep it from the earth."

"That day," said Bill Mellen, "will come if we get enough homesteaders to vote this place decent."

"That day," agreed Mitchell, "will come, with or without the homesteaders."

"What?" asked Bill Mellen, but Mitchell was smiling at the four children, and had drawn a smile from them.

He said, "I wish you luck," and moved back into Bismarck Alley. Coming out later to Willow, he found Ed Balder waiting by the mouth of Brinton's stable for him.

Balder said, "I could set my watch by you. You shouldn't be so damned regular in your rounds. Makes ambush too easy." This was his one attempt at friendliness, for he was in a sour temper and presently showed it. He was a long and humorless man, a merchant who knew his position and his power and liked others to know it too. He could be impatient and he could be critical—and now was. "I wanted to catch you alone. When I have a beef with a man I prefer to get it over with privately. You played hell last night. Buffaloing Cap Ryker was no business. The man's worth a million dollars in Texas. If he passes the word along to the big outfits they'll leave River Bend high and dry and drive elsewhere. Why didn't you pick somebody else to knock the brains out of?"

Mitchell teetered gently on his heels. He was a taller man than Balder, he was straighter and lighter. He looked at Balder without expression. He said, "Were you there last night?"

"No. That's a damned-fool question."

"Damned-fool question against another damned-fool question. I buffaloed Cap Ryker because he was pulling the crowd with him."

"You should have picked another man," insisted Balder.

"Maybe you should have busted up that crowd instead of me," suggested Mitchell mildly.

"That's the job you were hired to do."

"Then," said Mitchell, "keep out of it and let me do it."

56

Balder pulled up. He studied Mitchell over a long stretch of time as though the marshal were a stranger to him. Then he said, "That's a little bit tough, Dan. I don't like it. Uncalled for."

"Maybe you had better remember the grounds on which I took this job," pointed out Mitchell. "I was to be left alone."

"To keep order, not to break the town up."

Mitchell came back with a rough and instant query: "You want my resignation?"

It ground hard on Balder's pride and sense of authority. He showed it in the way his lips pushed together and self-consciously, in the widening of his eyes. All this Mitchell noted with an amused irony that made its faint appearance on his face, to further irritate Balder. The merchant held his peace with difficulty; he fought back his desires and said with a heavy sigh, "No, Dan, I don't want it. You're the marshal."

"That's right," was Mitchell's dry observation. "I'm the marshal as long as you can't find another. Or as long as you trust me. Or as long as I am necessary to you. Meanwhile, Ed, I'll run the town."

Balder said, "All right—all right. We'll forget it. Now there's another thing. Jett Younger stopped a herd outside of town and ran off with some beef. There was a scrap and this trail outfit lost a man. Come over to the store."

Mitchell walked beside Balder, cutting across Willow's powdered, trembling dust. Sun burned brilliantly against the store windows and the smell of heat began to rise all around resinous and acrid. The stage to Sioux Trail tipped sharp around the corner of Race and went away with a dry clack of its panels, and Irma Gatewood strolled up Willow, idly twirling her parasol and looking at the town with soft, eager eyes, as though hoping to find some unexpected break in the day. Mitchell lifted his hat to her as he swung into Balder's store. He followed Balder back to a rear office. Dug Neil was here with Bravo Trimble. Ford Green stood in a corner, silent and dry. He put a glance over to Mitchell and somewhere in his head new thoughts began to work. Mitchell actually saw those thoughts turn and interlace and cautiously make a pattern.

"Bravo," said Balder, "it won't do. We sent one outfit down the trail feeling tough against this town. We can't let another one pull out the same way. You've got to go after Younger."

Bravo said in his sighing voice, "All right, Ed."

But Balder turned on the sheriff, knowing exactly what was in Bravo Trimble's mind. "No," he said, "I mean you are to get him. I want Younger in jail."

Bravo's never completely hidden apprehension spread like sickness over his face. He made a full circle on his heels, scanning each man for some hopeful sign. Then he said to Balder, "What will Charley Fair think of that?"

Balder said, "I'm not responsible for Charley Fair's crooks." Yet the question brought him to a pause and he stood in the center of the room, thinking of the necessary politics of this thing, and a little later he turned to Dug Neil. "Drop down to The Pride and tell Charley Fair I'm after Younger. Tell him I want Younger."

Neil left the room. Ford Green, who had been standing, sat down in Ed Balder's desk chair. He dropped a hand on Ed Balder's paper-scattered desk and began to drum on it softly with his fingers. His head was tilted and his face seemed suddenly sallow and long. Mitchell watched some kind of hope warm Bravo Trimble's eyes. Yet in a moment this went away, for Bravo was an old hand and he knew how the game went, and afterward the sheriff grew hopeless and tired before Mitchell's eyes. Neil presently came back.

"He says Jett Younger will have to take care of himself."

Ed Balder nodded. "Charley Fair is no fool. He knows damned well Younger's stunt is apt to hurt the saloon trade as much as ours. I want Younger, Bravo."

Bravo Trimble spoke with an old man's dull anger. "Sure, that's easy to say. You want him. So I go get him. If you're so—"

"Bravo," broke in Balder, "you been drawin' a hundred and twenty-five dollars a month off this county for a long while. Maybe you better earn it. Go get yourself some men and swear 'em in. You come back with Younger or his scalp or don't come back."

Bravo Trimble murmured darkly, "Maybe I don't come back," and left the room. Mitchell, idly following in Bravo's footsteps, saw the sheriff cross Willow and move along Race at a loose, slow gait. Mitchell paused by Balder's doorway. Beind him Ford Green and Dug Neil and Balder were softly talking, the meaning of the words not coming to Mitchell. It made no difference, for at this moment his mind went ahead of Bravo Trimble and saw this man lying dead somewhere in the Aspens. In a showdown against Jett Younger the sheriff would not last.

In Mitchell's head was a constant awareness of his own position. His survival depended on a complete knowledge of the factions in this town, in the hidden motives which alternately pulled apart and pushed together the chief actors here. The merchants had their side of the argument, with Ed Balder speaking. Through Charley Fair passed the desires of Race Street and the alleys behind it and the drifting rustlers and horse thieves in the Aspen Hills. On most things Balder and Fair were at opposite ends, and watched each other and maneuvered for advantage. But on some things, as in this one, they saw alike. What hurt the town hurt them both. Therefore these two realists had made a deal. Charley Fair had thrown over Jett Younger. The outlaw was fair game if Bravo Trimble could get him.

Mitchell moved to Brinton's for his buckskin. Mounted, he turned back to Race and idly cruised the almost empty street. He passed Tom Leathers at the corner of Briar. Leathers leaned against a gallery post, bareheaded in the sun, a good-looking man made of rawhide and showing the world a spirit that had humor and gentle malice. The wisdom of many campfires made and many odd adventures showed at the edge of his eyes.

"And not drunk yet," commented Mitchell.

"Just standing here, thinking about same," murmured Leathers. "It is a big question. Should I get drunk in a hurry and feel like hell afterward? Or should I get drunk slow and feel like hell afterward?"

"A problem, for a fact. Must put a terrific strain on your mind. Don't stand up when you're in heavy thought. Sit down and take off the load."

"Ah," said Leathers, "don't bother me."

Mitchell said, "For an ordinary bum you talk large," and moved down the street.

Tom Leathers called after him, "I'll just stand here and soak up some sun. Takes a common man to enjoy the real pleasures of life."

The train was in, its bell rolling echoes across the town's housetops, and a homesteader drove up Race with a load of buffalo bones collected off his land, to be sold through the Breyman brothers to a fertilizer factory in Omaha. Beyond the corner of The Drovers', Mitchell found Bravo Trimble. He had come to a stop and stood with head and shoulders dropped, staring at the yellow earth. He turned when he heard the slip of the buckskin's feet in the dust. His face was a thousand years old.

"Dan," he said, "never make my mistake, which is to pack the star when your day is done."

"You've done tougher jobs, Bravo."

"Sure, when I was young and didn't care. I will go out there. I will say, 'I've got to take you in, Jett.' And that

60

will be the end of Bravo Trimble. Don't carry the star too long, son."

Mitchell put both hands on the horn and bent forward. In the game of politics the sheriff had always been on the other side of the fence, playing along with Ford Green. He was Ford Green's man and a hundred times in the last year, by one soft word or another, Bravo Trimble had tried to cut the ground from beneath Mitchell's feet. Yet he stood here now just a checker to be moved to a corner by Green, to be sacrificed if necessary. At the same time Charley Fair had withdrawn support from Jett Younger, who was his checker. The only difference was that Charley Fair was pretty certain he wouldn't lose his checker. That was how it went in River Bend.

Mitchell stared out into the yellow layers of desert sunlight lying upon the land. His heavy lips moved together and a resentment stirred through him, side by side with pity. This man wore a star and he was alone, nobody caring.

"Bravo," he said, "I'll ride along."

Bravo Trimble straightened. "Why, son, it ain't your fight."

"It will be someday. Might as well be now."

"He's got five riders in the Aspens."

"I've got another man for us, which makes three. That's plenty." He wheeled the buckskin back into Race. Tom Leathers stood propped against the Arcade wall, half asleep on his feet. Mitchell reined before him. "A little fun, Tom. Bravo and I are going after Younger. Maybe you'd like the ride."

"I had a ride," said Tom Leathers.

"Never mind," said Mitchell, "it was just an idea."

Bravo Trimble came up Race, walking fast, and passed around the corner toward Brinton's stable. Charley Fair emerged from the barbershop, his face turned ruby from its hot toweling. Mitchell moved the buckskin across the

61

street toward Fair. He said, "I'm ridin' along with Bravo, Charley."

Charley Fair made a full stop and jammed the tips of his fingers into his front trouser pockets. He made a blocky, dark shape under the wooden gallery; his glance moved around Mitchell's face and he weighed the man and seemed to put away the things he thought at that moment. "Might be somewhat of a ride."

"Charley," said Mitchell, "if I strung along with a man I'd stick with him. I wouldn't sell him out."

"You're giving the advice?" said Charley Fair, amused but not pleased. "Maybe it ain't a case of selling. Jett's no cripple."

"That's why I'm going with Bravo. Maybe he's the one being sold."

Charley Fair knocked the ashes from his cigar and replaced it, stolid throughout and showing nothing. "What side you think you're on, Friend Dan?"

"Mine."

"Lonely place."

"Maybe," agreed Mitchell and turned up the street. Ford Green and Ed Balder stood now on Willow's sidewalk, watching him as he passed on to Brinton's stable. Bravo waited there and Bravo's eyes touched Ford Green and came back to Mitchell, and showed a greater feeling than Mitchell had ever seen in them.

Bravo said, "You never know where a friend is, son. Never—"

Tom Leathers came around the corner on his pony, and was wholly displeased with himself. He said, "Pride is a damn-fool thing. Man never learns." He gave Mitchell a tough glance, grumbling, "What the hell you dallyin' for?"

"I thought you'd be drunk by now," suggested Mitchell.

"Remember," pointed out Tom Leathers, "this is just

a ride. I ain't interested in Jett Younger at all. Hate to see you get lost up in those hills, though."

"Sure," agreed Mitchell. "Big hills." He grinned at Leathers and saw the man's fertile imagination begin to work at the possibilities of the adventure before them.

Young Dick Lestrade came through a foot-wide gap between Webber's House and Poe's saddle shop and crossed the dust toward these three men with his head lowered to watch his square-pointed shoes furrow the dust. He stopped nearby and he lifted his chin and he surveyed them with a boy's wonder-working, unfathomed dreaming.

"Now," said Mitchell, "if we needed another hand we could take you along."

Young Dick's answer raced back at him: "I could keep up all right. I can ride."

"But it just happens," murmured Mitchell, "we only need three and Leathers asked first. Well, another time."

Bravo Trimble looked down on young Dick, and the boy was a mirror in which he saw his freer and better years, so that he said in an inexpressibly sad tone, "Kind of like to be a-ridin', wouldn't you, Dick? But don't ride too soon. Now there's the swimming-hole under the bridge and there's the cave out by Jordan's bluff and here's the whole long blessed day for loafin'. Don't ride too soon."

"Sure," said young Dick, understanding none of this but willing to agree, for it was one of his gods speaking.

"All right," said Mitchell. The three men swung around and moved out Willow into the prairie.

Ford Green turned on the walk so that he might face Balder; and for a moment he studied the big storekeeper with a close attention, as though it were important to him to know what went on in Balder's mind. Then he spoke in his quiet, suggesting way: "Wonder why he's going out with Bravo."

Balder displayed irritation. "Never know about that fellow."

"You gave him that job, didn't you? Your man, isn't he?"

"That's right."

But there was a ruffled, jumpy doubt in Balder's tone. Smart in all things, Ford Green was swift to catch that inner aggravation. He started down the street, high and square and a little ungainly in the manner in which he worked; and then, as though it were the purest afterthought, he turned and said in his dry way, "You sure he's still your man?" He didn't wait for an answer, but crossed Willow toward the courthouse, the sun brightening the freckles of his face.

Reaching the end of Willow, Irma Gatewood noticed that one homestead wagon remained at the temporary camp on the prairie. She went out there and found a woman and three children, one of them being a six-month-old baby. The husband, said the woman, was out looking at land. Mrs. Gatewood sat on the ground and held the baby, meanwhile hearing the woman speak of her hopes.

"We were always poor in the East," said the woman. "And we've got children growing up. Maybe you'll let me make you some tea. It is kindly of you to pay a visit."

Mrs. Gatewood had her tea, paid her respects, and walked back to Willow, grateful for the little interlude in the day and remembering the warm velvet hand of the baby as it had brushed across her face. She stopped at Gatewood's office.

He was quite busy on his ledgers and said so in his grave, absent-minded way. "After six o'clock, Irma, I am your man. But until then Wells-Fargo pays me for my time and I have got to give it to them. Did you need something?"

"No," she said. "I thought I'd just stop to smile at you."

"You smiled at me an hour ago, and will again at six o'clock. You have a very lively imagination."

"What shall I do, Will?"

"Why," he said, "I believe that is your particular problem. There's the house."

"Yes," she agreed softly, "there's the house."

"And the other ladies to visit along Antelope."

"I know."

"I should think," he said, "you ought to find ways of making it a pleasant day."

They never came nearer quarreling than this. He was always extremely quiet with his reproof and always certain that she saw his views, and for her part she had no capacity for real protest or anger. She could not make him miserable in order to awaken him. In many respects he was scarcely aware of her. She had her day in which to be pleasant and her time with him at the table. After that, in the evenings, they occasionally visited and sometimes strolled in the twilight; but he was a settled, inwardly absorbed man who liked best to stay at home and lose himself in a world of printed philosophy and at those times she sat still in her chair and listened to the dead silence in the house and gripped her hands together. Sometimes she wanted to cry at him, "Look at me, Will," but she never did. For he would have looked at her with his faintly surprised, courteous manner and would never have seen what she wanted him most to see—the thirst that had no quenching, the womanliness which soured for lack of being wanted.

Now she said, still mild and smiling, "I'll not bother you, Will. We're having cold beef for supper."

"I saw cucumbers in Lent's store. Let's have cucumbers with vinegar. I'm very fond of them."

"All right."

She continued down Willow. She stopped in at Lent's

and got three cucumbers and put the sack under her arm, going on to the depot. She passed Dug Neil and smiled at him and received back his very gallant gesture. Dug, she knew, was a lady's man and caused his wife some amount of grief. Yet she wondered—and was no longer shocked that she had vagrant thoughts of this kind—if a husband who sinned from an excess of human hunger was not more satisfying to a wife than a quiet one who put his wife in a corner with the footstool; at least the erring husband had some warmth left over for his wife. When she turned the depot corner she saw George Hazelhurst standing farther down the runway, his back turned to her.

Train time was an hour away and there were no other people here. Mrs. Gatewood strolled along the runway, and her heart struck its quick small beats and she knew, from the perfect stillness of his body, that he was aware of her. A lone passenger coach stood slightly ahead of him and he seemed to be staring at this. She passed him and reached the steps of the car; and now she was perhaps ten feet from him and her face was turned away from him. There was nobody else around the depot and nobody on the whole length of Railroad Avenue.

She spoke at the car. "You are very lonely and very bored and this is the best you can do, to come here and watch a car and to wish it were carrying you away."

"Yes," said Hazelhurst, "that's about it."

"Why don't you go, then? Nothing holds you back. You can run all the way across the world if you choose."

"It would still be the same," he said. "River Bend or Omaha or Chicago. If you are lonely and bored it makes very little difference where you are."

"I should think you'd find life exciting enough."

"Perhaps I wish for things that simply can't be. As you do."

"You have noticed me?" she asked in a voice that was

warm and indescribably pleased.

"Yes, Mrs. Gatewood."

She said, "I guessed you had but I was not too sure." Then she added one wholly impulsive thought: "It is rather nice to be noticed."

He said, "If you prefer, I'll walk back now. I should not have spoken to you at all. You realize we are on opposite sides of the town."

"How terrible a thing it is to be entirely alone. How wonderful a world of understanding can be. Are we so far apart? Is any living soul different from any other?"

He had suggested leaving but he had not gone. He stood silent behind her and she wished she might turn and see his face, resisting the urge because of the risk. Somewhere in this town eyes would be watching her. She put her hand to the side of the car and seemed to be interested in it.

Hazelhurst said, "Nor should I say this. You are a lovely woman."

Mrs. Gatewood wanted to cry, not for him but for herself. For now she knew what she would do. In her mind was one sad, forlorn question: *Why should it happen to me? Why couldn't my life be as other women's?* But she said aloud, "Sometimes late at night I walk alone. I come here and sit in this old black coach and imagine its taking me away."

His voice was rather fine in the way it rebuked her. "Mrs. Gatewood, I'll never come near that coach."

But, turning and passing him, she had a single glance at his face and she knew that he would come.

Chapter Five: In the Aspens

The three of them—Trimble, Leathers, and Mitchell—crossed the Spanish Fork by way of the covered bridge directly outside of town and swung southwest, thereby coming at the Aspen Hills in a slanting direction. Beside them and before them lay trail herds newly arrived from Texas and now awaiting their turn at the loading-pens in town. Deep in the south dust rose in thin straggling banners from the stretched-out columns of one more herd arriving.

"Be a hundred thousand head shipped out of this town before fall," prophesied old Bravo. He rode between the other two and was caught, as an unhappy man is, by the greener recollections of yesterday. "I remember very well how this started. Soon as the railroad reached River Bend—why, that was only five years ago—old Colonel Jack Vinson saw a way to make the town grow. So he took a trip to Texas and said to those fellows, 'Drive your beef to River Bend. You got good grass and water all the way and the railroad's there to meet you. We'll put up loadin' pens.' That summer two herds came up. Next year there was maybe ten or fifteen thousand head. Then she grew."

"Progress," said Tom Leathers, not much interested in the talk.

"Sure, progress," agreed Bravo in a lackluster voice. "I can remember this country when there wasn't a house nearer than Meridian, two hundred miles east. Then some buffalo hunters put up a cabin right where the courthouse is. Fall of '62. They moved out and after that Jack Vinson moved in, in '66. Sellin' trinkets to the Indians and catching a little trade with the overlanders. Pretty soon there was five-six houses. Then the railroad and a boom. I used to ride from Vinson's cabin across the hills to War Bonnet and never see a soul. Just antelope and maybe a wild horse or two. Mighty pretty country then."

"Still is," stated Tom Leathers.

"Not for me," answered Bravo. "When the feelin' of hell goes out of a man, when sleepin' on the ground gets to be a misery and the mornin' smell of coffee ain't like it was, when you'd rather just sit in the shade and let other men ride, then nothin's the same." He was in a dour mood and he looked upon young Tom Leathers with an older man's jealousy. "You wait twenty years."

The sun was half down the western sky, glittering on the mica crystals in the desert soil, changing the color of the sage, making the bunch grass a great yellow carpet all the way into the smoky distance. Heat lay thin and strong on the land as they angled toward the rolling, rising patches of the Aspen Hills. They came upon the irregular cut of Little Bear Creek and followed it into brown and bald footslopes and rose up a trail until, five hundred feet off the desert floor, the first line of timber stood in front of them. At this division between the elbow room of the open desert and the hills' piney coverts, Bravo Trimble made a stop and turned about to give the desert a final glance. "A man," he said in deepest regret, "never knows."

He was reluctant to enter the timber. Obviously he tarried here, as though he had his forebodings of evil and

69

now said good-by to desert and town. "I can stand here," he said, "and see the end of that place. All these cow towns grow from nothin' and have their time. Then they blow up and pretty soon there ain't nothin' left but a few ash heaps and broken bottles and some graves in the sagebrush." He faced the timber and pulled himself together, adding in a shorter, duller tone: "That way with a man. Starts from nothin' and goes back to nothin'."

"You sure give a man the dismals," observed Leathers. "Let's move on before I bust down and cry."

The creek's shallow gorge and its parallel trail entered the trees and moved upgrade by one quick turn upon another until at the end of another hour the trail veered away to its own destination somewhere in the higher levels. The trees made a close stand, free of underbrush, and a hot twilight lay beneath the pine tops and here and there a splinter of sunlight struck through the pines like a yellow exclamation point. Mitchell, second in file, saw Bravo's shirt darken from sweat. He saw Bravo's face turn steadily from side to side, pinched together by the care that was in him. They arrived at a meadow running its tan-and-yellow bay back into the surrounding dark green of the hills. Here Mitchell stopped.

He said, "Which way had you proposed to go, Bravo?"

"He got those cows near Antelope Butte. He'd run into the hills about there. I figured on turning south until we cut his trail."

Mitchell wasted time enough to build a cigarette. He cemented the smoke with a quick swipe of his tongue and lighted it. "Bravo," he said, "we're not out here for fun and I wouldn't like to go back to town with Jett's horselaugh behind me." He pulled in a good gust of smoke and expelled it and put a steady eye on Bravo. "Jett was in town this morning. He saw Charley Fair. Charley Fair probably dropped a word to you. What did he say, Bravo?"

Bravo Trimble sat on the saddle and looked down at the earth, darkly debating. Presently he said, very softly, "Said Jett would stay out of my road."

"Just so," drawled Mitchell. "A mighty comfortable game—and nobody hurt. You go south and cut his trail and he ain't anywheres near there. So we won't bother about that. Let's sort of guess where the gentleman might be taking his ease tonight."

"He'll still take that trail," pointed out Bravo.

"Imagine so. And he'll spot the beef in some convenient meadow. Might be up at the Little Fork. Might be at the old Casteen hut. If I remember right, Jett likes that spot. We'll try it."

"You're movin' right in on him?" questioned Bravo.

"I think," said Mitchell, "we'll fool him a little."

He took the lead and moved into the meadow, riding down its middle to the far end, there again entering timber and coming upon a trail. Along this way a rider had been not long before, the print of a horse's shoes fresh in the dust. The sun was far toward the rim, skimming its long rays above the treetops, and all the corridors of the forest began to darken.

Tom Leathers called forward: "We left a mighty broad track through that meadow hay, Dan."

"That's right."

"I get it."

Half an hour later, following the trail to the higher points of the hills, Mitchell came out on a knob from which the long major upland valley of the Aspens showed in the distance. The sun burned dark red and slowly sank below the horizon as they watched it. With its passing, the color of the world faded stage by stage and when they moved on again twilight ran in sirup-fluid bands of blue through the timber and the released heat of the earth came up with its vital odors of old soil and pine resin. Mitchell moved steadily through gathering blackness. He dipped into a shallow canyon and splashed across a creek and rose to a still higher trail. The stars were out and all the nebulae made their silvered swirl in the sky. Far off, as a single lonely note, an owl hooted. There was somewhere a pale edge of moon.

In full darkness they came to a meadow, with Mitchell pulling in. "Camp here," he said and got down. He left his horse saddled and moved back to rummage for pine boughs, and started a bright furious little fire. Neither he nor Bravo carried supplies. It was Tom Leathers who broke out his coffee pot and frying pan with some amount of grumbling.

"How'd you fellows propose to get along if I hadn't come? Kind of an absent-minded couple, should you ask me."

They ate bacon and drank coffee. Leathers and Trimble sat well back from the fire but Mitchell walked to the trees for another load of wood and threw it on the blaze, building it high. Tom Leathers started to speak and shut his mouth, and looked at Mitchell with a dry, understanding grin. Bravo was far back in his own thoughts, limp and old and disinterested. Mitchell lighted a cigar and stretched full length on the ground.

"Four miles to the Casteen cabin. If they're near it they'll see this fire—if they're looking. I think they'll be looking."

"Sure they'll see it," agreed Tom Leathers. "Then what?"

"Jett will think we're just notifying him we're around but don't intend to find him."

Bravo came out of his reverie. "You know, I kind of regret that. Never had much against Jett. We always got along. Wish I had some way of telling him it was Charley Fair that sold him out, not me."

"Tell him."

"No," said Bravo, "I bear no tales. But I'm kind of

72

disappointed in Charley Fair, and in Ford Green."

"Bravo," said Mitchell, thoughtful and soft, "you know your politics better than that."

"I have played my share of politics," agreed Bravo. "In my time I have sawed off many a man. But that man always knew when I was comin' after him. I never went back on my word." Bitterness came up in force. "This is a sellout. Me or Jett. It don't matter to the boys in town how it works. I never had that happen to me before and if that's the way the world goes I don't want to live in it. A man's got his word. If that's no good, what is?"

"Pretty stars," said Tom Leathers. "Mighty pretty. Breeze comin' up. Earth a-turnin' round. Just a cradle for the Lord's creatures. There's times when I can feel it a-turnin'. Mighty comfortin'. Pride sure kills a lot of men, Daniel my boy."

Bravo Trimble tossed up his hand and spoke across the fire to Mitchell. "Don't let 'em do to you what they're doing to me."

"Play my own hole card," murmured Mitchell.

"So did I. Look at me now. You can't buck the leaders. No man can play it alone."

Tom Leathers was small and idle and smiling on the earth. He watched Mitchell's length and breadth in the flare of firelight; he saw and slightly admired Mitchell's hard, tough shell. But he, better than any other man, knew the things lying beneath that armor of self-sufficiency, those things which might one day trap him and kill him. This man had a pride rising from convictions that would never let him step aside when trouble came, rising from an intense sense of honor, from a warmth and a need of warmth unseen by others. These things Mitchell had in him, and they would betray him.

Mitchell got up from the ground, saying, "Time to go," and swung to his horse. He circled the fire so that he would not make a traveling shape against it and led the other two across the bottomless dark of the meadow into the timber. The fire was a round orange stain in the night when they lost sight of it. Bravo's voice drifted forward.

"Dan," he said, "in case I forget to say this later, you had no call to help me. I'm kind of glad to know you're along."

"Sure."

The trail ran invisible before them through the timber. It rose slightly and it turned and dropped beside the clacking waters of a creek. It followed the creek and the creek's cool damp emanations and suddenly made a quick climb up a ridge into another small mountain meadow on which the vague moonlight and starshine laid a ghostly glow.

Bravo Trimble's soft and tired voice drifted forward: "You're near it."

The trail, once more entering timber, was a gray hole against the greater black of the trees. Mitchell avoided that hole and skirted the meadow's edge and faded into the timber by a pathless way, threading around the trees with the smell of firesmoke now in the air. Trimble and Tom Leathers broke the file and drifted abreast and the three sifted through the pines, moving down a gentle grade toward the creek and its restless clatter. The thick carpet of forest mold absorbed the sound of the horses.

One point of light winked and died and reappeared again. Mitchell moved out of the timber to the edge of a little clearing and faced the Casteen cabin with its single window and its open door showing their rectangles of yellow light. Woodsmoke from the cabin and two horses stood faint-shaped nearby. Back of the cabin the encroaching hills cut a ragged line against the blue-black sky.

This was fifty yards from the trees, with the creek between trees and cabin. A shape moved out of the cabin toward the creek and stopped by it and a second man shortly afterward came to the cabin's doorway, calling into the dark: "Nick out there?"

"No," said the man by the creek.

The man in the doorway was Younger. He turned back into the cabin. The man by the creek rose and strolled over the yard, but wheeled and went spooking around the dark, his feet scuffing the dry earth. Mitchell listened to that; he sat straight in the saddle and watched the man come out of the dark and enter the cabin. A chair scraped on the cabin's floor and the murmuring continued.

Leathers crowded his horse against Mitchell. "Somebody ain't here. Hear Jett ask about Nick? You want to be careful that fellow don't pop up behind us."

Mitchell stepped to the ground. He waited until Leathers and Bravo got beside him. He said, "Tom, you lay back. Stay by that creek and watch the yard. You all set, Bravo? We're going in."

The three left the trees, drifting downslope to the creek. Leathers stopped here and sank to the earth and was lost. Mitchell slid his boots along the creek's gravel bottom and felt them fill. Three long stretching steps took him across. Bravo came beside him again and they moved on in a small circle to avoid the lanes of light shining from the cabin's door and window. Mitchell reached the cabin's wall and put himself against it and listened to the run of talk inside and the clack of poker chips. Jett Younger was speaking of a bear he had killed. Bravo Trimble's shoulder touched Mitchell's shoulder and Mitchell heard the hard, rapid slugging of the older man's heart and the quickening of his breath. He laid a hand against Bravo's arm, whispering, "Stay here," and ducked under the window, coming to the door's edge. He checked himself, took one rapid view of the interior and moved through the doorway at a single long step.

It was a one-room cabin not more than twelve feet

75

square, with a stove and a bunk and a table. Younger and two of the other men sat around the table, and two men crouched against a far wall. He had a momentary view of a motionless scene. The following instant the two men at the far wall had come to their feet and one man at the table sent it over with a swift stab of his hand and yelled. Everybody was upright except Jett Younger, who sat in his chair and threw a dark, cutting glance at Mitchell. This was all. Younger turned his eyes to the fallen table and to the chips and cards scattered on the floor, and afterward stared at the man who had so impulsively done this damage.

"Torp," he said, "you're always doin' some damned rattle-brained stunt. One of these days the fool-killer is a-goin' to get you. Pick up the table. Pick up the cards. I had a good hand."

Torp grumbled, "This is no time to be lookin' at cards, Jett."

"Pick 'em up," repeated Younger, and watched his man slowly drop to his knees and crawl along the floor. He spoke to Mitchell without turning his head: "You maybe ought to whistle when you come up to this place."

"Never could whistle or carry a tune," said Mitchell. He was in the doorway, both hands full length beside him. He watched Torp collect the cards and pull the table upright. The men along the back wall remained dead-still.

Jett Younger rummaged the cards, until he found his hand. He bowed his head over it. "I've seen a lot of tomcats get their tails caught from tryin' to squeeze through places too tight for 'em."

"My tail went on the chopping-block a long time ago."

Jett spread his hand face up. "Queens on treys. I said it was a good hand. There was ten dollars and fifty cents in that pot. Get the chips, Torp." He was a bony, bulky, and awkward shape on the chair. He put both big elbows on the table and the light shining down from a ceiling lantern cast the black shadow of his upper body on the table. He was certain of himself, but he was crafty in the way he kept his talk split between the cards and Dan Mitchell; he was pushing this scene around, holding it away from him until he had it the way he wanted it. "In the first place, Dan, I didn't expect you. I figured it might be Bravo. In the second place, I didn't expect him. I got out of his way. You took a lot of trouble to hunt me up. What's the idea of lightin' a fire big enough to burn a barn if it wasn't to show me where you was—so I wouldn't bump into you?"

Torp stacked the chips on the table. Jett Younger counted them out until he had his ten dollars and fifty cents and he drew that little stack to the rim of the table beside him, his fingers lifting them and clacking them together. His attention clung to the stack; his eyes narrowed on them. "Or was that one of those fine-haired schemes? You figured I'd read it wrong. Which I did. You come alone, Dan?"

"No."

Jett Younger pushed his stack at Torp. "You're the banker. Remember it was ten-fifty." He rose and turned around his chair and now faced Mitchell. "You're a pretty big fool, Dan. Why you here?"

"Balder sent Bravo after you. So I came along."

"You talked to Charley Fair?"

"Agreeable with him."

Jett showed his first real emotion—an anger that had its edge. "You're lyin'."

"A deal," said Mitchell, laying out his words thoughtfully. "A deal between Charley and Balder. You tipped over the cart, which hurts the pocketbook of both those fellows. What's one man like you against the trail trade they might both lose? So it is you or Bravo. It doesn't matter much to Ed or Charley. Think it over."

"You're still lyin'," said Jett. But he was thinking of it; he was a bold man and a swashbuckler, yet he had his sharp self-preserving instincts and his mind followed these instincts in and out through their tricky variations. Slyness showed at the edges of his eyes. He seemed relieved. "Sure. Charley maybe said that. But he knew I could take care of myself, as against Bravo. It wasn't a sellout."

"I'm here," Mitchell reminded him.

Jett hit him with a blunt question. "What for? It is none of your business."

"To see it isn't Bravo that gets the sellout. I'll stick with the man that carries a star."

"Friend," stated Jett, "you better be sure you ain't the one sellin' out yourself." He stood still, alert to the night, slowly grasping the scene at last for everything it meant. He lifted his head, listening and his glance went around the room and then he was sure of himself and he was amused. "This looks like a pat hand to me."

There was a window on the far side of the cabin. Mitchell spoke over his shoulder, "Bravo, go around and knock in the glass of that window."

Jett's smile slid away. He moved one foot slowly along the floor and brought it back. Bravo Trimble's boot scuffed around the cabin and in a moment he hit the windowpanes with the barrel of his gun, breaking them out. The sound of this went clashing into the darkness, brittle and startling. Younger's four men waited, watching Younger who was, Mitchell saw, trying to tell them something without speaking. They were trying to understand—and failing. Younger called, "All right."

"I just want you," said Mitchell, pointing at Jett. "Move into the yard with me. Rest of you fellows stay easy. Wouldn't get nervous. Jett's been in jail before." He retreated from the doorway and wheeled out of the

78

land of light into the shadows.

Jett Younger released an odd laugh and now came to the doorway. He put his hands against the edge of the casing and balanced himself and he said in a voice soft for him, "All right."

Bravo's yell lifted: "Stop that!" The light died. Mitchell, jumping aside, heard Younger's great grunt as he threw himself forward. He heard the strike of Younger's hand on the hard butt of his gun. Mitchell threw himself in, low and swift. His hands caught Younger and were knocked aside and he made another sweep and caught the outlaw again around the waist. He felt Younger's arms strain as he bore him back against the logs of the cabin. Younger wheeled and tried to throw him away. Men rushed out of the cabin and a gun began to break the heavy stillness of the hills. Mitchell heaved at Younger, slamming him hard on the legs, and raised his knee and smashed it into Younger's crotch.

The big man had been a rioting animal in his arms. He ceased to be. A shouted cry rushed out of him and he turned heavy and momentarily soft against Mitchell, who ran his hand down along the big man's flank toward the gun Younger had not fully pulled from the holster.

Somebody in the yard kept yelling, "Jett—where you at—Jett, where you at?" Boots hit the hard earth and a quick firing pounded the meadow and the hills, rolling out and rolling back like minor thunder. That yell echoed again: "Jett!"

A man plunged full against Mitchell, shouting: "That you?" He had his arm around Mitchell's throat and, hearing no answer, he shoved against Mitchell. Mitchell turned, grinding skin from his neck; he pushed himself forward, throwing the man off his feet. He went down on top of this fellow and rolled away and got up, swinging back toward the wall. He had brought up his gun and when he heard the man rise off the earth and begin to yell he turned and fired full at the shadow moving against him.

All this was in a curdled blackness. Tom Leathers called from the foreground and potty explosions of gunfire continued back of the cabin. Mitchell made a run for the cabin wall and caught Jett Younger's leg. He had misjudged Younger's location and took a brutal blow from the wall when he slammed into it, but he tripped Younger and dropped on him, again searching for the outlaw's gun. Deep in the dust Younger moved and twisted and cursed up at Mitchell with a fury that came out of a senseless savage core, and out of that same inflamed and brutal rage Mitchell cursed back. There were times like this when a darkness moved as in an eclipse across every normal thing in him, so that he clawed and tore and had his lust to kill in order to survive. This was Mitchell in a fight.

He made a grab of Younger's holster. Younger's wild-flung arm caught him on the mouth, crushing his lips into his teeth. He quit trying for the gun and crawled nearer Younger and found the man's face and beat at it, with the man's yell growing harder and harsher in his ears, until something struck him on the flank and a hand caught at his coat and rolled him aside and a weight came down and stunned him.

He was never quite sure of what happened during the next half minute. Some other man roughed him up in the dust, dragging him and hauling him and reaching for his face with thick fingers whose nails tore the skin of his jaws. Mitchell got his arms over his face; he caught the man on the neck and pulled him in to smother and block those blows. Elsewhere, as in a dim distance, one voice called and he thought he heard his own name being repeated. Hanging stubbornly to this other man's neck, he found himself rolling, and then he found that the man was gone though he could not understand how it had happened. But the warning of it was enough and he kept rolling, and heard a gun's flat and deafening smash directly by him. He saw the little flash of pale light from its muzzle and caught the scorch of its burned powder. Then—all this occurring with the steady regularity of a ticking clock—another gun came in fast and hollow-sounding and steps trembled along the earth and horses rushed away.

"Dan," said Tom Leathers, "that you there?"

"Where's Bravo?"

Tom Leathers came up, breathing hard. He squatted on the earth, listening. Out on the meadow's edge Jett Younger's voice was a greater and greater shout: "Mitchell, this won't stand! I'll be after you and I'll make you crawl!"

Horses splashed in the creek and went grunting away and at last the echoes died. Mitchell stood up, a steady ache pulsing along his side, a fire burning on his slashed cheeks. Leathers was again searching the yard. A match made its bright flare between his palms and a little glow dropped down on a shape on the ground. The match went out. "That's Torp," said Leathers.

"Where's Bravo?"

"Bravo?" said Leathers, moving back. "Bravo's on the other side of the cabin dead. His time just ran out and all you got from this, my friend, is one hell of a big prospect of trouble."

The deep stubborn impulses still throbbed in Mitchell. "We're going after Jett, Tom. We're going after him."

"Why?" asked Leathers, bone-dry with his tone.

Mitchell pulled a hand along his face, and suddenly everything about this night became something that was a long time ago and all he could remember was the vague yell of his own voice; and now, his mind clear, he looked back on that memory with a strange wonder and was not pleased.

"No," he said, "we'll let that go for now. We'll take Bravo to town. I'll have the boys come back to get Torp."

"Torp and Logan Beggs." Tom Leathers had that dryness still in his talk. "Logan's lyin' out back there with Bravo. You made one more enemy in Jett. Ain't you got enemies enough?"

Chapter Six: An Old Fellow Goes Home

Mitchell and Tom Leathers climbed the ridge separating the Bear Creek meadows from the long narrow valley wherein the Cabin Creek Fork of Spanish River cut through the higher Aspens; once across the ridge they had sight of a late light in Mike Gault's ranch house. They came downgrade via the break-back loops of a mountain road, crossing a plank bridge that flung the footfall of their horses forward in hollow echoes of warning. Dogs sounded immediately in the Gault yard. When they rounded the house some man's voice boosted a taciturn question from the shadows.

"Who's that?"

"Mitchell and Leathers," said Leathers. "That you, Mike?"

"Ah," said Mike Gault, "you're ridin' late." The door opened and Sherry Gault came out. Mike Gault now moved forward. "Never know who's ridin' around here these days. Get down and have coffee." The doorway light was a gold-yellow beam touching Mitchell and Leathers. It went beyond them to strike the horse they were leading, and the body of Bravo Trimble lashed across his saddle. Mike Gault saw it and said nothing at all. He walked on until he was near enough to identify

Bravo, and turned back.

"You'll want a wagon to take him to town." He made a half turn, yelling into the night, 'Lake, put the two sorrels to a wagon." He watched Mitchell with a close expression but with no surprise, for he was a hard Scotsman who had come to this country young and had seen this story drift out of the hills too many times to be shaken by it. Sherry Gault, now at the edge of the doorway, had also seen Bravo. Still in the saddle, Mitchell saw darkness make its graphic sweep over her cheeks. Always he was interested in her, always he wondered at the strange flow of feeling in the depths of this girl. Outwardly she was reserved and sometimes hard, and sometimes her realism made her seem without feeling. In the year of watching, Mitchell had guessed other things about her and had never ceased to look for the little signs and inflections which betrayed their presence. She was to him a colorful and dramatic puzzle, with the power of drawing from him any other thought or preoccupation he had; she had the power of turning him out of the strongest channel.

What he saw now was sadness, and the sight of it pleased him. He got down and rolled a cigarette, watching Sherry move back into the house. When he raised his arms the long muscles of his back set up a stiff pull from the fight he had been through and the first smoke from the cigarette got into the cuts of his face with a nettlelike stinging. His lips were bruised, the inner flesh ripped. He took one more drag on the cigarette and dropped it, finding no pleasure in it.

Mike Gault's man came up presently with the team and wagon and stopped by Bravo Trimble. He gave the sheriff a close look but kept his place on the wagon, offering no help; nor did Mike Gault offer to help. These two remained silent, waiting Mitchell's word. Mitchell glanced at Leathers, briefly nodding; they went back to

Trimble's horse and unlashed the sheriff. They carried him to the wagon and laid him out on the bed. Leathers walked away from the wagon but Mitchell spoke up irritably: "This won't do," and returned to Trimble's horse. He took off the saddle and dumped it in the wagon. He got the saddle blanket around Bravo, wrapping Bravo in it.

"Lake," said Mike Gault, "you drive into town with the boys. Better coffee up before you go."

"Coffee ain't what I need," said Leathers and stepped into his saddle. "I'll go with the wagon, Dan. You catch up when you're ready." He went on into the darkness with the wagon, traveling the valley road toward River Bend.

Mitchell followed Mike Gault into the house. Sherry stood in the room's center, completely still, as though a thousand things ran darkly through her mind. She had been looking away from the door but now turned her head, meeting Mitchell's eyes and, as always, her chin lifted and she seemed deliberately to put up a guard against him.

Gault had gone on to the kitchen and called from there: "Here's your coffee."

Mitchell spoke to Sherry: "Sorry you had to see Bravo that way," and went into the kitchen.

Mike Gault said, "There's the cups on the shelf, there's the can of condensed milk—there's the coffee on the stove. Help yourself." He drifted to the far end of the kitchen and opened the door and looked into the night, and closed the door.

He turned, lamplight striking up a granite shine in his eyes. He was a square-faced man with shaggy eyebrows and a rough, burned-dark skin. He was a pure sample of a transplanted Highland Scotchman who had come to a rough country, had adopted its roughness, and had survived. He watched Mitchell drink the rank bitter

85

coffee and read some of the story of the fight in the lengthening silence, knowing better than to ask questions. He would have thought himself a fool to have pried into Mitchell's business.

Mitchell said, "Bravo went after Younger. Leathers and I tagged along. We didn't get Younger."

That was the story, and since Mitchell had opened the topic Mike Gault felt free to speak. "Looks like you tried hard enough."

Sherry Gault had come to the kitchen doorway and paused to hear this. Now she stirred across the kitchen, as though by impulse, and brought the coffee pot and refilled Mitchell's cup.

Mike Gault said, "Seems odd to me Bravo would bother about Younger."

"You know how the boys in town play this game."

"I know," agreed Mike Gault. "I can understand all of it, except why you tagged along. Bravo was no particular friend of yours."

"He wore a star," said Mitchell, "and needed some help."

"Ah," murmured Mike Gault. He gave Mitchell a prolonged study, both skeptical and thoughtful. "Maybe it was as simple as that, though my observation is that nothin's vurry simple in this country. I mean no reflection by the remark, of course." He had a short-stemmed pipe to his mouth, and took some time in lighting it, his glance dividing between Mitchell and Sherry. Very casually he strolled from the room.

Sherry said, "Would you like something to go with the coffee?"

"No."

She said, "Bravo was an old man. If you went along to help Bravo—if that was the only reason—I like you for it." She had turned restless. She circled the room, touching objects along the way, and eventually came to

86

the table. She stopped before him; and it was impulse again that made her lift a hand and run a finger lightly along a heavy scratch in his jaw. She pulled back quite suddenly and showed an instant self-irritation. "If that was really the reason."

"Not necessary for you to believe it."

Her answer came back instantly: "I don't. Everybody has his plans and private schemes. You have yours."

"That's right."

She said, again very quickly, "So it wasn't the real reason you went with him?"

"Yes, it happened to be."

She had been watching him with critical eyes. Hearing his answer, change went through her and her guard dropped and she was for that instant a full, charming girl with a faint smile in her eyes. "Would you have something more than coffee?"

"This is enough."

It may have been the brief way he answered her, or the manner in which he put down his coffee cup—it may have been one of a half-dozen small things of which he was really unaware—but the friendliness vanished. Noting it, he found the swift contrast unexplainable to him. Somehow she seemed to be at the mercy tonight of strong crosscurrents.

"You don't trust me very much," he told her, "and you have a pretty deep dislike for me."

"Yes."

"Why?"

"How can I trust you? Or why should I? You are in the dirtiest job in the country."

"Somebody has to do that job."

"Ah—somebody. Somebody who doesn't care, who doesn't mind if he dips his hands deep in the mud, if he plays the crooked against the crooked and stoops to them. Somebody who can make a lie out of his silence, or a

87

truth out of it, whichever suits him best." Then, once more one deep-rankling thought got out of her. "Somebody who can find his ease in Bismarck Alley when the day is over."

In that was a woman's jealousy, though it puzzled him to know why she should bother to be jealous when he pleased her so little. But he smiled at her and shrugged his shoulders and moved toward the door.

She called after him—very arbitrary with her tone: "Wait." She watched him turn. He could see that she really wanted to hit him hard. "Perhaps that's not the real reason I dislike you. Perhaps the real reason is you are too sure of yourself."

"It may be," he admitted. "When a man rides down Race Street confidence is all he's got. Thanks for the coffee."

He left the house and crossed to his horse. Mike Gault was somewhere else but Sherry followed him. She came up as though there were other things on her mind which needed to come out. She was willful, she was as sure of herself as she had accused him of being. Maybe, he thought, that was it: a proud woman hated the pressure of somebody else's pride. But she was beautiful in the lamp-stained shadows, she had a grace and a fragrance— she had a spirit that was an undertow all around him. He was moved by it and made restless and dissatisfied, and he had to speak.

"Remember that cowpuncher who stopped you on the street. When he touched you it was to see if you were real. You were the dream he had in mind, which most men carry but never see. What is a man, Sherry? There's the stars he wants to reach. Here's the earth that stains him—and feeds him. He's as dirty as the earth. He was meant for the earth. But he can look at the stars. Look at yourself. You feel the wind, and the wind goes through your pride. What are you thinking of? The same things I

88

am. People die. They cheat and steal. What of it? Your hand is warm. You're alive, and so am I. Somewhere inside you there's only one thing important. You'd give up every other thing for it. So would I."

She listened carefully. Her eyes never left his face, her lips stirred gently together. When he had finished she drew a small quick breath. She murmured, "You're a strange man. I wish—" She turned away without finishing the sentence. Ten feet on she wheeled and with a note of vehement restless impatience, "Don't come here again," and continued to the house.

Mitchell rose to the saddle and set out on the road to overtake Tom Leathers, the steady canter of the horse shaking up a good deal of pain in him. This was the first time he realized how much of a battering he had taken in the fight.

He was up at seven and had his breakfast, but this morning, crippled in every joint, he surrendered his trip to the Aspens and crossed Race at a stringhalted limp. He went into the back room of Fred Henkle's barbershop and lighted a fire in the wood stove and he heated enough water to fill the tub. Stripped down, he lay in the tub to soak out the stone-set muscles of his body. The steam in the little room, and the stove's fire, presently made him sweat and he got a cigar from his coat and lighted it and kept on adding hot water until he was buried in it up to his chin. He yelled through the closed door, "Bring me something to read, Fred."

Henkle brought in a copy of the *Omaha Bee*. Mitchell lay back, plunged in pure comfort, and read the week-old news while sweat dropped down his nose and cigar smoke and heat condensed in the room.

Ad Morfitt dropped in. "Early in the summer for a bath," he commented. "I always wait till middle of

August. No danger of a chill then." He considered the ragged scars on Mitchell's face and the purpling round bruise at his left temple. "Kind of a scrap," he suggested. "Tom Leathers told me." He had on a vest and a coat and slowly grew miserable in the room's heat, not yet knowing what made him so. "Charley Fair sent out some boys this morning to take care of Torp and Logan. You know what you've done, Dan?"

"Sure. Jett don't like me any more."

"I wouldn't be funny about it," admonished Ad Morfitt. He dashed sweat from his forehead with the back of a hand. Round bright beads of sweat streaked down to the points of his mustache and dropped like crystals of steady rain. He rolled his eyes around this cubbyhole of a bathroom and got irritable. "Jett never bothered you. But you horn in, and he's one more man on your trail. You sure do everything hard."

"It was Bravo, Ad. That's why I went out."

"Bravo," said Morfitt pointedly, "never was a friend of yours."

"No," admitted Mitchell, "he wasn't. He was an old man going out alone. Just a weary old fellow with a star."

Morfitt murmured in wonder, "From you," and watched Mitchell a long while, at last saying with an obvious worry, "Never tell that to anybody else, son. It shows a soft streak, which a lot of men would like to know about. Don't ever speak of it again." He was at last soaked in his own juices completely and suddenly realized the cause. "Good God," he groaned, "I got to get out of here."

"That's right," agreed Mitchell cheerfully. "You're beginning to smell a little ripe."

He watched Morfitt depart, finished his cigar in due time, and left the tub, brick-red up to the water line of his neck. Dressed, he lay back in Fred Henkle's chair and was thoroughly content. Now and then there were small intervals like this, in which a man reduced himself to the simplest things and discovered profound satisfaction in them; they were stop stations along the line of a man's fast-running life.

It was middle-morning when he emerged from Fred Henkle's. He stood bareheaded in the sunshine to let the sun dry his heavy black hair. He looked down Race with his eyes half closed, knowing he had a call to make that would bring him no satisfaction. He had had his content, and now would have his trouble; this was the way it went for a man. Turning, he walked to The Pride and entered its empty semidarkness. His boots made round, barking echoes in the great room. One swamper, bowed over his broom, looked up and looked down. Jim Card, who was Charley Fair's chief houseman, stood behind the bar counting up racks of chips. His lips moved as he counted, but when he saw Mitchell he ceased to count and laid the edge of a resentful stare on the marshal.

It was the small things that usually told Mitchell the story, and from the averted glance of the swamper and the single stare of Jim Card he understood how it would be with Charley Fair. The word was out on Race Street that River Bend's marshal had gone too far.

He said, "Charley in the back office?" He caught Jim Card's curt nod and walked on. He went into the back office and closed the door behind him and found Charley Fair. Charley Fair stood at a back window, the tips of his maimed fingers jammed beneath his trouser band. A cigar made heavy steady rolls of smoke around his head and when he turned his face was square and dark and unmoved, and this too was a warning.

Mitchell said, "Tell Jett to stay out of this town, if he wants to live."

"He'll come in, sooner or later."

"Tell him what he'll find."

"I guess he knows what he'll find and I guess you know

91

why he'll come." The softness of Charley Fair's words was a danger signal; it was a sign of stronger feeling strictly repressed. And now he added, equally soft, "But that ain't why you dropped in to see me."

"No," said Mitchell, "it wasn't." Meeting toughness, he could also be tough. Fundamentally he gave like for like, a smile for a smile, a blow for a blow. He looked down on Charley Fair, who was a full head shorter, and he was as easy and composed as Charley Fair would ever be, and as ready for a quarrel. "You've got a chip on your shoulder, Charley. Better get hold of yourself."

"Me?" inquired Charley Fair in a marveling tone. "You come into my place and tell me that?" The cigar smoke swirled thicker around his face. "I like smart men, Dan. I don't like fools and I don't waste time with suckers. These last twelve hours you've been both. A fool for talk, and a sucker for stepping into a fight that meant nothing to you."

"You made your deal with Ed Balder," said Mitchell. "You sent word it was all right if Bravo got Jett Younger. What are you squawking about?"

"You're not that dumb," answered Charley Fair. "As against Bravo, Jett was able to take care of himself."

"That's why I went along. Somebody was selling out Bravo, which he knew. He was an old man sent out to make a Roman holiday for you and Balder." He had a cold cigar in his mouth and now took time to light it. He didn't put much accent on his words and still they were effective. They bothered Charley Fair. Mitchell saw that they did. "If I were you, Charley, I wouldn't be so proud of this affair. It's all right with you if the old man gets killed. You figured he would, which he did. But it wouldn't have mattered much if he'd managed to beat Jett to the pull. It was just a bargain. No, I don't think I'd be too proud of that deal."

Dark color filled Charley Fair's cheeks. His eyelids

pulled together, shutting out all but the narrowest streak of light. "I been watchin' you a long time," he observed, "and I figured you knew what your job was. Maybe you're forgettin'."

"No, I haven't forgotten," answered Mitchell. "I'm the man walkin' down the middle of Willow, keeping a straight line between your people and Balder's people."

"Then, by God," blurted out Charley Fair, "you better do it. You ain't now."

"No? Why not?"

Charley Fair threw away his cigar with a sudden cut of his arm. "I've seen a lot of you marshals come and go. I have watched you mighty close. You been smart, up to now. As long as you know your place and toe the mark it is all right. But you're gettin' a little proud. Half this town is over there," pointing beyond Willow, "and half this town is down here. As long as you know that, I'd say nothing. But you went out of your way to help Bravo, which was against me. I don't trust men very much, and it occurs to me I don't trust you at all. You're goin' lone wolf. Your britches are gettin' a little tight. That is just one step before the funeral, friend."

"Whose funeral, Charley?"

Charley Fair opened his eyes fully. In them was an expression reminding Mitchell of low tide on a coastal river, bringing to daylight the cold, dank mud-slime. There was no bottom to mud like that and no mercy if a man got caught in it. There was no mercy in Charley Fair. "It might be yours," said the saloonman.

Mitchell was smiling, knowing how that smile would lift Charley Fair's fury; it would sting and poison Charley Fair, it would leave its scars. He knew that, yet he would not hold the smile back. For he was dealing with a man who respected no weakness and no softness, and he meant to hit Charley Fair hard before he was hit. This was the way the game went, rough and without sympathy.

"Not yet, Charley. You and Ed put me on this job. Now let's see you get another man. Where's another man, Charley? You know what happens when you get rid of me? Then it is the merchants against Race Street. One of you will lose. Where will you be then, Charley? No, you're not ready to get rid of me. So I run this town my way."

"I been waiting for you to say that," said Charley Fair. "For I have seen it coming. I guess you forget how you got your job and I guess you forget who's been behind you. But when Balder and I ain't behind you any more you're going to be mighty lonely on top of that buckskin horse."

Mitchell turned from the office. At the doorway he paused to look back to repeat, "But not yet, Charley."

Fair called out in a strong voice: "What the hell do you want?"

"Why nothing, Charley. Nothing you've got or Ed's got. Nothing anybody's got."

"Nothing," stated Charley Fair, "is not much to be dead for."

Mitchell left the saloon and noticed Leathers and Dug Neil and Lou Hambie this moment turning down Ute. At the same time the Reverend Lonzo Piatt passed the Arcade and the Bullshead with his head flung up, as though challenging the sin around him, and also turned into Ute. Mitchell followed, threading the north side of town. He crossed the tracks, seeing a wagon standing in the cemetery with a dozen people around it. When he arrived Hambie made a motion and the nearest men pulled Bravo Trimble's coffin from the wagon—Mitchell and Leathers and Balder and the town drunk, Chappie Brink. They had a little trouble getting the coffin on the ropes, and some difficulty in lowering it. Platt lent a hand and Dug Neil said, "A little easy, boys. A little easy."

Standing back later from the grave, Mitchell waited for

the awkward silence to break. Balder was here, but Ford Green was not; and Mitchell had a better understanding of both men then. Balder had a decent heart. Big Annie and Rita, and two other girls from The Dream, stood apart, with Big Annie's homely face all one generous wreath of sadness. Colonel Jack Vinson's widow, who lived on Antelope and was River Bend's first citizen, stood between George Hazelhurst and Chappie Brink. Someone else rode across the tracks and dismounted. Turning, Mitchell saw Sherry Gault.

She came up to stand beside Mitchell. Chappie Brink dashed a hand across his blurred, half-destroyed face and looked around this crowd and seemed to see things others did not see. These people, good and bad, stood together under the hard downpour of sunlight on the empty plain.

Mitchell heard Lonzo Piatt say, "One way is the bullet and the other way is the Word. The bullet is the easy way, the Word is the lasting way. Why is man so cruel to his fellow man?" Mitchell felt the pressure of Sherry Gault's hand—unconsciously placed there—on his arm; and looking down he noticed that she wanted to cry but would not.

Lonzo Piatt said a few things more, then the group broke. For a moment these people had been completely together, making a small circle of warmth and defense against the great lonely arch of the world, and the meaning of it went fugitively through the mind and passed away before he could seize it, leaving behind the momentary heat and light of its passage. All humankind had its brotherhood. Sherry Gault quickly dropped her hand from Mitchell's arm, returned to her horse, and rode away. Mitchell watched the sway of her shoulders in the sunlight. Once, at the turn of Willow, she looked back and her eyes met his.

Ed Balder came up to Mrs. Vinson and took her arm. They went forward a short distance and then Mrs. Vinson

95

said something to him and sent him on alone. She came about and waited for Chappie Brink. Reaching her, Chappie removed his hat, shabby and small and derelict in the harsh sunlight. Mrs. Vinson smiled at him and spoke and Chappie gave her his hand for support and these two survivors of an earlier day walked in the direction of Willow. Mrs. Vinson had lived in the town's first log house and Chappie, once respectable, had operated its first store. As he watched them, the strange feeling came again—a second and mysterious warning of fraternity—and fled as swiftly as before.

They had reached Willow and there they stopped at the invisible deadline. Chappie raised his hat and stood bareheaded while Mrs. Vinson spoke. He shook his head slowly. Mrs. Vinson continued across Willow and in a little while Chappie wheeled and headed for Race, where he properly belonged. His pace quickened, as though thirst got into him. In another hour, Mitchell knew, he would find Chappie dead drunk in Race's dust.

Chapter Seven: The Very Clever Man

Ford Green's office was on the second-floor front of the courthouse and from this elevated spot he had his excellent view of Willow and Race. Patient in all things and having infinite faith in the power of scheming, he liked best to sit back in his chair with his feet on the desk and watch River Bend's people meet and pause to talk, and move on, and make their little crisscross journeys. A town was like an anthill, except that the people in it had less logic than ants, did more foolish things and wasted more energy. With rare exceptions none of these men who walked abroad in the sun had any really driving emotions to carry them along, any burning ambitions to justify their lives. They were nothing so much as shapes pulled about by appetites and greeds and fears and prejudices. Upon these emotions a clever man played.

He was clever, and knew it. He was also sly, but though he knew this too and had some self-scorn because of it, he never allowed himself to look that fact squarely in the face. A complete opportunist, he sat in this corner room by the hour and studied the people passing below him with his attentive interest, storing the revelations of their little acts back in an unforgetful brain. For he was one man in a small town on the farthest barren edge of the state. The state, whose complete attention he meant to have, now knew him not. This obscurity was a great rock blocking his progress. The way to move that rock was not by battering himself against it, but by finding the one spot beneath which a small pressure, skillfully placed, would roll it aside.

He had a sallow freckled face which no amount of sun could burn or color, and coarse black hair and a long nose and chin never meant for smiling; he was an awkward, rawboned plowboy, with a tremendous strength never used publicly and therefore never known. He sat now deep in the chair, a dour and ingrown young man whose lack of human and appealing qualities made him hate those who possessed them; whose drudging boyhood had made him early run away from home, to scheme himself forward to this little place of power as the county's district attorney; whose terrible hunger for a place in the world had at last centered itself in the one ambition to be a senator from his state. Inching himself patiently forward, he saw how he might achieve his will, and forecast some of the ruthless and unscrupulous things he would have to do—and looked upon those things with a bloodless fascination, certain that he was hard enough to do them, yet not altogether certain.

He saw Chappie Brink advance along Willow and throw a glance at the courthouse, and because he knew Chappie thoroughly he was not surprised when the town's drunk came down the hall to his office and stood in the doorway, his burned-out eyes dull in a face that once had been rather fine. Chappie said, "Maybe you've got an extra dollar."

"You tapped me last week," said Ford Green.

"Once a week ain't bad."

"You're pretty thirsty," said Ford Green.

"Sure—sure," agreed Chappie, made irritable by his craving. "Don't talk so damned much about it. How much I got to crawl to get a dollar?"

"Mitchell was in The Pride awhile back. Just smell around there. See if he talked to Charley Fair. See if you can find out what happened."

Into Chappie Brink's lackluster eyes came a resemblance of pride. "I'm no damned eavesdropper."

"You're a bum," said Ford Green, "and you'd do anything for a drink."

Chappie Brink lowered his head so that the little look of shame would not show, and he went through his private torture, to at last murmur, "All right, Ford. All right. But I can't go in there without money to buy a drink. They'd throw me out."

Green took a half dollar from his pocket. He said, "Catch," and deliberately threw the coin beyond Chappie's reach. Chappie Brink reached for it and fell, and crawled to it on his hands and knees. He got it and rose up and for that instant the pride he could not entirely forget caused him to throw a complete feeling of hate at Green. He turned and went out of the room.

Chappie Brink's weakness was whisky and his price was a dollar. Chappie Brink was the lowest level in this town, not much better than the brindle dog that hung about Big Annie's door; but all men were on one level or another, each with weaknesses, each with a price. Ford Green thought of this, watching Ed Balder come up Race. Balder's big weight presently groaned on the stairs. He came into Green's office.

"Not at the funeral."

"No," said Ford Green. "I was busy."

He knew immediately he had said the wrong thing. He knew he had made a mistake in avoiding the funeral and despised himself for being clumsy. Ed Balder gave him a queer glance and Green could see that the man's sense of right had been offended. Balder was big and slow; he was proud of his authority and in many ways he was narrow.

But somewhere in him was a streak of kindness.

Balder said, "You're mighty sharp, sometimes. No time to be sharp when a man's dead. He was your man. He liked you, depended on you, and did your chores."

"Better get the other county commissioners together and appoint a new man, Ed."

Balder's mind didn't shift that rapidly. He said, "Now and then I make a deal with Charley Fair—when I've got to. This one went bad. I'll never make another with him. Mistake to try to get the two sides of this town to work together on anything. He knew he wasn't promising a thing. He was just laughing at us. Jett Younger did the rest."

"Was that Charley's fault?" Then Ford Green added his afterthought: "Bravo had a good man along. He had Mitchell. Why not send Mitchell out again, with a posse?"

"No," said Balder. "Forget it. He's got trouble enough in town."

"Funny," murmured Green. "He goes along but still Bravo is killed."

Balder gave him a narrowing glance. "What's funny about it?"

Chappie Brink moved up the stairs to Green's doorway. He stood there with four-bits of liquor giving him a little life. It made him forget a great deal and it made him more sure of himself. He said, "Hello, Ed," and then he said to Ford Green, "Yes—and they had a quarrel about something. Where's the rest of the money you owe me?"

Ford Green took a dollar from his pocket and laid it on the desk. Chappie Brink came to the desk. He studied the dollar and lifted his glance to Ford Green. "The bargain was a dollar," he said, turned furious. "I got half of it already. You only owe me fifty cents. I don't want more than I asked for."

100

Green said, "Only change I got. What's the matter with you, you damned drunk?"

Chappie Brink picked up the dollar and went to the doorway. There he turned and suddenly said, "Catch," and threw the dollar with all his strength at Ford Green's head and stumbled down the hall.

Ed Balder said, "What's that all about?"

The dollar was on the floor. Green started to reach for it and changed his mind, his sallow face flushing. "Nothing," he said. "Chappie's getting insolent. Ought to be run out of town."

"Not in my time."

"All right." Green looked up at Balder. "I discovered something. Mitchell went to see Charley Fair and they had a quarrel. Did you know that?"

"No," said Balder. "I'm not his guardian."

But there was a revival of doubt in him which Ford Green saw. Green thrust his further talk into that doubt. "He's supposed to be on your side, ain't he? You sure he is?" Then, softly and with the cleverness he had, he added one more idea: "He never did like Bravo. Bravo wasn't his friend. Kind of strange he should go out with Bravo on that chase. And kind of funny Bravo should get killed. I been wondering all afternoon whose bullet got Bravo."

Balder said nothing. He turned from Green's office and tramped down the stairs. From his window, Green saw the big merchant cross Willow to his store, walking in heavy thought. Lying back in the chair, Ford Green had his weaving calculations. Mitchell was the law, tolerated by the gamblers and backed by the merchants. But in twenty-four hours Mitchell had made an enemy of Jett Younger, had turned Charley Fair against him, and had left himself wide open to a charge of playing both sides for his own benefit. The soft suggestion of treachery had unsettled Balder and Balder's faith would be disturbed,

101

and the whisper of doubt would go around town concerning Bravo Trimble's death. One by one, Mitchell lost his supports. Riding this town on the buckskin, he was a greater and greater target. Sooner or later he would be killed and the town, bereft of its authority, would go wild. That was the way with all these towns. When that happened, Green foresaw, it would be the exact moment for him to step in and clean up River Bend. Dramatically; so that his reputation would rush like fire across the state. This was how it was done. And now he was thinking ahead to one thing: he had to have a tough sheriff to step in when Mitchell fell—an outlaw with a gun and a star who would fill this town with terror. That had to be managed.

The train, two hours late, arrived at the depot and passengers stepped down from the cars and Bill Mellen hurried along Willow to meet the homesteaders who would be there. In a little while Mellen had a group around him on the platform depot and his arm lifted and pointed southeast into the flats. It was five o'clock, with the sun striking across the parapet of Willow's buildings. Mitchell came up Race on his buckskin. Ford Green lost interest in Bill Mellen, and looked down on the marshal. His lips, never very expressive, slowly moved together until they made the thinnest cut across his face. His green eyes lightened and began to glow with deep, cool fire.

Mitchell ate at his corner table while the light of day faded from the dining-room windows and the lamps began to gleam against their crystal ornaments. Sherry Gault came in with Ford Green and then Dug Neil and his wife and Harry and Juliet Sharpless—from the Star and Crescent Ranch in the Aspens—and all six made a cheerful group in the room; and once Sherry's eyes lifted, as though reluctant, and her glance came to Mitchell with its sober search, rousing in him an emotion stronger than any other human being could produce. At this moment she was for Mitchell the only living thing in the room, her face softly lighted and softly shadowed, her shoulders straight and graceful, her presence creating its beauty and its imperative call. When he passed her table on the way out she dropped her glance and deliberately ignored him. All he saw in that brief interval was the dry face of Ford Green turn to him and to Sherry in a careful appraisal.

Night came black and soft and warm to the town. Shadows lay solid against the unlighted walls of Willow, respectability once more drawing its skirts clear of the renewed bawdiness on Race. He went on to the stable, brought out the bucksin and moved into Race, into the yellow heat of its outshining lights, into the boiled-up dust of arriving Texas men camped on the edge of town, into the quick and wild and free calling of voices, into all the old smells and odors which emanated from men in their loose moments. This town had two characters, one by day and one by night, and those characters lived uneasily together by necessity; and someday would openly clash.

There was no difference in this night from a hundred nights that had gone before. His fight with Cap Ryker had seemingly made its little ripple in the current and had dissolved. Each night was a new night with new faces and new voices, with new quarrels and new laughter. Yet this newness was a deception; it was only a repeated echo of man's old hunger for release after long and lonely times on a dusty trail; and the voices said the same things and the quarrels rose from the same white-heated sparks of primitive vitality and pride. And beneath this apparent forgetfulness, old grudges lay solid and changeless, and of all these grudges the most enduring was the Texan's hatred of a trail town—and of the man who sat on a horse and enforced its law.

Nobody saw this or felt this so acutely as the man on the horse. Idling down Race, he watched the faces before him and beside him. He listened to the laughter and to the resonant tones of those voices speaking—seeking to catch in this confusion some meaning for him.

Jim Card stepped from The Pride and said to him, "You seen Hazelhurst?"

"No."

"He ain't shown up," said Card. "Time he was at his table."

Passing beyond Briar, he noticed a man at Naab's shooting-gallery. This one took up a .22 and dropped the moving ducks one upon another and put down the gun, swinging about. His glance came directly to the marshal and though that face was only one more face in the ceaseless tide of faces coming steadily out of Texas, Mitchell saw the man's lids immediately creep together. In one more moment Mitchell had pased on, but warning flowed from that man and rang its clear bell in Mitchell's body. After a year in the marshal's saddle, he had come to catch obscure changes like that; there never was any doubt, never any need for reasoning. In this little world he was the center, surrounded by the rush and play of hidden emotions. They were warm breezes blowing against him, and then one cool current came across his face out of nowhere—and by that he had his signal.

He turned at The Drovers' and cruised up Bismarck Alley, hearing the long, strenuous laughter of men in Straight-Edge Lizzie's. Coming out by Brinton's stable, he saw a fire burning on the prairie beyond the end of Willow, illumining the homesteaders and wagons camped there. Over the distance he heard them singing. He wanted to go out there but the bell was still ringing in his head and he pushed the buckskin to the head of Race and looked down it. The Texan who had been at Naab's now moved slowly across the dust to the Arcade's front. He stopped there and swung his head, scanning the lower end of Race. Observing him, Mitchell discarded the notion that this man had come up the Texas trail. There was nothing tangible on which he could pin this change of mind. This too, like the original warning, was only a cool current in the warm light, but it was sufficient. Then the man, quite slowly searching the alleys feeding into Race, at last faced the head of Race and saw Mitchell and realized Mitchell had been watching him. The man dragged his cigarette makings from a pocket. He lowered his head and built himself a smoke.

The big bell in the courthouse tower struck its sullen nine-o'clock curfew notes. Mitchell reversed his course and rode through Antelope's serene stillness. Now and then some sharp sound javelined over the parapets of Willow Street's buildings to disturb this genteel quiet—a single warning reminder of the live and trembling lava of human behavior on which the town was built. The blinds were up in the front room of Balder's house. In there, all grouped in idle comfort, were the Balders and their guests, with Sherry Gault among them. Mitchell pased on but that picture remained, clear in every detail—the picture of grace as seen by a lone outsider riding by. The town, young and raw as it was, had its social barriers. Willow Street was one barrier, meant for the toughs; but here on Antelope was another, across which no man or woman passed to enter those comfortable rooms unless silently approved by the genteel. He had never been in Balder's house. He was a marshal who rode on Race Street, who was touched by its dust and evil, who had that dust and evil on his boots; he would never enter Balder's house. Respectability had its rigid code. Needing its chores done, it hired a man to do them, yet once giving that man pay to do those chores, respectability closed its

105

social doors on him.

He passed Gatewood's house. The door was open and Gatewood made a small, narrow-shouldered shape in it. Gatewood said, "Wait, Dan," and came down the walk. He put his hands on the gate pickets and looked up and showed Mitchell a puzzled face. "Have you seen Irma?"

"No, Will."

"She went out for a walk. She likes to walk in the evening. But it is later than usual. I wish she wouldn't do these things. After a long, hot day I'd think the comfort of a porch would be good enough."

He was an urbane and polite man with some notions of culture. He was one of the town's steady and faithful citizens, the kind to worry about its schools and its water, the kind to form a library committee and to complain about broken sidewalks. He had his education, which he would never forget, and in his quiet way he would feel himself a crusader in a far raw land for the gentle and neat and ordered treasures of living. When he died there would be a dozen small, useful monuments to testify to his worth, none of which would bear his name; for he was the little, civilized man who worked his way in diffident background from sense of obligation alone and denied himself ostentatious display as he would have denied himself a sin.

"If you see her," he said, "please tell her it is time to come home."

"Will," said Mitchell, "the night's for walking."

"What?" asked Will Gatewood.

"Heaven's up there somewhere," Mitchell said. But he quit on that, for there was no way of reaching this good and sober and heatless man's precise mind, no way of bringing to him the fire and sweep and disordered, prodigal wonder of life that his wife Irma now walked abroad to feed her soul upon. He added, "I'll tell her," and moved down Antelope. Then he recalled that George

106

Hazelhurst was missing from The Pride and for a moment he thought of Hazelhurst and Irma Gatewood, recognizing them both as lonely ones who had no real place in this town.

He circled the depot, listening to the dying simmer of the engine, and rode the middle dust of Railroad Avenue. There was nothing but the track and open prairie to his left, but on the right side the black walls of buildings were against him and the blacker mouths of alleys made their ink-dark stains. As he rode he sat deep in the saddle, with his legs pushed against the stirrups and his rein hand lifted and ready to swing the horse. For a moment tension caught up with him—in memory of the other time he had been ambushed here; and tension remained until he reached the foot of Railroad and pursued Cattle Street to the foot of Race. In passing Race, he gave the street a long survey and found the man he had earlier watched now gone.

The night was mild. Race, swinging into the heart of the revels, had so far offered no trouble. Out on the prairie the campfire of the homesteaders burned its round disk against the black and he went that way, hearing voices, roughened and turned drowsy by weariness, come across the earth.

Irma Gatewood had been in the coach perhaps a quarter hour when she heard Hazelhurst come along the cindered runway and pause at the coach steps. He would be struggling of course with his own sense of right, for she had watched him a great deal and had come to believe that, either in spite of his trade or because of it, he had a very strong sense of honor.

She had never doubted he would come. She had never doubted, since speaking to him, that she would meet him. This was a part of her life surely marked out to happen, regardless of her marriage or her feeling of self-respect or of what the world might say about it. So deep was this

107

feeling of inevitability that when she asked herself if she felt shame she could not honestly say that she did. What she actually felt was a great content, as though, after silence and oblivion and a blind threshing around for some kind of glory in her life, this was happening. It was nice to have a man look closely at her and see her as a woman.

He came into the back end of the coach. She said, "I am at this end," and listened to him move on. He stopped beside her. She saw him vaguely against the car window. She said, pleased by the warm, full happiness his presence brought, "Sit down here."

"Mrs. Gatewood," he said, "I have done some foolish things in my life. You must know that. But if I should in any way hurt your reputation I'd never forget it. I shouldn't be here at all. Do you understand?"

"Then why did you come?"

"You asked me to come," he said.

"You could have stayed away."

"No," he said. "You knew I couldn't stay away."

She said, "Sit down," and watched him turn in the dark and take the opposite seat. She had not been mistaken in him. Whatever else he was and whatever his past had been, he possessed his sharp rules of right and wrong. They were not the gentle and flexible rules of Will Gatewood. They were the hard-formed rules of a man who had lived a dangerous life, had made his errors and saw them very clearly. A sinner, she thought, knew so much more about morals than a saint. But he had noticed her and her word had brought him here and the sense of that importance and power was like drink, filling out her tissues and making her giddy. She had been unimportant and unnoticed so long.

"This is our train," she murmured. "Where is it taking us? Would Paris be too far?"

He said, "Better not let yourself dream, Mrs. Gatewood. You will be badly hurt in the end."

"I do a lot of it."

"So have I. You see what I have become from it."

"What else can I do?"

"No use building a better world in your mind. If you do, you'll be living in it half the time and feeling miserable when you're not. Make the best of the world you've got—the world made by the folks of River Bend. You can't get away from it. You'll just get hurt if you try."

She said, "Which is real, my world or theirs?"

"Don't ask me that, Mrs. Gatewood."

"You ought to know," she told him. "River Bend's no more your world than mine."

"I made mine," he said. "You see how poor a job I did of it. If you want me to be bitter about these blind and selfish and petty people walking up Race and down Willow, I can't oblige you. Maybe some of them are blind, some of them stupid and selfish and little. But they're as happy as I am. Happier. They live more useful lives. They will die in peace."

"No," she answered, "I don't want you to be bitter about anything. What's the use of that? But if this isn't our world why can't we find one that is?"

"Escape?" he said. "I have tried that too. You can run to the bottom of the earth. It will still be like River Bend."

"Then," she said, "the difference is in me and in you. If there are only two of us, that's enough. Two people can make the biggest world of all."

He said very slowly, "You should not have asked me to come. I ruin whatever I touch."

"I have often been sad, often ready to cry for want of somebody to speak to, somebody to feel in the wind the things I feel. But I've never been afraid." She reached out her hand in the dark, toward him, and her voice was musical and warm. "Touch me."

Mitchell rode out to the homestead camp and found Bill Mellen squatted at the fire, spinning stories of the land's richness to the half-dozen men around him. Women stirred in the background and somewhere in a wagon a baby cried, the strangest and most gripping sound to Mitchell.

He said at once, with concern, "Sick child?"

One man drawled, "No, just cuttin' teeth."

Mellen said, "This is Dan Mitchell, marshal of the town."

"I wouldn't want your job," spoke up another homesteader. "A hell of a town. A sink of rottenness."

"Good and bad," said Mitchell.

"What's good in it?" asked the homesteader.

"The same good that's in you," said Mitchell.

"What?" said the homesteader and thought of that remark carefully. Bill Mellen looked up at Mitchell with interest.

Mitchell said to the homesteader, "This man Mellen lives in the town. You think he's bad?"

"That's different," said the homesteader.

"Everybody's different," said Mitchell. "Everybody's good—and bad."

He was a mystery to them and he was saying things they didn't understand, for they remained silent in the way of people who, disagreeing, do not wish to argue. They had never ridden through the heart of a town night after night, watching the actions of people with the eye of care. They had never seen blackness and whiteness live side by side in the same woman, or courage and fear alternately surge through one man. They didn't understand him. Mellen, who saw all this as he saw it, smiled

110

and shook his head, whereupon Mitchell idly changed the subject.

"Where are you taking these people, Bill?"

"Chickman Flats."

"Only eight miles from town," commented Mitchell. "That's coming close."

"Everything on Bear Creek is just about taken up. Country's filling."

"My father," said the most talkative homesteader, "homesteaded Iowa. I never thought much about it, but it is a fine thing to stand on your own ground and sift the dirt through your fingers. Poor man's country."

Mellen rose from the fire. "I'll be by before sunup in the morning. I'll lead you out."

The fretful child had ceased crying. One of the men said, "Let's have some coffee," and a young woman moved up from the wagons. She looked at Mitchell steadily. She had a broad, undisturbed face; she had deep yellow hair and a strong shape and for a moment Mitchell saw her against the land, against the sun and the hard winds, untouched by it. She still held her eyes to him when he turned away and moved townward with Bill Mellen beside him.

"You're a funny one," said Bill Mellen. "I just don't think you give a damn."

"For what?"

"For anything."

"Solid lot of people back there."

"Someday you'll see something."

"What's that, Bill?"

Mellen shook his head. "I've been called a damned fool too many times. So I won't say—until it happens. Look, Mitchell, what happens to you when the trail's gone and your job's gone?"

"Another job, I suppose. In another town."

"You see? You don't care." Bill Mellen had always

111

held a reserve toward Mitchell and now said so frankly.
"I don't know whether I like you or not. Maybe I could if
I tried. Some point there I never took time to think
about."

"Not important, maybe," said Mitchell idly.

"You see? You don't give a damn. You don't tie to
anybody. Man that wants friends has to open up. I get the
impression you sit four feet above this town, laughing at
everybody."

"No," said Mitchell, "not laughing."

"The nearest I ever heard you speak out was tonight,
about people. Maybe that's why I'm talking like this now.
Of course, there's another difference. I'm an Easterner
at heart. Never fired a gun in my life. You're something
else. Dig right down and that has some unpleasant
aspects. A killer, for instance."

Chapter Eight: Heartbreak

They had reached Willow. Bill Mellen continued on to Webber's House while Mitchell turned into Race. For a little while at the homesteaders' fire he had been relaxed and off guard. Now the weight of the town came hard against him again, like a voice on his shoulders. It was 11:30, with all the hitchracks crowded and the deep, strong rumble and shout and cry of the crowd passing from the saloons and dance halls. Riding abreast The Pride, he saw a Texan come out and pause on the walk. He wheeled over at once.

"Riding or staying?"

The Texan looked up, deviltry shining in his eyes. "Maybe I'll stay."

"You're wearin' a gun. If you're staying, go back and leave it at the bar."

"Maybe I'll leave," said the Texan, amused.

"You're not sure?"

"Hard to make up my mind."

"I'll make it up for you. Pull out."

"Why," said the Texan, "now I know I'll stay, and to hell with you."

Mitchell put the buckskin onto the walk. The buckskin, clever in all this, wheeled against the Texan

113

and flattened him to The Pride's wall. Mitchell reached down and caught the Texan at the back of the coat collar and swung the buckskin into the street. He had the Texan at a drag and he moved up the street with the Texan cursing at him and turning under his arm like a loose pole. Mitchell rode the buckskin to the jail-office door and stepped down. The Texan stiffened for a fight but Mitchell hit him on the ribs with an elbow, flung him around, and pushed him into the jail office. The Texan backed away, his eyes shining yellow in the light. Mitchell gave him a careful look and saw that he wasn't really dangerous. He moved in suddenly and lifted the Texan's gun. He hauled out his keys and opened the cell door.

"Sure," he said, "you'll stay. You'll stay until morning."

"I've heard about you," said the Texan. "I've heard a lot about you. See if you can put me in that coop."

"Friend," said Mitchell, soft as wind, "don't make me do that."

He hauled up in the middle of the room and stared at the Texan with an expression completely unreadable. The Texan sighed. He looked down at his hands and he shook his head and stepped into the cell. Mitchell locked the door after him. He grinned at the Texan.

"When you buck the tiger, friend, you've got to figure to get scratched."

"You're the fellow that busted up Cap Ryker. That's it. Why, now, I wouldn't like to be you at all."

Mitchell crossed toward the door and suddenly he was thinking of the other man marching somewhere in the night. Maybe this was a play. He turned around. "You got a partner in town?"

"My crowd's in The Pride."

Mitchell swung to the buckskin and cruised down Race, passing a group of men at The Pride's corner. They had seen him handle the other Texan and now they watched him in suggestive silence, nursing a pride of clan into stronger shape. There might be a break come from this, maybe on the next round after they had plenty of time to steam up. When he skirted The Dream he saw Tom Leathers stand with a shoulder against the dance hall's doorway. Texans moved in and out and brushed him as they went by. Leathers paid no attention, being completely engrossed by what he saw. To Mitchell he seemed less cheerful than usual, and he was sober. Mitchell crossed Sage and cut the corner of The Drovers'.

Leathers, having no better use of his time, made a swing around the outer edge of town and came down Race to take his stand at The Dream's doorway, watching the crowd. The Texans made hard work of their fun. They boomed into the dance hall as though time would presently end, claimed some girl standing on the floor, and began to shout for the music, which was a piano, a guitar, and an accordion. When the music started the Texans whirled and stamped and collided and cut their little jigs, serious as death and howling as they moved. Precisely at the end of two minutes the music ceased, regardless of melody, and the girls automatically swung their partners to the bar. The girls drank ginger beer, which was harmless, the house got a quarter, and the Texans, glistening with sweat, once more began to shout for music.

There was only one girl Leathers bothered to watch and he watched her with the sharpest interest of which he was capable. These girls were necessarily robust for the work they did and all of them had been trained by Big Annie to smile and be gay. Rita was the lightest of the group and her smile, Leathers observed, was a thin, mechanical glow, soon dying. When she went whirling around in the arms of a Texan she closed her eyes, as though exhausted. Leathers endured that for a brief while and moved straight across the hall at her. The music was on point of beginning and another Texan came in beside Leathers to claim Rita. Leathers simply moved the Texan aside with a straight-armed shove. He had the makings of a first-class quarrel on his hands at once, for the Texan promptly surged back to Leathers.

"Hell with you," he stated. "I'll tear your damned ears off."

Leo Soames, who was The Dream's bouncer, stepped into this immediately. Knowing Leathers, Soames shoved the Texan out of the way. Soames was six feet four inches tall and weighed two hundred and eighty pounds and he simply put his hand on the Texan's chest and walked him straight out of The Dream.

Rita looked up at Leathers, expecting to be seized and hurled around at the break of the music. Leathers waited for her quick, meaningless smile to come, but she only watched him, pale and black-eyed.

"I'll sit this one out," he said and led her to a table at the back end of the hall.

"Ginger beer?" he asked.

"No."

"Then the house will get no percentage out of this deal."

"You're not drinking?" It was only a way of making talk. She sat back in the chair, at his pleasure for the next two minutes, docile and uncomplaining.

"Came to town to get drunk," he said. "Something keeps delayin' it. Man's got to be in the humor to make a sucker of himself. I started out with some mighty magnificent intentions. What happened to them I don't rightly know."

She said, "I guess you've always got to have good reasons for doing things."

116

"Me?" said Leathers. "I'm just a fellow the wind blows around." He thought of nothing more to say, and so sat still.

Rita's shoulders were round and dropped and her energy seemed to die. She looked down at the table, waiting for him to speak, and presently, when he let the silence run, she lifted her eyes and gave him her black, soft glance again. "Do you want me to talk, or do you want to dance?"

"No," said Leathers. "You don't have to entertain me."

"That's what I'm here for."

"I'm wonderin' about that."

She showed her first animation. "Don't ask me how I got here."

"No," he said, "I never ask questions. The fool-killer gets people who do that."

She put her elbows on the table and bent forward and caught his attention with her eyes. They held a thousand years of pain and trouble, they had things in them that should have made her tough and bitter but he had never seen bitterness rise to the surface of her resigned face and there was no mark of this brutal life on her. It was that fact which struck him most of all.

"If you're through with me, I'll go."

"That's all right," he said. "I'm no spellbinder."

"It isn't that," she told him. "I guess I'm afraid of you. You make me remember too much."

"Never knew I was anybody's conscience."

"I know what you're thinking. You're thinking I shouldn't be here. You're wondering how good I am and how bad I am, and how it happened, and whether there's anything in me worth bothering about. It is just the way you look at me. I wish you wouldn't. If you've got to watch me, do it like these other men do. I'm used to that."

"I might look at some women like those fellows do," he

117

said. "But not at you."

She shrugged her shoulders. "If there isn't anything more—"

He said, "No, nothin' more," and watched her leave the table. She stood in the center of the floor, small and yielding and patient. A Texan ran in from the door and seized her, crying shrilly through the hall, and as he whirled her away she closed her eyes. Leathers got up suddenly from the table and left The Dream by a back door.

It was near midnight when Mitchell rounded The Drovers', and some of the Texans had now collected in the street to ride beyond the river to the held herds. He threaded Bismarck Alley, passing the glow of Big Annie's curtained windows. A man came through a between-building space and arrived at the alley and fell flat in the dust, groaning softly. Mitchell reached the back end of Naab's shooting-gallery and rode near its black margin. The buckskin, stepping at a steady pace, flung up its head and in the dark Mitchell saw its ears strike forward. Weight pushed its way through him again and in the uneasy quiet of this alley—down here where came the backwash of Race Street in formless echoes and strange, faded laughter—a warning rubbed across his skin. He was abreast the back area of Brinton's stable; and here the buckskin halted and swung around, its head pointing straight at the back area.

Everything turned fine and this and the run of time stopped; and in these suspended moments he lived the fullest parts of his life, waiting for the unexpected and the unexplained—waiting, too, for his own one clear impulse. That impulse arrived when he heard the buckskin exhale a strong blast of wind; his heels came down hard on the buckskin's flanks and he pushed fast into the area. The buckskin stumbled on a roll of wire and swayed aside and up from the pitch-black earth came a roar and a short thread of blue-tawny muzzle light, foreshortened because of its nearness. A man lay on the ground hard by and now fired a second time and seemed to be rolling to gain his feet. Mitchell hauled the buckskin close about. He had his gun free and he fired three times, spotting the shots on the earth. He hit nothing, for he heard no cry following; but the buckskin, whirling like a dog, charged again and its feet struck solid material, and it bucked aside and was brought back by the quick pressure of Mitchell's arms, and its feet struck that shape again and brought up a short yell of agony.

Mitchell dropped from the saddle and hit the man below him full in the belly. The buckskin, trained and responsive as it was, backed nervously away from any further contact with man. Mitchell flattened himself full weight against the ambusher. He let his weight remain and he brought one forearm across the man's windpipe and held it there until resistance died. Reaching along the man's arm he cauaght hold of the gun and got it and threw it into the deep rubbish beyond him.

A shade flew up from the window of Big Annie's house and a woman looked out and pulled the shade down again. Men were running through the between-building spaces and one of them called, "Who's there?"

"Ad," said Mitchell, rising from the earth, "give me a hand. Send one of those fellows behind you for Doc Utten."

Somebody dogtrotted back through the dark toward Race Street. But he had no need of going far, for the sound of firing had reached through town with its signal and now somewhere in the alley Doc Utten's voice calmly called, "Trouble here?"

Mitchell said, "Pack this fellow to where we can get some light on him."

119

Ad and one other man joined Mitchell. They lifted the still man on the ground and lugged him down the narrow way of Briar Street to the corner of Race, and up to the jail office. People came out of the saloons and a crowd moved in and collected around the door.

Mitchell said, "Put him on the floor," and stepped back. This man was the one he had earlier seen at Naab's shooting-gallery. The buckskin's hoof, striking him hard on the head, had left its round, swelling bruise; it had knocked him out so that he lay insensible, with his eyes open and unrecognizing on Doc Utten, who bent down and searched him with inquisitive fingers.

Mitchell said, "You know him, Ad?"

"He's been in town before," said Ad Morfitt.

"New to me," said Mitchell.

Tom Leathers pushed his way through the door and took one indifferent look at the victim. "Name's Irish Jones. I saw him couple weeks ago out in the brush."

"Alone?" said Mitchell.

"No, he's one of Jett Younger's crowd."

Mitchell had been interested in this man but suddenly no longer was, now that the ambush had been explained. He said to Utten, "A bad bump?"

"He'll come around."

It was beyond midnight. Mitchell said, "Your town, Ad. Tell him to clear out when he wakes up."

"Better lock him up," suggested Ad.

"If we locked up everybody that wanted to shoot me," observed Mitchell, "we'd be running a full-sized boarding house." He reached the street and swung onto the buckskin, who had followed him from the alley. The town was emptying and here and there lights went out and darkness slowly crept into Race. He turned about, riding toward the head of the street, and his eyes lifted and he saw Sherry Gault framed in the window of her second-story room in the hotel, watching him. He raised his hat

120

and all the dark weariness went out of his face and he smiled at her, that smile a long flash against the bronze of his skin.

For her part, looking down at him, she saw the strangest most unsettling picture at that moment. The lights and shadows of Race Street made a sullen glow and dust rose heavily like sulphur smoke—and out of this glow and smoke and evil he rode, a man emerging from the pit of hell. Each day he descended into those depths and was lost in the slime and heat, surrounded by the crying and the lust and the malevolence of sinners—and each midnight, the long tour done, he reappeared; and now his shoulders lifted and he smiled at her and turned to Brinton's stable. She watched him disappear in the stable and presently emerge and go down Bismarck Alley.

She had admired him. She had felt the tremendous pull of the picture he made against Race Street; for a little while she had been more than a spectator, and for a little while she had shared his pride and deliberate insolence toward the shapes waiting around him to pull him down. But as he walked into Bismarck she lowered the blind of her room and wheeled away with a long breath; and then she hated him and all her distrust rose and all her doubts about him grew strong.

Mitchell started down Bismarck but turned back and stood at the edge of Brinton's a moment to watch a single shape moved forward from the depot, well shadowed by the wooden gallery along Willow. When this lone shape reached the lights of Webber's, he recognized Irma Gatewood. She came slowly abreast of him, on the farther side of the street, and she had her head lifted and she seemed to be watching the sky. He had a fair view of her face for a moment and it struck him that she walked in a dream and was aglow with that dream's goodness. Once in a rare while he had seen a completely free spirit; and she was such a one, detached from the earth and forgetful

121

of it, and happy. She passed on around the corner of Neil's, toward Antelope.

Looking back on Willow, he now saw Hazelhurst come along. Hazelhurst arrived at Race and had some impulse to turn into it, but presently he continued on. He stopped near Brinton's to light his cigar, and by the matchlight Mitchell noticed the bare, stonelike set of the gambler's features. The match died and afterward Hazelhurst discovered Mitchell.

He said, "Evening, Dan," and started on. He had not gone three paces before he swung around aroused by some thought, and came back. He stood before the marshal and he looked into the marshal's face with one steely, searching glance. He said nothing and Mitchell said nothing, but there was between them a passage of understanding. Hazelhurst threw his cigar into the dust and made a strange, shaking gesture with his head and walked away.

The last outflung shouts of the departing Texans pulsed over River Bend's building tops and faded. Mitchell followed Bismarck and turned into Big Annie's parlor. A bell tinkled somewhere in the back quarter of the house and Big Annie's voiced called, "I'll be right in with the toddy." Rita sat on the stairway, arms tightly hugged across her breasts. Hearing him come, she looked up to show him the bottomless despair in her eyes.

Mitchell stopped before her, looking down without speech. She had been a pretty girl and still was pretty except for her eyes; in them was a gray forsaken stillness. Out of somebody's home she had come to be one of the girls in Big Annie's, but of all the girls she alone still remembered what she had been, still had some remnant of self-judgment which came terribly into her mind.

He was a man in whom the sight of suffering left its broad painful track; behind all his toughness, the soft spot lay. For that reason alone he had gone into the hills

122

with Bravo Trimble. Now, when he saw Rita so cramped and tortured by her thoughts, so brutally caught in a world too big for her, his pity came again and, without speaking, he set himself down on the step beside her and took her in his arms as he would have taken a little girl and listened to her sudden burst of crying rise out of her hopeless heart.

He had heard women crying before; in this town it was no novelty. He lived his days in the midst of broken people and the wreckage of dead faith. Yet he had never heard crying so deep and hopeless as this. The girl's tears dropped on his hand and her body shook and turned in his arms. Big Annie came in with the toddies and showed her instant resentment at Rita's troubling Mitchell. She started to speak, and was stopped by Mitchell's expression. She went on to the front room and put down the toddies. She came back to the hall, standing formidably there.

"When a girl cries," she said, "she's got regrets. And when she's got regrets she don't belong here. A dance hall is no place for tears."

Rita pulled herself away from Mitchell. She sat lumped over, staring at the floor. "That's all right, Annie. I just got to thinking. Hard to stop that."

Leathers came in and saw all this and stopped at the door. He held his hand on the door and looked at Mitchell. Neither Mitchell nor Big Annie paid any attention to him and Rita didn't see him.

"Thinking you could go back and start fresh?" asked Mitchell.

Rita shook her head. "I know better than that. But still I can't help thinking."

"Maybe it wouldn't be so hard to do. Starting fresh, I mean."

"How?" asked the girl and lifted her head. She noticed Leathers and her face changed. She put a hand across her

123

eyes and flattened the tears. She looked at Leathers as though he were a stranger, so that he said, "Maybe I don't belong here," and started out.

Rita said, "It doesn't matter."

Leathers turned back to say something, but once again the others disregarded him. Mitchell was speaking.

"Move two hundred miles away from here and who would know you? Out on the desert there's a thousand men mighty glad to have a wife, no questions asked."

"What would I tell a man like that?"

"Ah," said Big Annie, "tell him nothing. What would he tell you? Tell him nothing."

"You can't start by cheating."

"The bargain starts after you marry him not before," Mitchell answered. He had his mind on this, he was planning it out deliberately. "Annie, you rustle around Race Street the next few days and raise five hundred dollars for her. We'll send her to Omaha. She'll take a train from there to Texas."

"What would I do in Texas?" asked Rita.

"Find a man and marry him. Take care of his house. Raise his family. Fair enough bargain, isn't it?"

"He'd know," said Rita. "Even if I didn't tell him. He'd look at me and know."

Mitchell shook his head. He was trying to think of the right words. There was no hard and fast distinction between right and wrong. Sitting on the buckskin, he looked down upon this town and saw the mixture of sin and purity, saw the white that was in people, side by side with the black. "Looking at you," he said, "no man would ever know. Listen to me, Rita. If one mistake damned a man or woman there'd be nothing but hell down here. If we couldn't start fresh every morning this would be a sad place full of sinners."

Big Annie, thinking along practical lines, said, "I'll raise that money in five minutes."

124

It was Big Annie and Mitchell who did the talking. Leathers said no word at all. He stood in the background, a careless man turned grave. He watched Rita with so close a glance that it made him seem severe; and it was to him that Rita turned. She looked at him a long while and then she said in her colorless voice:

"What would you do?"

He shook his head. "Don't ask me."

Rita put her eyes on Mitchell. "It is too late," she said in a dull, all-gone way.

Mitchell made a shrewd guess. "Maybe there was another man once."

"Yes."

Mitchell shook his head. He turned away. "There's nothing you'll be able to do about that."

"Ah," contradicted Annie, "a man's a man. One husband is as good as another. No man in this world is worth a year's thought."

"Wrong there, Annie," said Mitchell.

"You're sentimental," said Big Annie. "All men are, as long as it costs them nothing. If there was but one man for one woman, or the other way around, where would this world be? A woman takes the best she can get— which is sometimes a terrible choice—and does the best she can."

"You can't wipe out what's in your head," murmured Mitchell.

Leathers said, "Wish you'd both get out of here."

Mitchell and Big Annie stared at Leathers, who stood solemnly by the door.

"Go on," he urged. "You're both talking like a couple of damned fools."

Big Annie snorted. "From you," and disappeared into the rear of the house. Mitchell shrugged his shoulders and left.

Leathers went over to the toddies. He said, "A favor to

me. Drink this. I can't drink alone." He was himself again, cheerful and not caring about much. "This has been hangin' over me a long while. Drink it, sister. Never was a medicine like it."

"I don't like it very much," Rita said.

"Right now," he said, "you're doing a man a favor. How."

He watched her sip at the toddy; he watched her quite a while before he took his own drink. She had to sit straight when she drank, and she gave him a shy, doubtful glance and at that moment he saw one pure shine of innocence that struck him so powerfullly he had to take his eyes from her. She wasn't accustomed to whisky; it took very little to bring color into her face.

He said, "Move over," and sat on the steps beside her. "Those people mean well," he added in a confidential voice, "but they take life mighty serious. What's to grieve about? This earth still turns. Why water it with tears when there's rain enough in the sky?"

She said, "I feel strange."

"That's the halfway mark on a glass. When you get to the bottom you'll see something you never saw in your life. I'm just taking you on a little journey. You're holding my hand. I'm the old man that's been there before."

She had her head averted from him. She asked, "Are you looking at me like you always do?"

"No," he said, "I'm just goin' along with you. You're three-quarters down the glass and you ain't dizzy any more. I know. This is the place when the doors start opening and you're seeing things as they might be if folks hadn't set up such a damned-fool set of rules. Kind of pretty, everything is. Take that rug. Ever see such a nice shade of red? Well, it is like being a little girl again when you didn't have anything to worry about and you could do anything. You could walk in the sky, you could run

126

faster than the wind, you could lie in the grass and watch a grasshopper's eyes get big as plates."

She turned to him. She watched him closely. Her lips loosened and he saw dread and shame and old memories thaw. She was just a girl, a pretty one who had traveled alone too long. There were no scars in her, not one. She said—and would never have said it without this whisky—"I can tell you why you look at me that way. You want me to be better than I am. Why do you want me to be?"

"I guess," he said, "you didn't read right. I have been wonderin'—what made you think you got off the track? Listen to the old man who's just takin' you where he's been before. I see a girl who's got white teeth and black hair and a way of makin' a man remember her by her eyes. Nobody—this is what you sort of forgot somewhere along the road—nobody who knows what goodness feels like has ever been bad."

She said, "Where did you come from?"

Half an hour later Big Annie, having climbed the back stairs, came along the upper hall and stared down. Leathers had found a bottle of whisky in the house. He had emptied half of it and he sat cross-legged on the floor. He was telling a story and making Indian motions with his hands and his face was full of laughter. Rita sat on the step with a shoulder against the newel post; she watched Leathers and she listened to him and she was smiling at him with a relaxed, soft forgetfulness. Big Annie studied the girl's face for a considerable time and marveled at it and went quietly back down the hall.

Here and there in the saloons a few men played a last game and occasionally a gambler came out to stroll quietly along the shadows and Ad Morfitt cruised Willow's farther block, his boots clacking into midnight's silence. Mitchell entered Webber's House and climbed to his room. Lighting a cigar, he stood at the window, looking down on a town whose goodness and evil alike slept.

When day's vigil was done and the tight strain of nerve and muscle began to go, he had his time of reflection. Standing thoroughly alone at the window, he saw the town more clearly than anybody else saw it and wondered about its ending—and his own ending.

For his life was inseparably connected with the town. He was tied to it by a thousand things, by the enmity of Charley Fair, by the endless intrigue of Ford Green, by the pity he had for Rita, by the affection he bore Chappie Brink and the trust that broken little man had in him, by his pride and his hatreds and his loyalties, by a streak of compassion which other people had never seen in him, a compassion for all these people of River Bend who worked their little ways on the hard soil of the prairie and had their longings and hidden tragedies and their courage.

He saw both sides of River Bend. The merchants of Willow and the genteel families living in Antelope's quiet had their moments of narrowness and greed, yet according to their own lights they were just people, conscious of their obligations and laboring to keep the town alive. Living in sun and dust on the raw edge of civilization, they dreamed their dreams of goodness and had their desires, and were practical enough to make their bargains when bargains had to be made.

Race Street, too, was part of this town, catering to lusty appetites that called to be fed, and in this same sun and dust Chappie Brink lived with his memories and his moments of decency and Rita had her hungers for goodness. Standing above the dark and quiet streets, Mitchell felt the presence of all these people, and knew of their silent crying and of their unspoken words and of the things that were common to them all, high and low. He knew them better than anyone else; the deeper he saw into them the more tolerant he became of them.

But no town stood still and no deadlock lasted. Little by little the silent maneuvering went on, isolating him. Cautious and unrelenting in the background, Ford Green slowly cut the ground from beneath him. He had lost the grudging neutrality of Charley Fair, he had made an open enemy of Jett Younger. One by one his supports fell away, leaving only Ed Balder. Even Balder had his doubts and those doubts would grow and someday Balder, seeing a better way of running the town, or believing the steady whisperings of Ford Green, would turn against him.

. . . *I should turn in my star now*, he thought, and moved from the window. But he knew he never would. The memory of the little people held him—and one other thing held him. Having been marshal during the town's fair weather, he could not run before the storm. Lying in bed, he considered these things, listening to stray small sounds move through the hotel. At the end of the hall Sherry Gault slept—and the thought of her broke through all other thoughts as a cold, tonic wind.

Mrs. Balder was giving a tea and she had tables on a porch which ran around three sides of the house; and here in the shade the ladies of Antelope, very pretty in their summer dresses, idly sat and exchanged the little things they had to say, and made those little things important by the inflections and dramatic pauses they used. At the head of the steps there was a bowl of lemonade for the youngsters who had come along with their mothers, which was a bribe for decent behavior. Young Dick Lestrade knew it and sat on the ground in the angle between steps and porch with his hat pulled down over his forehead and thought of the shadows the big bridge cast on Spanish River and of the deep cool pool under the bridge. There was a stringer on the bridge which stood twenty feet above the water's level, so that one long straight dive took a fellow deep down. His mother had said, "For my sake I want you to stay in Mrs. Balder's yard and be nice to Estelle Louders. She's your age. Why don't you like her?" Estelle and the other children were somewhere behind the house but Dick Lestrade sat here, hidden from the women, and thought about the river. Now and then the sudden gusts of talk came down to him and went away.

Sherry Gault sat on the south side of the porch, watching the blue-and-brass shimmer of heat along the horizon. Great streamers of dust rose on the river road where trail herds moved slowly toward the loading-pens. Beyond the river other gray-raveling clouds showed where new herds moved up from the south and threw off to wait their turn. Drinking her tea, she considered the ladies idly and smiled and was polite and selected the little bits of gossip that interested her in the steady chatter.

Irma Gatewood moved up and paused. She said, "I thought you'd be in the hills, with weather like this."

"Warm there, too," said Sherry. "And lonesome. All the men are in the timber, riding trail."

Irma Gatewood said, "I know," and when she smiled her eyes had a kindness. Her face was soft and she moved along the porch and didn't really seem to be with this group; her mind was somewhere else. After a while she made her excuses and departed. Sherry watched the girl adjust her parasol and go along Antelope, small in the hard sunshine; and for some reason which Sherry had no way of explaining she felt sorry for her.

Louisa Pallette spoke in the lightest voice: "Will Gatewood's a nice man, but I think I'd prefer a more

130

robust husband."

Marion McNab murmured, "He's most courteous."

"Ah," replied Louisa Pallette, "but that seems to be all." Some of the ladies smiled, whereupon Louisa Pallette blushed. "What a silly thing for me to say."

"Well," put in Sherry, "I suppose we must have our gossip."

Mrs. Balder had been standing attentively by, large and formidable. "Gossip's gossip," she said, for whatever it meant. "More tea, Sherry?"

It was three o'clock. Estelle Louders came from the back of the yard and whispered some shocking atrocity in her mother's ear, and was sent away. Mrs. Louders murmured carelessly, "Georgie, it appears, tripped her," and gave Mrs. Snow, who was Georgie's mother, one of those smiling glances in which venom dwelt. Dan Mitchell came into Antelope on his high buckskin and moved down the middle of the street. Abreast Mrs. Balder's porch, he lifted his hat and passed on.

Sherry looked at him with that swift and complete interest his presence always brought. He sat straight-legged on the saddle, one arm full length, one arm lifted a little with the reins. He seemed very long and the sun turned his face deep-bronze and the edges of his hair showed a heavy black beneath his hat. The hat lay raked on his head and his body moved with the horse and seemed to have no weight to it; he was a grave man who seemed to smile and to be apart from them and yet to be judging them by his own standards; and so he turned the depot corner and was gone.

His passage had left its effect. Sherry noticed that Mrs. Balder followed him with her glance as long as he remained in sight, very clearly hating him with all the power of her solid will; and it was not heat alone that lifted the color of her cheeks, for she said, "Why does he ride down Antelope? Race is where he belongs."

131

Sherry said one sharp word: "Why?"

Mrs. Balder, surprised at the tone, lifted her brows. "That's the part of town he's hired to keep order in, isn't it? Those are the people he touches. He's one of them. Everything they are, he is also. I do not like him. I never have. Ed picked him for that job and you'd think he'd be grateful to Ed. But he has talked to Ed as though Ed were no better than Charley Fair. Ed shouldn't put up with it a moment. I've told him so. But it isn't only that."

"Then what is it?" asked Sherry, now roused. She wanted to know. Anyone connected with Mitchell summoned her instant attention—as though she wished to see him for what he was, as though there were parts of him dark to her which had to be illumined.

"He's as bad as anything on Race Street," said Mrs. Balder. "Never—never once has he lifted a finger to clean it up. The same crooked men are here that were here a year ago. The same women. Where does he go when his job's done? To Big Annie's. He's hand in glove with all of them. He's one of the crooks."

Sherry didn't answer. She was surprised at the resentment she immediately felt toward Josephine Balder. This big, ample woman had a truculent nature; she had tremendous energies and she liked to be fighting. She had, Sherry knew, tried to organize a reform movement in the town without much success, and her failure only deepened her antagonism against everything on Race Street.

Josephine Balder looked around her and said in a lower voice, "Why do you suppose Mitchell went into the hills with Bravo Trimble? He was no friend of Trimble's. Trimble was Ford Green's friend—and Mitchell hates Ford."

All the ladies glanced at Sherry. There was a moment of discomfort on the porch. Sherry said, "Then why did he go?"

"Hasn't Ford told you all this?" asked Josephine Balder.

"I don't ask about Ford's business."

"It wasn't Jett Younger that killed Bravo Trimble," said Mrs. Balder. "It was Mitchell who did. He wanted Bravo out of the way."

Sherry rose and spoke with a thorough irritation. "Who told you that? Ed?"

"Ford," said Mrs. Balder, "told Ed. Not outright, of course. He simply let it drop as a hint. A hint is enough, isn't it?"

"Is it?" said Sherry. "Why should Mitchell want Bravo out of the way?"

"A deal," said Josephine Balder. "A deal with Charley Fair. Mitchell is very close to Charley Fair. Bravo did something Charley didn't like."

"What was it?"

Josephine emitted a slicing breath of exasperation. "How would I know that?"

"You seem so sure of everything," pointed out Sherry.

Mrs. Balder cast a sharp glance on Sherry. "It is odd to me you'd doubt something Ford said. After all—" She let the rest of it stand as implication.

Sherry said, "I do not know that Ford said it. If he said it I do not know that I believe it."

"He's your man," pointed out Josephine Balder.

"Perhaps," said Sherry. "But he didn't see Mitchell shoot Bravo."

"There are ways those things get around."

"Yes, there are. And some of those ways I don't like." Sherry, never anything but blunt, put her feelings into the briefest of phrases. "It is the same as shooting a man in the back. Mitchell's a very broad target. It is very easy to stand in the dark and ambush him. I wouldn't be very proud of that. If I had something against him I'd meet him face on."

The rebuke took effect. Mrs. Balder's color deepened and her anger grew plain. "Why don't you tell Ford that?"

"I will. I'd tell anybody that."

Mrs. Louders, wishing to break the growing embarrassment, said, "Josephine, could I have some more of that delightful cake?"

Hidden in the angle between steps and porch, young Dick Lestrade dreamed of the pool under the bridge and heard nothing until the mention of Mitchell's name broke through his dreaming. Mitchell was one of his silent worships, and Bravo Trimble had been one of his gods. Now in complete stunned attention, he listened to Mrs. Balder's revelations. He knew these were things he shouldn't have heard and presently he got on his knees and crawled along the base of the porch wall until he was on the far side of the house. Rising, he circled the house and walked toward the depot.

He reached Willow and went slowly along the street with his head down, struggling with the terrible wreckage those few words had left behind him. He was twelve years old and his loyalties were great loyalties, without which he felt empty and forlorn. He came up to the arch of the Wells-Fargo barn and stopped, so deep-sunk in his thinking that he had not realized he had stopped. A voice came from far away, saying, "Hello, Dick," and he raised his head and found Mitchell on the buckskin in the middle of the street. Mitchell was smiling at him.

"Hello," said Dick in the hollowest voice possible. His face was pulled together and there was no light in his eyes. This, from a boy who had always seemed to glow in his presence puzzled Mitchell.

"Trouble?" asked Mitchell.

"No."

"You know," said Mitchell in his conversational tone, "a friend's a friend. Anything I can help you out on?"

134

"Nothin'," said Dick, and turned away. But he only took a step, and swung back. Loyalty died hard but the words of his elders were words he had never learned to doubt, and Mrs. Balder had said everything plain. "You didn't kill Bravo?" he asked. "You didn't do that—even though you didn't like him?"

"Son," said Mitchell, "who said that?" He had been smiling, and no longer was. He said, "We've got to talk about that," and started to leave the saddle. Dick Lestrade turned away and broke into a run. Mitchell called after him, "Son—wait a minute. Wait up for me." But young Dick was crying and would not turn his face to Mitchell. He ran down Railroad Avenue, out of sight.

Chapter Nine: The Tiger Growls

Mitchell stepped from the saddle, watching young Dick Lestrade run away; and then he swung back to the saddle, every instinct pushing him to ride on and overtake the lad and mend his heartbreak. But he did not. He sat still, knowing that he would do no good now. Realizing this, a feeling of pain passed through him with the cut of acid. Nothing, not even the tragedy of Rita, hit him as hard as the lost faith of young Dick.

The boy's disillusion was his disillusion. This one scene, crueler than any other had been, brought home to him the fact of his vulnerability and his isolation. When a man wore the star he opened himself wide to slander and doubt, to whispered hatreds and jealousies and dark suggestions; a man with the star was a target. All this he had earlier realized and had closed his teeth firmly against making any answer. He had learned to smile and be silent, he had come to know the things behind other men's eyes when they watched him—the soft, quick, fugitive things running there even as they spoke and were friendly. All that he had toughened himself against. But Dick Lestrade's destroyed faith broke through and got at him.

He turned down Willow. Sherry Gault came from

Antelope and moved toward him. The sight of her brought him out of his preoccupation and when he noticed that she was closely watching him he swung over to the walk and lifted his hat.

She said, "I want to talk to you. I have heard—"

She stopped the sentence. Looking across Willow, he saw Ford Green come from the courthouse at a long-legged and slightly hurried gait, as though he meant to break up this scene. Even at the distance the signal of dry jealousy showed on his pale freckled face. Sherry said, "Tonight, as soon as it is dark, I'll ride out to the bridge."

Ford Green arrived. He removed his hat and divided his pale-green glance between these two people. Suspicion showed in the glance and suspicion edged his voice and made it arrogant. "I'll walk along with you, Sherry."

She was an independent girl, she had her own will. Ford Green's suggestion hit her wrong, for she lifted her head and gave him a full stare. "I had not said I was ready to walk along."

He showed a greater irritation and a more stubborn insistence. "When you're ready to walk, I'll go along."

She made it a point to delay. She said to Mitchell, "Why was Dick Lestrade crying?"

"He'd heard bad news."

"Maybe," she said, "I could help."

"Someday," he said, "it might be mended, but not now."

She turned on Ford Green. "If you are still in the humor, come along."

Mitchell lifted his hat. Green, stung by the rebuke, put both arms behind him and marched beside Sherry Gault, past Balder's store toward the depot. Mitchell turned down Race for another circle of the town.

It would be, he realized, Ford Green who had started the rumor of his killing Bravo. This was the way Ford worked, moving toward his aims with all the noiseless

137

stalking of a cat. He passed Poe's saddle shop and nodded at Poe in the doorway. Poe was usually a pleasant man; now he only nodded back and in his eyes was a reserve that had not been there before. The rumor had reached Poe as it had reached others. All through this town, in the past twelve hours, Mitchell had found that strange withdrawing from him and had not understood it. Now he did. He turned down Race, one sharp ache in him when he remembered young Dick's face. At the foot of Race Street, just before he circled The Drovers', Chappie Brink came out of Horsfall's livery, violently shaking and terribly in need of a drink; and though he said nothing he was silently begging for help.

Mitchell said, "Chappie, I owe you four bits for currying my horse," and got a half dollar and dropped it into Chappie's hand. Chappie had not curried his horse; it was a fiction which both of them understood, meant to save that little shred of pride still burning in Chappie's ruined body.

Chappie said, "You know what's goin' around about you?"

"I know."

"You know where it started?"

"Yes."

"By God, Dan," said Chappie in his rasping voice, "somebody ought to go after that man." Then he said, "I believe I'll go get a bite of breakfast," and turned up the street, traveling faster and faster toward The Pride. His breakfast would be four whiskies and a free lunch.

Sherry Gault strolled along the galleried walk, past Balder's and Tarleton's millinery. Ford Green's attitude had roused her ready anger and now his sulky silence infuriated her. She said, "Ford, I want to talk to you. Did you tell—"

138

He said, "Not here, Sherry," and looked carefully around him.

Gatewood moved up the street and said, "Hello," and passed on.

Ford Green's eyes inspected this street and he murmured again, "Wait."

This caution rubbed Sherry Gault wrong. She said with a cutting scorn, "What are you afraid of—your shadow?"

Ford Green sank deeper into his balky temper. His jaw lengthened and his long legs stamped against the walk harder than before. They passed the butcher shop and crossed Willow's dust to the depot and walked along until they were well beyond it. Ford Green would have gone farther but Sherry stopped.

"Now, Ford, what have you been up to?"

"First," he said, "there was no call for you to make me cool my heels while you chinned with Mitchell."

She threw the challenge back at him without delay. "When did you become my guardian, Ford?"

"Ain't it understood—"

"Nothing's understood. Maybe there's one thing you ought to know. I'll talk to whomever I please at whatever time I please, for however long I please. You came across the street with the idea of carrying me right away from Mitchell."

"The man's no friend of mine," said Ford Green.

"Makes no difference," said Sherry, carrying the attack to him. "You're not to interfere with me. Don't you know that yet?"

He didn't answer and he didn't meet her straight glance. He looked past her into the drenching late sunshine on the desert, his eyes half closed. He was silently resisting everything she said, listening to her but not agreeing and never meaning to agree. Behind his softness was a stubbornness, she observed, as great as her own. More than that, he now showed a streak of surly ill nature. She had not particularly noticed this in him before; the pressure of the last few days had begun to pull out the things he had so long been careful to conceal. She didn't like what she saw.

"If you were a woman you'd be pouting," she pointed out. "It's the same kind of a look and has no place on a man's face. Buck up, my friend. You don't like to be crossed but you had better make up your mind to take a licking gracefully when it comes. This time you're taking one. You don't run me, Ford. Never try."

"Let's just forget it," he said, very dry and disagreeable of voice.

"That's not my style. What have you been telling about Mitchell around town?"

He looked at her for the briefest of moments, quick and searching, with his eyes springing open; and again looked away. Slyness made a momentary appearance. "What?" he said.

"Ford, don't beat around the bush with me."

He seemed to debate with himself and when he spoke it was in a balanced, thoroughly cautious manner. "I simply said that I wondered why Mitchell, who was certainly not Bravo's friend, should go into the hills with Bravo. Let's walk back."

"What else did you say?"

"Sherry, let well enough alone."

When aroused she had the ability to rough a man up with her talk. "Don't crawl and creep and duck, Ford. Stand straight."

His sullenness grew in the increasing projection of his lower lip and he spoke as though the words were wrung out of him. "I said how could we be sure it was Younger who killed Bravo. Let's walk back, Sherry." He turned away, expecting her to turn with him. Five feet away her voice came after him.

"You walk away now, Ford, and you'll keep right on walking as far as I'm concerned."

He wheeled, half crying, "What do you want out of a man!" He came back, so stirred that he forgot to be cautious.

Looking deep into his eyes, she saw that he had danger in him, physical danger. It pleased her a little to see this and took a part of her contempt away. "You must be pretty proud, Ford. Whispering sly little things behind the man. There he is, out in the open. It's very easy, isn't it, to skulk around him, out of reach of his fists?"

"You think I'm afraid, Sherry. Afraid of him?"

"What I really think is that you've been cautious and clever so long that you've forgotten how to stand up and fight straight. You know you have nothing to base those whispers on. You know nothing more about that fight than I do."

"I told you once," he reminded her, "he was in my way and I proposed to get him out of my way."

"If you want to fight him—fight him. But do it straight!"

He said, "You think he'd fight straight?"

"As far as I know him—from what I've seen of him—I think he fights no other way."

"Fine, fine," said Ford, full of unhappy irony. "Which man are you marrying, him or me?"

Always she met her challenges head on, and met this one so. "If you are unsatisfied, Ford, we'll call it off right now."

She was astonished at his reaction. He came down all the way from anger to a worried answer: "Oh, no, Sherry. Good Lord, how is it possible for you to talk that way?"

"I'm not too pleased with you right now."

He stood silent on this, high and lank and ungainly, his freckled dry face pointed with thought. He wanted to

141

express himself in the right words. She saw his struggle to find those words. Presently he said, "I have a great ambition, Sherry. I'll let nothing stand in my way of it. Politics is never too clean. In a town like this it is pretty dirty. But that's the game—the only game I know. I started pretty low in life. I mean to go pretty high. A man doesn't mean anything unless he puts out all he's got to get someplace. Don't judge too strong. I do what I've got to do."

"Why," she said, really pleased with him for a moment, "go as high as you please and do what you've got to do to get there. But don't scurry and don't duck. Stand up."

They went along the cinder path, with nothing more to say to each other. They walked up Willow as far as Balder's store. She stopped here and Ford Green removed his hat, coming as close to a smile as it was possible for him to do. His courtesy was unexpected, for he was not a particularly courteous man, never thinking of the little gestures. Paused here, she really had her first complete view of Ford Green. They had gotten all the way to an engagement without her ever knowing the deeps of his nature, without her very great interest. Now that she thought of it, this lack of interest was a strange thing, and when she analyzed it in her logical mind she was somewhat shocked. Perhaps she had never really cared too much, perhaps all this had been a matter of indifference to her, never really touching her heart.

"I'll see you later," he said, and went away.

She watched him cross the dusty street and asked herself one very pointed question: *How much do I care?* and suddenly closed her mind before the answer came. Love, to a woman, meant the world turned over, it meant the difference between living and not living, the difference between light and dark, cold and heat. It meant a full heart, a wild, strange, and ever-changing feeling, it meant all the colors and all the sounds, it meant a thousand unexpressed thoughts; it meant talking and giving, it meant feelings that ran all the way from rich goodness to cruelty; all things full and nothing empty; it was something proud and abject, something like a slashing winter wind and something as hot as a bed of fire. If it was anything it was all of this. She still watched Ford Green move across the street.

Mitchell, making his swing of the town, came into the south end of Willow and then her glance whipped away from Ford Green and she forgot him completely. Mitchell was a black shape against the yellow light and his shoulders swayed a little as he rode.

The secret sense of power so necessary to Ford Green had been pretty well knocked about during his talk with Sherry Gault. Now he returned to his office and lay back in his chair, watching the street below him until the feeling of personal strength came again. Within the four walls of this office he was always a bigger man than he was any other place.

For a little while the scene with Sherry kept troubling him, so that he rehearsed it, giving her silent answers and better answers in his justification of himself. Then he at last put all this away and thought of the man he must have in River Bend to take charge when Mitchell was knocked out. It was up to Balder and Dug Neil and Tom Franzen, who were the county commissioners, to appoint a new sheriff, but he foresaw that they would abide by his word if he presented the proper man.

He meant to get one of those men common on the frontier, one who wore a star yet was hardly better than the outlaws they were sworn to take, a rough one who had a killer's reputation and gloried in it and was always ready to add to it. With this kind of fighter, Ford Green proposed to lay waste Race Street, to tame it and destroy it. It was essential to him that he destroy Race Street so thoroughly and dramatically that the news of it would sweep across this state, an example of swift and terrible vengeance made upon sin by one incorruptible district attorney. When he killed Race Street the town of course would die; for there was no other great trade remaining to support it. But that was an immaterial by-product.

It was late afternoon, the sun near the western rim. A homesteader's wagon pulled down Race Street, filled with a family heading out toward Chickman's Flats under the escort of Bill Mellen. Back in a corner of Ford Green's busy mind a side-thought had its brief play: there were a lot of homesteaders drifting into town these last few weeks. Then the thought gave ground to the things more urgent. He had his man in mind. Tonight he would catch the stage for Pawnee and see Bill Bexar, who was the marshal there. Time was growing short. Mitchell had about reached the end of his tether and one of these days would hang himself or be hanged.

He picked up his hat and left the office. He crossed to Balder's store in the sudden still clear light that precedes dusk and met Balder at the doorway.

"Ed," said Ford Green, "I'm going out tonight to see a man you might want for sheriff. I'll bring him back for you to look at."

"No rush," said Balder. "The county can run without a sheriff for a few days."

"Might be later than you think—right now," commented Green in his suggesting, mysterious voice.

"Why?"

"You might want a strong sheriff on hand pretty soon," said Green. "Where would you be if anything happened to Mitchell? Suppose he quit, or was killed? Suppose he turned against you? Suppose Race Street just rose up and went wild, with nobody to stop it? Where

144

would you be then?" He was again sliding his doubts into Balder's slow head. Knowing his man, he dropped those little acid fragments into the stream of Balder's thinking and then changed the subject. "I'll bring this man up. Do what you please. But no harm in looking at him."

The southern stage was making up by Neil's big barn and would leave in another half hour. He had time for dinner and so turned himself toward Webber's. As he turned he saw Mitchell swing out of Brinton's stable and also advance toward Webber's. Green moved steadily on, now reminded of that earlier scene in which Sherry had rebuked him in front of Mitchell. Without his knowing it, his pace quickened, and this man who was usually a complete master of the things in him now became a puppet of those things, never aware of it. In the space of three steps he had decided he would enter Webber's before Mitchell.

It was a small, obscure desire rising out of pride and jealousy. When Mitchell came before Webber's door, the late-arriving Green reached forward and caught his shoulder and flung him away. Not until then did he realize how every cautious precept of his life had gone out in one single tide, how completely he had turned into that kind of man he so much despised, at the mercy of old savage instincts, of thoughtless rage and sheer ego.

It was then too late to turn back. Mitchell straightened and surprise showed on his face and was covered by tight amusement—as though this was something he had wished for and never expected. "Ford," he said, "you have been eating meat."

There was no answer Ford Green could make, no logical thing to say, and for this he hated himself and saw himself in a poor light and grew more greatly enraged. He stood still, blocking the doorway with his angular shape, without reason for doing it but powerless to give ground. All he saw now in Mitchell's eyes was that growing brightness, that complete understanding. Mitchell knew. Mitchell, who dealt with the errant and the proud and the sinful and the violent, looked straight into him and fathomed the queer promptings which had placed him here.

People moved up from the darkening street and one sharp voice seemed to send a call all down Willow. "Look at that!" This was the oldest story in town but it was new now, because it was Ford Green who prowled River Bend's dust and looked for trouble instead of a wild puncher off the Texas trail. He saw Balder in the background. He saw Chappie Brink staring at him with the greatest expectancy he had ever seen on a human face. He saw Dug Neil. There were others around him, for the smell of a fight went through River Bend like lightning. It sickened him to think of it, yet he could not move and he could not shake away from the blind, ever-heating rage that grew into obsession.

Suddenly Mitchell quit smiling, and spoke one actually gentle phrase: "Never mind, Ford. Turn around and go get your supper."

Mitchell stood above him, seeming to look down from a height. He was a flat and serene man, taking this situation securely within control, and now he was offering Green a way out, he was giving ground deliberately to save Green's pride. Everybody, Green understood, caught this humane impulse. It changed everything, it turned the evening black, and Green's hatred grew to fury because he could not endure this other man's unhurried mastery. There was still nothing for him to say but he could no longer remain still and so, obeying the oldest of impulses, he dropped his head and rammed himself at Mitchell, his arms going out in a great sweep to imprison the marshal.

Behind Mitchell was a four-by-four post, supporting the wooden gallery of the hotel. Mitchell lifted his arms, knocking Green's arms aside; he had stiffened himself for

146

Green's plunge but Green's weight, thrown out in the one violent lunge, carried him back against the post and the post gave way and fell and the two men went down in the dust with the dust rolling around them. Green let out a pure yell—of anger, of relief, of animal exuberance, that had no meaning. He was on his knees, clawing in the dust and half blinded by it, seeking Mitchell, who had vanished.

Mitchell was on his feet, speaking from a distance. "All right, Ford. All right."

Green hauled himself up. He swung, seeing Mitchell balanced beyond range. He dropped his head again and ran in. Mitchell hit him full on the cheek and stopped him. Green set his teeth against the raw streak of pain that cut all the way through him to his legs. Mitchell was a shadow before him. He put out his hands, catching Mitchell's blows. Mitchell moved around him slowly. Mitchell's smile was gone; there was a dark, drawn steadiness on the man, a thin ever-watching glow in his eyes, an infinite patience that could wait for the kill to come.

Green, pivoting to match the marshal's steady circle, suddenly felt rage again and flung himself forward. He took Mitchell's swinging fist on the head and he heard the magnified crack of Mitchell's knuckles. He brought up his hands and knocked down Mitchell's arms and closed in. He hit Mitchell in the belly and drove him across the dust. Mitchell struck a wall and the wall echoed all down Race Street. Mitchell came away from the wall, elusive in the first evening shadows, and closed in and beat him across the temple and seemed to fade, and came out of the shadows once more and slashed him in the neck and over the bridge of his nose.

Thunder rolled through Ford Green's head and the light of day faded. Reaching out without vision, he caught Mitchell's arms and clung to them and closed in and drove his knees up into Mitchell's belly. He roughhoused around the dust until his head was clear, and sprang back. He hit the edge of the collected crowd; he half turned and struck at the crowd, and turned against Mitchell once more, lowering his head and charging. A barrel—a water barrel that had been standing at the edge of the courthouse—came rolling out of nowhere, catching him at the knees. He went over the barrel, falling into the dust. From the distance again he heard Mitchell call at him:

"Here, Ford. Up here."

He was blinded, he was stunned; but he was not beaten. He had ceased to feel hurt and he had no fear. He got on his feet, crouched low, watching Mitchell move slowly sidewise. He gritted his teeth and dropped his head and drove up. He reached Mitchell with his fists. He felt the solid, wonderful impact come back along his arms and he felt good because of it, he felt new and fresh and unbeatable. He lashed out, straight at Mitchell's head, seeing that head bob aside; and thereafter one great smash landed on his mouth and a hole seemed to open in his stomach and his breathing stopped and there was no power in his arms and no strength in his legs. He fell to the dust.

Somewhere men began to talk and a boy's voice yelled: "He's gettin' up!" He had not known this until the boy spoke. But he was on his knees in the dust and he looked down and saw that he was in this position. He saw blood dropping steady from his face to the dust. He lifted his head and wanted to rise but could not. He said:

"Mitchell! My legs won't work! God damn you—I can't get up! If I could get up I'd fight you all the way down this street to The Drovers'!" He turned to cry at the astonished crowd around him. "Balder, there—give me a hand! Don't stand there staring! Get me off the ground! I can lick that man! By God, I will!"

148

Mitchell was still before him, his hazel eyes round and very watchful. "Your judgment was poor for once, Ford. You're pretty sly and mighty clever. Stick to that. Don't pick a fight with a man who knows nothing but fighting. Walk through Webber's door and eat your supper. That's what you started to do."

"I'm not finished," ground out Ford Green. "Oh, no! I'm not through!"

He talked to a crowd slowly dispersing. The novelty had left this scene and darkness stirred like a tide and lights broke yellow into the dust and Texans began to arrive on Race Street. The crowd drifted away and Mitchell moved off into the darkness. Ford Green pulled himself to his feet and braced them until strength began to return. He watched Mitchell go and he was proud of himself for what he had done; and he knew he would never again possess those faint small doubts of his own courage. That was gone. He could do anything.

The southern stage was now in front of Webber's, waiting out the last ten minutes. Ford Green started toward the courthouse and cut through Ute to reach his house on the edge of town, intending to clean up before the stage left. Crossing Bismarck, he saw the shape of a man break out of the darkness lying so heavily against Brinton's. He heard Chappie Brink say:

"You got a lickin'. Never thought I'd ever have that pleasure. You know, Ford, I'm drunk, and when I'm drunk I see a lot of things I could do and maybe ought to do. Here's one of 'em—"

Green watched Chappie Brink's arm lift, and he saw that Chappie had gotten a gun. He stepped forward, saying, "Just a minute, Chappie," and his arm came down in one hard cut that knocked the gun out of Chappie's hand. He pushed Chappie back and he lifted the gun from the dust. He came up against Chappie, watching Chappie's white face rise.

149

Chappie said, "I guess I'm too old to do what I want to do." That was all he said.

Ford Green, remembering the insolence that was in Chappie Brink's eyes, hit him over the head and watched Chappie drop. Then he turned back to Willow and got aboard the stage and in a little while he was on his way south.

Mitchell walked back to the jail office and found Ad Morfitt there. He said, "What you doing here this time of the day?"

Ad, so usually weary and in need of sleep, displayed a rare burst of feeling. "I'd of slugged that damned crook if you hadn't busted him down. You took a lot of time doin' it."

"The man's tough, Ad. Tougher than we think." He washed at the sink and brushed his clothes and combed his hair. He had scuffed off the skin on his knuckles and he had taken a couple of bad blows on the face and chin. After every fight and after every night's run of this town a let-down always came, bringing its wonder. It came now. Standing in the room, he took time to light a cigar and make his little speech to Ad:

"What's a man do these things for? There's better things in life than to roll in the dust like a dog. There's easier ways of living. There's fun in the world somewhere if a man could only look for it and get at it. What am I doing, Ad?"

"That's what Tom Leathers has been tellin' you," pointed out Ad. "It is what I have been telling you."

"Someday," said Mitchell, "I'd like to pull out. Someday I'd like to go up to my ranch in the Aspens and sit on the porch and let the world go by. That's a man's proper life. Not a bad ranch if I ever took time to run it. At night I can look down into the desert. I can see the lights of the train forty miles away. I can see the glow of this town. You know, Ad, I'd like to quit."

"Why don't you?"

"No," murmured Mitchell, "not now. I can't."

"Sure. They all say it. Time comes when a marshal gets to thinking he's the only one to run the town. Nobody else can handle it. I've seen a lot of marshals. They all think the same thing. You know what it is?"

"What is it?"

"Pride," said Ad. "A marshal's got to have a hell of a lot of it to stand the job. If he didn't have it wouldn't last at all. But it gets the best of him finally. He's on parade all day and pretty soon he can't step down. Pride."

"It may be," agreed Mitchell, "but I can't quit now."

"No," admitted Ad, "you can't. Things have gone too far. Most of the ground's cut from beneath your feet. Now you got to stick it out, come good or bad. I told you that too. Your time for quittin' ran out a while back."

"Sure," said Mitchell. "That's it." He moved to the door, watching dusk and dark sweep into the town, watching riders boil up dust as they pased, watching lights strengthen all along Race. "Pretty in a way," he reflected. "A damned sinful street, Ad. But still, it is made up of people. All kinds of people and, bad as they are, most people are good. A lot of these folks on Race deserve a square deal. That's why I'm staying on the job."

Ad said, "Where you going now?"

"Out for a little ride on the desert."

"Be careful where you ride," warned Ad.

Chapter Ten: Under the Bridge

Mitchell returned to Brinton's and took out the buckskin. Full dark moved rapidly over the land and he knew Sherry would be waiting for him at the bridge. As he left the stable, Neal Brinton said, "You ain't had supper."

"No," answered Mitchell and moved toward the end of Willow. It was an idle question asked by a man who was his friend, yet it drove home a point to Mitchell. All his acts were under close scrutiny. Many eyes in this town closely watched him throughout the day, some with liking and some with hate. Between sunrise and bedtime he was a target for the town, so constantly before all these people that he ceased to be a man and became instead a symbol to be defended or destroyed.

Night was soft and warm. He passed the campground and noted that several fires burned on the earth, illumining the scatter of wagons and homestead people bedded down for the night. He had come to accept the casual stream of immigrant settlers; it had gone on day after day, causing no particular stir in town. But tonight, seeing this group, he was suddenly aware of the fact that these people, so quiet in their passage, had grown into a steady current. The desert was filling up in certain districts, and now he recalled the idle phrase of Bill Mellen's: "Something's going to happen to this country. I won't say what that will be until it happens."

The big wooden bridge across Spanish River was a faint bulk in the night. Beyond it, wide-scattered on the prairie, the many cook fires of the Texas trail herds made their round-orange spots. Half a moon threw its dull-silver glow on the ground and wind breathed out of the south with its blend of bitter-strong earth odors, driving that salty vigor deep into Mitchell, so that his weariness and the dark aftermath thoughts of the fight and his black speculations concerning River Bend went away. Nothing stood against the raw and good smell of life; to whatever depths a man descended and to whatever impassable abysms he came, this smell of the earth was the one reviving tonic. The earth was man and man was the earth and dust was his portion and out of the dust he got his strength, his fertility, and the prime fire for all his dreams.

He cut a circle on the prairie, watching his back trail with a close eye, reached the river, and dropped down its bank to the edge of the water. He came in this way to the dark area beneath the bridge decking and saw Sherry Gault's horse vaguely standing before him. He dismounted and moved forward and saw her; she sat on the ground, silent and waiting, and when he dropped beside her, coming within the circle of her presence, he saw her face turn and make its pale glow.

Now that he was here he had nothing to say immediately, nor did she seem in a hurry to break the silence. The fragrance of her nearness revived his acute hungers, so that he had to bring his will upon himself. She was like no other woman he had known. Beyond the bridge the river was a silvered flat shining between gray banks and its steady motion came against the sand shore and made small liquid echoes. A pair of riders ran off the prairie and took the bridge townward, the plank boards roaring above them and fine dust sifting down. Mitchell removed his hat and covered her head with it. His shoulder touched the soft point of her shoulder; the sweet smell of her hair came to him.

She said, "I saw the fight."

"I'm sorry."

"I respect him a good deal more than I did."

"Didn't think he had it in him."

"Then," said Sherry, "we both learned something."

"He's your man," said Mitchell. "Don't you know what's in him?"

"Do we ever really know what's in anybody?"

"You've been with him long enough to know. You've watched him long enough."

"I haven't watched you as long as I've watched him—but I know you better. I know more about you than I do about him."

"One thing," he said, "you ought to know—"

She took his hat from her head and handed it back. She moved her shoulder away. "Never mind, Dan. That's not why we're here. You know what's being said around town about you?"

"Yes."

She was long silent, struggling with some hard question. Since she was Mike Gault's daughter, he thought he knew what it was. Mike had taught her never to interfere in the affairs of other people—and to permit no other people to interfere in hers. Now, he guessed, every impulse collided with that training. Therefore he said:

"Young Dick Lestrade asked me that same question, and ran away before I could answer it. No, Sherry, I didn't kill Bravo."

She sat still. Other horsemen boomed across the bridge, once more loosening the dust upon them. Again he put his hat on her head to protect it. After the sound had died she said, "That hurt you a great deal—Dick's running from you. I saw it on your face when you came up the street. Would it help if I found Dick and told him?"

"Not now. He'll have to kind of struggle it out for himself. Then maybe I can talk to him—and maybe he'll believe me. This is his first introduction to the miseries of living. I hated to see it happen to him so soon. Tough enough to grow out of being a boy without making the change in a hurry."

"Suppose," she said very softly, "he won't believe you?"

"A bad break for me. Nothing to do about it though."

She removed his hat and gave it to him. It was as though she wanted to keep him away so that no part of his personality or his will touched her. She was self-reliant; she had always maintained a barrier against him. She murmured, "I hate to think of it," and rose. She turned to him, near enough for him to view the unreserved feeling on her face. "Josephine Balder told it this afternoon. That's where Dick Lestrade heard it. But it came from another source."

"I know."

"Do you know? You're sure?"

"Yes. From your man."

"That's the second time you've called him my man. Don't do it again."

"Isn't he?"

"Don't talk about it, Dan."

He went at her with a rising energy: "If he is, what makes you so shy of it, or afraid of it, or ashamed of it?"

"Maybe—" she began, and stopped. Later she added in a changed, subdued voice: "Is it that clear, Dan? Is it that certain? Can't I have any doubts at all? Can't I wonder, sometimes, if I'm doing the right thing? Can't I wonder how it might be if—"

"Maybe," he said, quite dry with his answer, "I don't know anything about it."

"How should it be?" she asked. Her voice held a reluctant note, a note of wanting nothing from him and having been forced to this question against her will. It made her voice somewhat sharp. "Tell me, since you seem to be so sure."

"Why," he said, "I ride in the dust, and I mix with sin, and so I guess I shouldn't know. But as far as I'm concerned, if you love him then heaven and hell are all the same, right where he is, and you're right with him all the time. If it isn't that it is nothing at all—and I wouldn't want it."

"Do you think," she said, now unaccountably angered, "you'll ever find that in any woman on earth?"

"Yes."

A long string of riders thundered over the bridge and Sherry Galt faded into the muddy gloom and he thought she had gone. But afterward, when the hard echoes had died up and down the river, he heard her say in a half voice, "Dan," and he walked on half a dozen steps and found her near her horse. Moonlight came in and touched her. Her shoulders swayed and her face was round and open, without coldness. "Why don't you leave me alone? Why don't you stop saying things like that?"

"The only way I know is to say what I feel, to go after what I want."

"You don't really want me. Any woman would do."

If she meant to hurt him she did it well. He said, "Good night, Sherry," and turned to the buckskin.

She called after him and when he didn't stop she ran after him and pulled him around. "I'm sorry." Then, exasperated at this quick change in herself, she cried out, "How am I to know what you are? There never was a man so contradictory. You can be cruel enough to beat the living lights out of Ford or cut a man down with the butt of your gun. You can take your ease in Big Annie's. You can smoke a cigar and stand on the street and smile as though you were a king. How should I know what goes on in your head? How can I tell what is in your heart?''

"It doesn't matter, does it?"

She drew a great long sigh. "Yes," she said, "it seems to matter. I wish you'd give this job up. Move on to another town or go back to the Aspens. But turn in your star. There aren't many days left on your calendar. Everybody knows that but you. When I stand in the hotel window and watch you go down into the shadows at the foot of Race I wonder if you'll ever make the circuit and come back alive. It takes you fifteen minutes to reach Brinton's stable. Someday I'll count off those fifteen minutes—and you won't be there."

"You've done that, Sherry?"

"Yes, I have." But she covered it with a quick explanation. "So does everybody. Why not? You're a gambler, shaking dice for your life. It is the biggest gamble in town and the town's got its bets up—on how long you'll survive. Get out of it, Dan. Doesn't it hurt you to know that people wonder if you're honest or if you're one of the crooks? Doesn't it cut you pretty bad to know some of them are lying about you and believing the worst? That's why it matters to me—because Ford started this rumor. You two are fighting for survival. That's what it amounts to. I don't mind the fighting. Men were born to fight. But I'd not like to know it was Ford's tongue that killed you. Not that way."

"Sherry," he said, "there's only one thing I want. You know what I want. But even if I could have that, I wouldn't resign now."

"Why?" she said. "Why?" Her voice was strong and alive and disturbed. Its echoes ran deep into the full silence of the night.

"I never rode around a shadow. If I ever do there won't be much left of me. That's about all I've got—just the knowing that I won't duck."

"Oh, you great fool! Proud men die just as fast as humble ones."

"Sure—but they die proud." He moved forward to her and he let his will slip so that it no longer disciplined him; and since he wanted her he brought her in until her warm and cushioning body was close with him, and he kissed her and took her wild, fiery flavor from her without restraint and had his moment of free entry into the full and deep and passionate values of this girl. He had that entry with her consent. Taken by surprise, or suddenly willing—this he never knew—she gave him all he asked for and pulled herself away. Afterward she seemed to understand how completely he had broken through and how open she had been to him during that interval. She hit him in the chest and wordlessly ran to her horse. In a moment she was racing back toward town.

He stood fast. Every edge of the night was sharp and biting and every sound had its melody in the dark and every odor came to him for his keenest relish. He was pleased. He felt free and great; the day's irritations vanished. He had done what he had long wanted to do and had done it well. Swinging to his saddle, soundlessly laughing at the night's goodness, he started back to River Bend. Tonight, for this little while with Sherry Gault, he had found what wonders life could hold for a man.

Other things were happening in River Bend this night and other people were weaving their little separate strands of circumstances that were to make the red-and-black pattern of fortune for the town and for Dan Mitchell. One lone light burned on Willow Street in the office of Bill Mellen near the depot, and Mellen sat in talk

158

with three homesteaders who had come from the camp at the edge of town.

"Be ready to travel before sunup," he said, "and I'll be there to lead you out. We'll go beyond Bridget's Coulee. All level land, not far from the river. Anywhere along there a drilled well ought to bring you water within a hundred and eighty feet. You people can join hands in the expense of the first well. That's the way it is done."

"I've heard about Chickman Flats," said one of the homesteaders. "Why don't we file there?"

"The best of that district has been taken," said Mellen. "The rest of it isn't good. I don't want to see you starve out on poor soil. I don't want to see a string of busted homesteaders moving back East in their wagons in a couple years." He was a sincere man; he had the hot zeal of a good cause in him. "These Texans come here and raise hell and make a big show and a lot of noise all in one night. Then they are gone. The homesteaders have got to take it slow and patient. One day, friends, you'll have your fences up all across this country and the wild trail bunch will be gone."

"Glad to see that day come," said the homesteader. "This is a wicked town. I would not care to bring my family up Race Street now."

"Race Street will die soon enough," said Mellen. "The gamblers and the toughs will go. Wait and see. It is people like you who make a country. I'm the only one who sees it, but every day the tide grows. There were twenty-five prospects off the train this noon. Look at the horizon to the east in the mornin'. You'll see wagons coming. Minnesota, Illinois, Wisconsin—they come from every place. Folks who want poor man's land."

"You think winter wheat will grow here?"

"It grows in Minnesota, doesn't it? Then it will grow here. Fellow down in Heister's Coulee is going to sow winter wheat this fall. Fellow by the name of Wallin.

Then we'll know. This land will grow anything. Someday River Bend will be a little city and you'll se the day when a cowpuncher will be a stranger in a crowd of farmers— looking for a saloon that isn't here."

"You're sure?"

Mellen said, "The history of all these towns is the same. They start wild and then they grow tame. It won't be long. The cowpuncher and us homesteaders can't live side by side. The open trail and the homestead fence are two different things. The fence always wins."

The homesteaders went away and Mellen killed his lamp and left the rear of his office, coming into Antelope. He passed the Balder house and saw its lights strong-shining in the front room.

In there Josephine Balder, a woman who had her convictions and pushed them ceaselessly, now lectured her husband. "Ed," she said, "I know you too well. You have your authority. Why don't you use it? You can tell Dan Mitchell what he is to do. You can tell him to close up Big Annie's. You can tell him to clean out Charley Fair's. Don't tell me you can't. Why don't you do it? You're too easy."

Ed Balder gave her a bully-ragged husband's futile glance. When Josephine was in one of her moods Ed Balder, from long experience, trimmed his sails and tried to work through his heavy seas.

"You're not afraid of him, surely," said Josephine, well aware of her husband's vulnerable pride.

"Josie," said Balder, "for the love of God stick to reasonable argument. Don't go flying around on this and that. Why should I be afraid?"

"Then why don't you do something about Race Street?"

"You know where the mearchants of River Bend get their bread and butter. From these Texans full of money to spend. From these herds that come here and pay

160

stockyard charges, from the trail bosses who buy supplies, from the train crews who put up here and take care of the cattle cars. Where would we all be without that trade? Suppose the trail moves away from us? Suppose it goes to War Bonnet? Then War Bonnet would have the railroad shops and the big barns for the stage lines, and the warehouses and stores. Pretty soon War Bonnet would have the county seat—and this town would dry up and blow away."

Josephine, having used one line of reasoning, now jumped to another—caring nothing for strict consistency. "You said yourself," she argued, "that Mitchell was too rough with Cap Ryder."

"True."

"Then why don't you call him to heel?"

"I spoke to him about it."

"We don't have to deal with crooks and we don't have to close down our blinds every sunset. We can get along without Race Street. We're decent people. We don't have to make our deals with Charley Fair. What a repulsive thing that is."

"I make no deals with Charley Fair," pointed out Ed. "We just get along, best as we can. What is good for him is good for me, to a certain extent."

"Maybe then you ought to be running a joint on Race Street."

"Josie, for heaven's sake—"

"It amounts to the same thing. If you agree with a crook on anything you're the same as a crook, aren't you?"

"All right," retorted Balder, "close down the town, then. What do we do without trade?"

"If it goes to War Bonnet, we'll set up shop in War Bonnet."

"So you'll follow the crooks to War Bonnet," said Ed Balder, finding some satisfaction in tripping up his wife.

161

"Oh," said Josephine, "you just talk in circles. You don't face me straight out. I'm telling you Race Street is getting worse. I'm telling you that Dan Mitchell thinks himself master of this town, and of you. And there you sit, letting him think it. Talk about your trade all you want. One day you'll wake up and find that Charley Fair's running this town and it will be so bad nobody can live in it. I wish I were a man. I'd stop it. I'd drive them all out. I'd burn Bismarck Alley. If I had to live in a shack in the middle of sagebrush and live on potatoes, I'd still do it."

Balder, knowing Josie, thought differently, but contained himself. But his wife's taunts struck old bruises and he settled back in his chair and irritably considered the ceiling.

At this same hour Will Gatewood, having read his apportioned chapter of Marcus Aurelius, waited for his wife to return from her walk; and when time ran on he began to put his mind to her with more interest than in many a month, so that at last the philosophies of literature ceased to be a refuge. When he heard her come up the steps, quite late, he took the book and seemed to be reading it.

She said, "I thought you'd be in bed."

He laid the book aside. His wife had an even and rather musical voice that faithfully recorded her moods and it was a new thing to him that she should speak with so strong and lifting a tone. Her eyes were bright and there was color in her cheeks. She faced him and seemed very happy. He had not remembered this much outright happiness in her before.

"You must have walked a long way."

"Out of the valleys of doubt and up to the hills of promise."

He said, "I don't seem to place the quotation. What

have you been reading lately?"

"A very big book, Will. One you couldn't hold in your lap. The sky—the sky at night."

"You know," he reflected, "if you like nature that well it would be good for you to read Thoreau." Then he said, perceiving the freshness and the spirit in his wife with a most thoughtful attention, "Some night perhaps I ought to walk with you. But not too far out on the desert. You know this country is full of snakes. You should stick to traveled roads."

He had a certain fatherly air toward her, he had a good man's feeling of better judgment, and so it disturbed him now to see that she smiled down at him in this new and free way, listening to him but not believing, seeing him but not seeing him as he wished to be seen—And her tone, gentle as it was, made him seem old.

"Shouldn't you go to bed, Will?"

Afterward in bed he lay long awake, very much puzzled, and now and then stray impressions came to him, to be put harshly aside but to be remembered, so that he was troubled.

From her room in the hotel, Sherry watched Mitchell swing down into Race, black and tall as the saloon lights reached him. Riders came up the street in great clouds of dust and broke against Mitchell and veered aside, and Mitchell, never moving from his steady pace, disappeared around the corner of The Drovers'. Sherry looked at the clock on her bureau and waited as the slow minutes dragged by.

Deep in Bismarck the buckskin shied away from something and came to a halt. Dismounting, Mitchell came upon a figure in the alley and lighted a match, and found Chappie Brink sitting dazed in the dust.

"What's up, Chappie?"

"An accident."

"What kind of an accident?"

He helped Chappie to his feet. Chappie groaned and shook his head. "Nothing much," he said. "Just a fool thing I'll remember. I got a good memory, Dan. That's my biggest trouble—always had too good a memory."

Chapter Eleven: Hard Choices

The meeting between Sherry and Mitchell had been on a Wednesday night. Three o'clock Friday afternoon the southern stage rolled up and deposited four passengers, one of whom was Ford Green. Riding out of Bismarck, Mitchell saw Green step stiffly from the stage and wait for a second man to join him; and then these two walked on to Balder's store. That second man turned as he got to Balder's doorway and gave the street one sudden backsweep with his eyes and when he did so Mitchell recognized that lithe and muscular shape and that face, soft as a woman's, with its great tawny mustache. This was Bill Bexar. Bexar gave Mitchell one moment's attention and passed into Balder's.

Ford Green found Balder in the back office. "Ed, this is Bill Bexar. Ed Balder, Bill."

The two shook hands. Balder settled back in his chair and favored Bexar with a good steady stare. Bexar's reputation he knew. Bexar was a bad man who had turned town marshal; his reputation stretched up and down the trail. Bexar had big blue eyes, fully open and quick in the way they absorbed all surrounding things. He was completely certain of himself and gave no ground before Balder's insistent attention. Actually it was Balder who broke the inspection first and who first spoke.

"Traveling?"

"Remains to be seen," said Bexar. "Friend Green here had a talk with me."

Balder was nettled. "Ford speaks for himself, not for me. Thought you were marshal at Pawnee?"

"Am," said Bexar, "but the town is quiet." Then he added with the simplest, completest self-assurance: "I made it quiet. I hear that's what you might be wanting in this place."

"Maybe," said Balder, committing himself no further.

"I'll be around for a couple days," said Bexar, and turned away. His was the manner of a man who had nothing to explain or concede, who could wait for others to come to him.

Green waited untl Bexar had left the store. "No harm done in looking at him, Ed. If you want a man, there's the man."

"A damned killer," said Balder. "I know all about him." He was greatly irritated. Green had brought up strong doubts in his mind concerning Mitchell, and though he tried to discount them because of Green's obvious cleverness, still they lingered and grew; and Josephine had never let up on him. Hating to be hurried or pushed, outraged that others should use him as a battleground, and increasingly troubled, he let out on Green. "Keep your damned schemes to yourself, Ford. The commissioners will appoint the new sheriff when we get around to it."

"Sure," agreed Ford Green with that yielding stubbornness which Balder could not circumvent. "Sure, Ed. But he's here if you got to have a man."

He went out, pausing to watch Bill Bexar as the latter walked down the middle of Race Street toward The Pride. Mitchell rode into Race and followed Bexar's path. At The Pride Bexar swung about, leaning one elbow against

166

a post of the overhanging gallery. Mitchell turned the buckskin and moved up to him. All this Ford Green saw with the closest attention, and as those two men faced each other he drew a long breath and his thoughts went ahead with a catfooted sureness, so that he saw their eventual collision. The picture was a certainty in his mind. All he regretted was the inability to hear what they were saying now as they stood by The Pride.

The train, late again, came into the depot. Green, who seldom smoked and never drank, now permitted himself the luxury of a cigar because of the satisfaction he felt and watched, with a mild surprise, the number of settlers coming off the train. Never a man to overlook any political chance, he would have put his mind fully on those settlers had not his attention been so completely attracted by Mitchell and Bexar; and so he dismissed the settlers and went over the dust to his office. From his window he saw Bill Mellen come down the street with the crowd behind him.

Mitchell put the buckskin up to the gallery of The Pride and faced Bexar. "Your town peter out on you, Bill?"

"Just on a little trip," Bexar said. "Man gets tired of the same thing. Thought I'd come up for a drink and some poker—and maybe ride back."

"You'll get good whisky and a good run for your money," observed Mitchell. "If you're lonesome for your trade I'll lend you the buckskin tonight and you can ride the town. Anything to oblige."

"Mighty nice," said Bexar, and smiled, thus revealing his mouth and his white sound teeth. The smile brought its quick lines up against his eye corners. This man was soft in all his features; his fingers were long and white and supple. He spoke slowly with a let-down drawl. But this was a surface of deception beneath which a swift mind moved in a ceaseless range of readiness and all muscles lay waiting for a call. His reputation spoke of a wild, slashing, terrifying rapidity of motion. "Mighty nice. I'll just sit by and watch you go about your business."

"Anything to please," said Mitchell. He was easy on his horse. He had no care; he held the buckskin not quite head-on to Bexar and the buckskin stayed there. He said, as the idlest afterthought, "You'll be taking your drink in The Pride. There's a little rule in this town. Give the barkeep your guns."

"Down my way we don't bother with that," said Bexar, still smiling. "I like to lèt the boys have their fun. Of course, they know me—and I know them."

"Different here," murmured Mitchell. Bexar was old-style. He carried a gun on either hip, slung low in black, worn holsters. There were only two kinds of men along the trail who bothered about that much weight, the greenhorns trying to look tough and the occasional wild one who knew his business and knew it well. "Just leave those things in The Pride."

He waited for his answer, not knowing what it would be. For a man like Bexar, to be disarmed was to be naked. All his strength was gone; all the terror of his reputation was nothing. And for a man like Bexar, with the thousand enemies he had at every turn, it was almost the same as being dead to go without his guns. Mitchell waited.

Bexar quit smiling. He said, "If it is the same to you, friend, I'll have my drink and drift back to the hotel. I'll keep 'em there."

"Your choice," agreed Mitchell and rode on.

This was the beginning of something, not the end. Riding around the corner of The Drovers', Mitchell speculated on the new move in the old game. Green was looking ahead to the reckoning day. What was it Green foresaw, and planned for, and schemed toward? Little things like this all added to something. The game was running on, the pace quickening. The arrival of Bexar meant that the end, obscure though it might be, was not far ahead. In the middle of one of these dark nights the powder keg that was River Bend, ignited by some small bit of casual match light, would blow up.

When he came into Willow again he stopped before a string of homesteaders trudging out toward the camp beyond the edge of town with their boxes and valises and their filled sacks. Behind them rolled one of Dug Neil's dray wagons, loaded with their baggage from the train. He had grown accustomed to these daily groups, and he had been aware of the steady increase; yet this crowd—men and women walking steadily through the dust with their children crying and running ahead—was a sudden exclamatory note of warning. Bill Mellen passed him and looked up, and Mellen's face was lighted and there was a look of laughter in his eyes, as though this were the revelation of a secret he had long carried. Balder, Mitchell observed, was on the porch of his store, studying these people with a puzzled expression, and other storekeepers had come out to observe. Something new was happening to the town.

He followed Willow north. Balder looked at him and Balder said, "Dan, what you make of this?"

"World's changing," Mitchell said. "Your world and mine. Mine mostly."

"What's that?" asked Balder. But Mitchell grinned at him and went on.

Dug Neil stood in the arch of his big warehouse. Neil said, "A funny thing is happening here. You know that, Dan? A funny thing—right under our eyes. What's it going to do to us?"

It struck everybody. Mitchell swung about on his horse watching the string of people along Willow, black against the sunlight, with the sunlight drenching them and the sunlight shining on the bare heads of the women and the children. Dust rose up around their feet, turning the air to gold—and through this gold film they moved, and one woman was crying, and Dug Neil said, "My God, why?"

Mitchell softly said, "Looking at the promised land and crying because she's glad. But she's thinking of everything green and nice back home and of her friends and of the graves of her people in the cemetery, a long way off from here, and maybe she's thinking of the old furniture she couldn't bring—and part of her cryin' is because she's sad. That's the way people reach the promised land, Dug. It started a long time ago. Moses was the first one. Now it is Bill Mellen, leading them out toward the sagebrush."

"Why," said Dug Neil, "you damned philosopher."

Mitchell laughed at him and went on down Willow. Other homesteaders still moved up from the depot and Irma Gatewood stood on the platform and looked at the train and saw nothing else. She was, Mitchell thought to himself, a long way from River Bend. Down Railroad Avenue he found Rita idling along the walk, taking her little hour of sun on this back street of town before night came. She was at the big area near Durham's rear lot and there she stopped, her face lifting and shocked. A man—a new man from the homestead crowd—broke down Railroad Avenue, saying, "Lila! Lila Durrach!"

Some of the straggling homesteaders turned to watch. A few townsmen swung about, also watching. Mitchell brought the buckskin to a stop and he had one great desire at that moment, which was to sweep this street clean of spectators so that these two people, Rita and the young man, might be alone.

He knew how this was at once. The young man was decent in every line, and he had called Rita by another name, by a name she had undoubtedly once owned and had abandoned; and so this was the story of a girl once good now meeting someone she had once known, he thinking her still good. Mitchell remembered what Rita had said in Big Annie's when he had asked her if there had been a man; he remembered her answer. He saw the young man reach her and remove his hat. The young man's face was full of pleasure; it had on it a clear expression that cut back through time and destroyed whatever absence there had been between them and made everything as it once was. That was the man, Mitchell thought.

The young man's fine and tremendous smile was steady-shining on her. He was so engrossed by his own happiness that he was blind to the misery she showed him; and suddenly he reached down and caught her at the waist and kissed her. Mitchell saw one tragic thing happen then. He saw Rita's hand lift and press ineffectually against this young man, and then her arms fell and she was silent and unresisting and passive. This was all he saw, for he wheeled the buckskin sharp about and cleared his throat and rode into Willow, the street growing dim before his eyes.

John Poe, who ran the saddle shop, stepped to the edge of the walk, saying, "Dan, if you've got a minute—"

Mitchell said, "I'll see you later," and kept going. There were times when the cruelties of life came up from the surface like splinters of glass to slash him.

Young Henry Dreiser stepped back from Lila with reluctance, still lost in his own personal joy. "Why, Lila, what you doing here? Last I heard you was in Freeport, Illinois. I came all the way down there, but you weren't there. I never got any answer from my letters. You come out here to homestead? Your folks come out?"

"No," said Rita.

"You been living here?"

"Yes," said Rita.

"How's your folks?"

171

"They're dead. We went to Kansas from Freeport. They died a year and a half ago."

"You alone out here?" asked Henry Dreiser. Then one vast dark cloud went over his face. "Married?"

She hesitated, she looked down, trying to think how best to answer. She was confused, she was in deepest misery and wanted to run. She said, "No—not married."

"Lila," he said, "I came to Freeport after you. That was our agreement, wasn't it? I was to wait a year till I made some money, then I was to come. But you quit writing and when I came you had just gone off, leavin' nothing but a hole in me big enough to drive a team through. What'd you do that for?"

She shrugged her shoulders. "Things happen, Henry. A lot of things happen."

"What happened?" he wanted to know. Then he added, "But what you doin' here alone?" When she didn't instantly answer, he had his own answer. "Maybe I can guess. You always liked to work with a needle. So you learned to be a seamstress."

"Yes," she said, "that's it." One great quick worry made her say, "You're not staying here, are you?"

"Goin' homesteading. Everybody's going homesteading. Half of Iowa seems on the move out here. Nothing for me to stay in Iowa for. Ed's going to get the folks' farm. Mabel's married to Beek Kadden. So I lit out."

She said, "I'll see you later, Henry," and turned away.

He caught her arm, greatly laughing. "Oh, no. I'll see you home. Why, Lila, what's happened all this time? What about me? Why didn't you write?"

She gave him a dark half glance and dropped her head. They moved to Willow and turned down its east walk toward Race. "Oh, I guess you were a long way off, Henry, and things got awfully crowded for us and I had to work hard, and there wasn't any time to think of the things we had talked about. Dad went broke in the feed

172

business. When he died I had to work to keep Mother. Then she died. Things change, Henry."

They were passing the Wells-Fargo barn. Dug Neil happened to be here and gave her a strict glance because she walked the open street with a man, contrary to the rules laid down for dance-hall girls. He was about to speak to her but when she looked up at him he closed his mouth. The sunlight pressed hot against them.

Henry Dreiser said in a solicitous voice, "We'll cross to the shade, Lila."

She stopped at the mouth of a little alley by the Wells-Fargo barn. In the middle of Willow lay the deadline she could not cross; the cool shadows under the farther board gallery marked a place she had never walked and never would walk.

She said in a hurried, hard voice, "There is something I forgot to do, Henry. Wait here a moment." She ran down the between-building alley, passing the back end of the Arcade and the Bullshead, and came to Ute. Here she turned the corner, ran over Race and continued to Bismarck. She threw herself into Big Annie's and stood a moment in the middle of the front room; and dropped to the bottom step and crouched over, hard-breathing and pale and making little gasping sounds in her throat.

Big Annie, coming out of the back end of the house a quarter hour later, found her there. Big Annie said, "What's wrong?"

On his next round in the late afternoon, Mitchell came upon Henry Dreiser at the foot of Race Street, round-faced and solid and without deception; the kind of a lad, Mitchell thought, whose mind would not run ahead and piece the puzzle of Rita together. This boy had his faith and it remained unshaken. But he was puzzled.

He said, "My name's Dreiser. I met a girl I used to

173

know back in Iowa. You saw me with her. Where's she gone? She said she'd come back—but she ain't. This is a right small town to get lost in. You know her?"

Mitchell said, "If she wants to see you she'll come back."

"Sure she wants to see me," insisted Dreiser. "You don't up and change, after everything—" He moved his large hands and his stout shoulders. "Think anything could of happened to her down these alleys?"

"No," said Mitchell, and moved on. Henry Dreiser called after him. "Where's she live?" but Mitchell went around the corner of The Drovers', into Bismarck.

Big Annie stood before her house waiting for him, and said, "You know what's happened, Dan?"

"I know."

"Well," she said, "I guess we've got something to do."

"Nothing left to do, is there?"

"You get off that buckskin and come in here."

It was last sunlight when he entered Big Annie's. Twilight was soft and warm on the town when he left the house, moved through Ute again, and crossed Race. Turning into Railroad Avenue, he came to the house where George Hazelhurst kept bachelor's quarters, and found Hazelhurst on the porch, smoking his evening cigar before beginning work at The Pride.

"George," said Mitchell, "I want your house for a few days. Rita's going to move into it. She's a seamstress and this is her house, you understand?"

"The lad—the chunky lad with the look of devotion written all over him—that one?" asked Hazelhurst. "I saw him. I saw him meet her." He was groomed and pale in the evening dusk, he was a still and disillusioned and cool man grasping the little enjoyment of his cigar. "What are you trying to do? Make him believe she's a good woman?"

"Isn't she?" asked Mitchell.

174

"Ah, my friend, let's not touch the philosopher's stone. Does he know anything about her?"

"Seems they were engaged back East. Folks took her to another town and they died. Something happened. She quit writing to him and drifted here. He comes here to go homesteading and finds her. As far as he's concerned she's still the girl he knew back East."

"Life and its little joke," murmured Hazelhurst. "Now you propose to pull the wool over his eyes and make a match, so that everybody will be happy." Being a gambler, he was interested in the odds and found them unfavorable. "It is a bad bet, Friend Mitchell. If they go homesteading around here he'll have her story inside of a week and he'll leave her. Everybody will know about this thing by tomorrow morning. You know River Bend. Your young friend will find out."

"It is up to her to get him out of the country—some other place a long way from here."

"We are being practical," observed George Hazelhurst, slightly amused. "But it occurs to me the lad is getting a deal from the bottom of the deck."

"George," Dan pointedly asked, "do you know anything against her?"

Hazelhurst said, very slowly weighing his words, "It is a little odd for you and me to be debating morals, is it not? No, I know nothing against her. But I know something about her." His cigar tip gleamed red in the gathering black. He was a nerveless, detached man whose pity and passion were well buried. "It will not matter so much about the man. He will be getting a woman who will make him a wife, no worse a wife than she would have made him when she was a kid back East. But it will matter to her. She has a conscience." He rose to his feet. "The house is hers, Dan. I will pack a grip and move down to Jack Spain's rooming-house within ten minutes." He paused to give Mitchell a long, close look. "You are an

175

odd fellow. I do not believe I quite know you. In any event, do not let the affairs of these people take your mind from the main chance. Things are happening around here."

Mitchell cut back through Ute to Big Annie's and left word. On the next round he reached Railroad Avenue in time to see Rita standing at the open doorway of Hazelhurst's house. She had her belongings in a valise; she had just arrived and had not yet entered. The light coming through the doorway burned yellow against her, creating for Mitchell a biting picture of complete aloneness.

Mitchell came up. He paused to say, "Go on in. I will send that young man to you." Continuing down Railroad, he heard her call after him.

"It is too late."

He circled to Race and moved up through a gathering tide of Texas trail hands. Light burned from Sherry Gault's window. In the courthouse light also burned through Ford Green's window, one late signal of scheming. Mitchell found Henry Dreiser on the porch of Webber's, so posted as to watch both Willow and the length of Race.

"You will find her on Railroad Avenue," said Mitchell. "That is the street facing the depot. It is the sixth house down."

Henry Dreiser's broad face lightened and without a word he wheeled and walked down Willow. Mitchell got off the buckskin and was in Webber's doorway when Leathers came across from Race and stopped him. Leathers said, "What the hell's going on?"

"Go talk to Big Annie."

"I know about all that," said Leathers. He wasn't cheerful, he wasn't himself. "When are you damned-fool people going to quit trying out nutty notions on that girl? It won't work. You keep pushin' her at something she don't want to do. Pretty soon she'll do it because she figures you think it is right. Then she'll be sorry she did it."

"Look at who's talking," commented Mitchell. "You got a better idea?"

"Let her alone."

"Why?" asked Mitchell.

Leathers stared at Mitchell and was about to make an answer. He never made it. He opened his mouth and suddenly showed a very strange expression, and closed his mouth and walked away.

Mitchell crossed Webber's lobby and climbed the stairs, passing his own room. He knocked on the end door. When the door opened, with Sherry standing before him, he said, "Could I see you a minute?"

Her hand was on the door's knob and for a little while he thought she intended to close the door on him. The memory of the night before came to her face and made her resent him, or fear him. He was not quite able to fathom the expression she wore—but it was there and it gave him no encouragement. After a considerable pause she said, "Come in."

Chapter Twelve: "I Had to Eat"

Charley Fair watched the first crowd into The Pride. He walked the length of his bar to see that all was in order, he cast an eye at the tables, and stood at the bar's end, knowing that this would be another good night. To start it right he let his affable voice boom through the house.

"Everybody up. This one is on me. I want everybody to be satisfied." Spotting familiar faces—for he was a man who remembered these trail people from one year to another—he pushed through the room, shaking hands and dropping casual words of welcome, and pausing to drop his big hand on a man's shoulder. In this manner he reached the back of the saloon, slipped through a rear room, and let himself into Bismarck. He strolled out to the end of Willow, there catching view of the home-steaders' fires a quarter mile away. In the silvered half moonlight these fires were beautiful, but it was the number that engaged his attention, not the beauty. Earlier in the day, seeing all these people move down Willow from the train, Charley Fair had grasped at the edge of something that deeply disturbed him and now was giving it the benefit of his full thoughts.

These settlers had been nothing more than shadowed shapes on the land, only vagrant individuals drifting through town and vanishing. It was no longer so. Each day the train dropped more of them and each day more wagons rolled up. Wide and deep as this country was there would be a time when the homesteaders and the trail would meet head-on. It always had been so in Charley Fair's experience; and his experience was broad. So he stood beyond the edge of Willow, piecing together the story as it might affect him, and at last turned back to his saloon. Going through the barroom, he saw that it was filling and was pleased, and went on to his own office, closing the door behind. He sat down at his desk and lay back in a chair. He put his feet on the desk, watching the ceiling through the steady ripples of his cigar smoke. A good deal later—a full half hour later—having canvassed the whole scheme of things and having arrived at his own answers, he simply lifted his voice.

"Jim."

Jim Card came in. Fair said, "Shut the door," and when the door was closed, Charley Fair said, "Ride up to the Aspens tonight and tell Jett to slide into town tomorrow night without being seen."

Sherry said, "This boy knows nothing of what she's been?"

"No. He's thinking of her as she was back East, a couple years ago."

"After all that's happened do you think she still loves him?"

"If she did once, she still does. Those things don't change."

She gave him a strongly personal glance. "You have said that before. You are so sure of it. Even if the earth turns over, even if a man or a woman goes through every kind of torment, you still think that one thing remains constant—the love of one man for one woman."

"What else is certain?"

She said, "I don't know," and continued to watch him, so close and dark and completely interested. "That belief tells more about you than anything else could. How wonderful it would be, if it were true. How simple life would be and how complete and satisfying." She turned away from him. "I'd like to think it true, but is it? Now and then I get a little glimpse of it and for a moment I think it is possible. That would be the answer to everything, wouldn't it? Nothing else would matter. But how can it be true?"

He said, "Sherry," and waited until she faced him. "If you doubt it, you're wasting your time with Green. If he can't make you smile, and cry. If he can't—" None of this got near what he was thinking, and the lack of words made him angry. "I have seen your eyes smiling. You're a shut door. Has Green opened it? Is it comfort you want? Just to eat and sleep and drink your tea at three o'clock on somebody's porch? Listen to the wind blow in the Aspens. Listen to a coyote howl. Any of those things make you think of Ford? There's a puncher coming up the street now, full of hell, ready to squeeze the last drop out of the night, as if maybe there never was another night coming. That boy is filling his cup to the top. He's afraid of nothing. He's reaching out because it is swell to be alive. There's no caution in him, no penny-counting. He's laughing, he smells the night, he feels his blood run through his heart." Then he said, "Were you thinking of Ford last night, under the bridge?"

She took one step away from him and thrust her hands behind her. She put up her head, defending herself against the steady beat of his presence. She was on the alert, she was fighting back with a darker color in her eyes, with a quick in-and-out run of breathing; she was disturbed and unsure, she who so seldom was. "Dan," she murmured, "please let me alone."

"Why," he said, "perhaps I will. For there won't be

many more nights like this for me. You'll not be standing much longer at that window counting the minutes while I come up Bismarck."

"Why?"

He shrugged his shoulders. "I saw a motto on a sundial one time, which I never forgot. *It is always later than you think*—that was the motto."

She stood still, measuring his words and troubled by them. He could make her glow with anger and he could bring the shadow of trouble across her face. Those things he had done. But he could not make her smile and open her arms to him, and so he shrugged it all away. Fatalism, new to him and strange to him, had its way tonight. Like Hazelhurst, he had played his chips and sat silently by, knowing he had lost and gritting his teeth together so that she would never see that it mattered.

She said, "You are kinder than I thought. Why should you be kind at all? If this girl loves the boy she'll tell him the truth—and he'll go away."

He said, "That is what Hazelhurst said, and Leathers. So both sides of Race Street see it the same. There's your town, Sherry—the good and the bad both looking in on this, both with the same answer. I guess I'm the one wrong."

"But don't you see? She would be cheating. If she doesn't love him, it wouldn't matter. But if she does—"

"All I see is Rita. She deserves better than she got. I wish some woman would talk to her. Maybe—"

The door rattled to quick knocking and came rapidly open. Ford Green said in a voice rancid with jealousy, "You've got no business in here, Mitchell."

"Ford—" said Sherry.

But Ford came before Mitchell with his green eyes betraying the latent impulse to kill. Nothing could be more easily read. Mitchell, now softly laughing, made his turn.

"You may be right, Ford. But you are a fool, as I have

told her. I would take her from you if I could. Maybe she
likes it your way—soft and sure and never a chance of the
wrong thing said or done. You will do well, both of you,
figuring everything out safe, never getting dirty and
never letting the rain touch you. A very pleasant life. I
wish you luck."

He was at the door, not knowing how openly his anger
showed. He had entered this room in one frame of mind,
and left it in another. Change had swept over him without
explanation and futility came and everything was
different from what it had been. In his own mind he said
good-by to Sherry. Strange currents were running
through the town and he had lived so long by the
intangible scents and sounds and rumors drifting across
River Bend's housetops and up its streets that he never
doubted them now. They were bringing him messages of
disaster and ruin. He was returning to Race Street; he
would never come out of Race Street again. Then he
smiled, turned quiet, and regretted his hard talk. "Best
regards," he said.

Sherry called, "Dan, why do you say that? Come
here!"

He closed the door behind him, hearing the rapid
break-in of Ford Green's voice, half wild with its
suspicions. Sherry Gault's answer cut at him and beat
him down to complete silence. In the lobby Mitchell
stopped to light a cigar. Josephine and Ed Balder came
late from the dining-room and moved by him. Josephine's
eyes met him and hated him in her formidable way, as
though she had the desire to use her hands on him. This
was the way she always looked at him and was not new.
But Balder dropped his head, not looking at Mitchell at
all; on his face was a sulky, embarrassed expression.
Mitchell remained in the lobby a little while after these
two had gone, thinking of Balder's evasion, and he knew
then—even though it was not yet an accomplished fact—

hat Balder would soon go against him.

He went out and stepped to the buckskin. Race Street was a yellow glow of light and the dance-hall music was in full, steady swing and dust rolled heavy on the street, through which men moved and laughed and launched their exuberant crying. Somewhere a gun made its dull breath in the alleys beside Race. The buckskin, trained to follow that one sound like a retriever, pricked up its ears and paced forward rapidly. Mitchell slanted the cigar upward between his teeth and looked above him to the darkly silvered sweep of sky and its clouded froth of stars running across emptiness. Up there was a cold and still beauty untouched by dust or the sound of men's hard voices or the pulse of men's fears and ambitions and heartbreaks. The thought moved in through him, very strong because of his own black mood. Then the buckskin turned at Briar and walked into its darkness. As he left Race, Mitchell looked behind him and saw Sherry Gault posed at the yellow square of her hotel window.

Henry Dreiser turned down Railroad Avenue, counted the houses, and knocked on the sixth door. It was a very small house with a light shining through a single front window; and not until he knocked a second tme did he hear footsteps move slowly over the floor. Rita—or the girl he knew as Lila Durrach—opened the door and stood before him with a pale, unmoved face. Had he been an observant man he would have at once noticed this constraint, but his own happiness at finding her again shut his eyes to it. His own imagination jumped the two-year gap and for him she was the girl he had planned to marry and everything was as it had been.

He said, "I had a hard time finding you. What did you run off today for?"

She said, after long thought, "Come in."

He entered the house. "I expect," he said, "you were busy."

"Yes."

He took a chair and stretched his long legs before him. He filled and lighted his pipe, a stout and broad young man with slow ways and an unruffled disposition. "I been thinking," he murmured. "I been thinking about you and me. We had everything settled—and then you went away and pretty soon I didn't hear from you any more. Why didn't you keep on writing to me, Lila?"

"I told you. Things changed."

"Yes," he said, "that's what you said this afternoon. For me, nothing's changed. How've they changed for you, Lila?"

"Two years is a long time."

"Awful long," he agreed, and looked at her thoughtfully. "Why didn't you come back home when your folks died? I was waiting there. All your friends were there."

She backed into the corner and faced him as though afraid of him, and her answer was long in coming. "Oh, things just happened."

This recurring phase troubled him. He turned it in his mind, studying her. She was small against the lamp glow. She was a dark girl, unreadable and beyond his understanding. Her lips were soft and she had a prettiness that stirred him, but she hadn't smiled at him and there was trouble in her eyes. "Yes," he said, "things happen. But what things, Lila? That's what I wish I knew."

"It is very hard to explain, Henry. Maybe, when people get a little older they don't feel the same as they did before."

"That," he said, "is what I want to get at. You don't feel the same toward me any more? That what you mean?"

She stood still, now long silent. Her lips came together

and her head dropped and her shoulders trembled faintly until she tightened them. "Oh, Henry, just let's not talk about it."

"Why I guess I've got to talk about it, Lila. Not about you—if you don't want to. But about me. I can't say hello and good-by. Not even if I tried. I sure went through a bad time when I tried to find you and couldn't. I couldn't tell you how bad a time. Now here you are. I ain't leaving this town until you either take me or send me away." He looked at her with a tremendous solemnity. "It was the not knowing that hurt worst. I don't think it would have been quite so bad even if I'd known you were dead. This other was worse—the not knowing."

She said, "What will you do now?"

"I'll go out somewhere on the prairie, homesteading. You think that's a good idea?"

"Why ask my advice, Henry?"

"Ain't I talking clear enough?" he asked, freshly puzzled. "I would have gone from house to house and door to door. I wouldn't have left this town until I found you. You know it. You ought to know why I'm asking your advice. You're in whatever I do unless you tell me to leave."

She spoke in a strained way: "I don't like this country very well."

"What country do you like better?"

"Texas," she said. "I think I'd like it in Texas somewhere. Or Montana. Away in the corner of Montana."

"Texas or Montana," he agreed, following her talk with a dogged patience. "Which one is it? If that is what you want we'll do it."

"But you like it here best," she added quickly.

"I always depended on your advice when we were going together," he told her. "You always had better

185

judgment than me." He bent in the chair, placing both long arms across his knees. He looked down at the floor, the pipe smoke rolling back over his round, strong face and his short half-curly hair. "Main thing is to have you with me. That is everything. I guess you don't know how lonely I have really been. If you knew what I've been through these two years I think you'd really be sorry for me."

She watched him, holding back all that she felt.

Not hearing her speak, he looked up. "Not blaming you, Lila. I guess you've had your troubles, too. Matter of fact, you don't look happy. I guess you have been through a lot. You'll never need to any more. Which is it to be, Texas or Montana?"

"You don't know much about me, Henry. Not much about the last two years."

He said, still clinging to his patience convictions, "You're the same girl. I'm the same man. That ought to be enough." He straightened in the chair. "Maybe you are trying to tell me you don't want me at all now. That it?"

Backed into the corner, she wanted him to go before he found out about her; and this was the easy way—to answer his question and send him off. Yet when she came to say what seemed so easy, she couldn't say it. Instead, dumb and heartbroken, she only shook her head.

Henry Dreiser rose, smiling his relief. "It was the thing I been fearing all afternoon. I'd rather be shot than hear it. Well, Lila—"

She faced him, she drew upon her strength and spoke as quietly as though there were no hurt or shame in it. "This is not my place and I'm not a seamstress. They got me this house so I could fool you, so you'd think everything was all right. I live in a house with other girls over on Bismarck Alley. I work in a dance hall, and have for six months. I met a man in Freeport after the folks

186

died. Then he went away. I've got to tell you that. Now do you want me, Henry?"

He stood before her and grew sick around the mouth and she saw it and said in a still quieter voice, "I told you things had changed, didn't I? You don't know what happens to women when they're alone and haven't got any money, when everything's gone and nothing matters. But you don't want me now, do you?"

He took his pipe from his mouth. He held it cradled to his big palm. He stared at it and reversed it and shook the ashes into his hand; they were red hot but he seemed to feel nothing: He rubbed the ashes cold and put them in his pocket. He put his pipe in his pocket and pushed his palms together. Now he lifted his face and she saw that his eyes were a kind of pale, burning hazel and that one heavy vein stood out on his forehead. He wasn't really thinking of her so much as of the man she had known in Freeport. He wanted to kill that man. He turned, walking with an old man's gait, and opened the door.

She called after him, "Remember, Henry, I told you the truth."

Absent-mindedly he nodded and went through the door. On the porch he turned, asking his question in a small, colorless voice. "That man—he tricked you? He said he was going to marry you, and then he fooled you?"

She squared herself and answered him with a thorough honesty: "No, I was hungry and I had to eat."

The sick look crossed his face again and he moved up Railroad into the shadows. She listened until his steps ceased to telegraph back on the loose boards, and then left Hazelhurst's house, cut through town by way of Ute, and disappeared in Big Annie's.

Standing in the shadows of Railroad, Tom Leathers saw Henry Dreiser leave, and later watched Rita go back toward Big Annie's, which told him how the meeting had gone. He sighed greatly, and he murmured, "Sure—I was right." He rolled a cigarette and lighted it and he walked across town and reached Bismarck, once more stationed in the shadows. "Dam' right. What else they figure she'd do?" He drew a great breath, as though relieved.

Half an hour later, when Mitchell threaded Bismarck, Big Annie stepped from her house to tell him the result. Big Annie was angry at Lila but it was the kind of anger near to tears and it made her voice loud and it made her swear. "Men—" she said, "men are fools. They're ignorant, they're cattle. They deserve nothing. By God, Dan, they don't know good women when they see 'em. I hate the breed!"

Sherry, Mitchell thought, had been right and so had Hazelhurst and Leathers. He had been the wrong one. He reached Brinton's and looked along Willow and saw Henry Dreiser come forward with his head down and his hands swinging heavy beside him. He passed Mitchell, not seeing him, and he was crying openly, tears running down his cheeks and great windy gusts coming out of his throat—so continuing on toward the flare of home-steaders' fires on the desert.

Mitchell circled into Antelope and for a moment was glad to be in this quiet back eddy. Lately the cruelty of the town, or the cruelty of people toward one another, had bitten into him harder than it should, so that he rode these streets with too many things in his mind and was therefore less watchful than he needed to be. It got this way with a peace officer. Things piled up and distractions pulled at him until one day, buried in some piece of thinking, he failed to see the danger signals on the street and walked straight into a gun.

It was eleven o'clock then. At twelve, cutting through Ute Street on his last tour, he paused in the black shadows and watched Bill Bexar stroll down from Webber's House, cut back into darkness, and disappear. In a little while Bexar showed up in the alley adjoining

188

Charley Fair's saloon, found the rear door and entered it. The night crowd had started to leave town and the dance-hall music quit and here and there gamblers began to walk Race Street toward The Drovers', where they liked to gather for a midnight meal and a last cigar before going to bed. Ad Morfitt appeared on Race and entered the jail office. At twelve-thirty, Bill Bexar slipped out of the saloon's rear door and took to the shadows again.

Mitchell crossed to the jail office, said good night to Ad Morfitt from the saddle and continued to Brinton's. This night, he varied his routine by going straight to his room. He could not face Big Annie, he could not face Rita. Lying in bed, he thought about this girl and saw no future for her, and had his fiery hatred for the brutality of the world; and then his mind went to Bill Bexar and he lay long awake, fathoming the man's motives in visiting Charley Fair, and slowly going again through the complex web of the town until he thought he knew how things went, and fell asleep.

By seven the next morning he was on his way to the Aspens; at noon when he returned he met Tom Leathers at the head of Willow.

Leathers said, "News for you, my friend."

"Good or bad?"

"What would be good news in this town?" asked Leathers. "No, it is bad. The homesteaders finally made entry six miles straight south of town. There is a bobwire fence directly across the cattle trail. A two-mile stretch of it, thrown up yesterday sometime. Know what that means?"

"Yes," said Mitchell. "Yes, I know."

"The world," said Tom Leathers, "is fallin' in."

Chapter Thirteen: World Falling In

The news of the building of the homesteaders' fence came in on the fast heels of Hale Margrath's pony. Margrath, a rider for the big Laughlin and Donlevy cattle ranch twenty miles south of the river, shouted the news down Willow much as he would have announced the imminence of an Indian raid, for to him it was, as Leathers had said, the world falling in. What he yelled into the morning quiet of the town was:

"Bobwire all across the trail! Dam' scoundrels ought to be shot! Bobwire—three miles long of it! What the hell—what the hell—"

It was news in every house and building in River Bend within twenty minutes. South Peters carried it to Charley Fair and to every other saloon on the street. Having done that, he headed for the Aspens to notify all the ranches along the War Bonnet road. For cowhand and cattle owner, for saloonman and trail driver, for every man whose money came directly or indirectly from beef, this news was a great red comet flaming down from the sky. It shook the town out of the usual early drowse. Brinton walked along Willow, in and out of the stores, repeating the information and adding his question: "What the hell we going to do about it?" Dug Neil came up from his stage barn and stopped Brinton, the two talking a little and falling silent, and talking again. Balder stepped from his store and joined them.

In a little while Mrs. Balder came from Antelope and said, "What's this I hear, Ed?" As soon as Balder gave her the story, she turned about, going back to Willow. As she left she flung a last shot over her shoulder: "You're so good at watching and waiting and trusting people. Now what will you do?"

Balder said, "Dug, call in Gatewood, will you? And Ford Green. Bring in the rest of the crowd. We've got to talk this over."

In a little while the dozen or more men who ran Willow Street stood and squatted in Balder's back office. Brinton said, "Three miles of fence means a bunch of homesteaders put in and fenced together. It sure went up in a hell of a hurry."

"According to Hale Margrath, they took a block of land against the river."

"Can't fence out the road. They'll have to leave that open."

Pete Godefroy said, "A road ain't enough. No trail driver's going to run cattle down a fifty-foot lane of bobwire. Where'll these held herds graze? You put bobwire within ten miles of this town and you've spoiled the town for the trail."

John Poe said, "They can skirt the homestead wire and come in."

"No," said Brinton. "If there's three miles of wire today there'll be thirty miles of it next week. The whole flat will be in fence. There's the end of free graze. It will scare hell out of the trail men. You've seen the end of River Bend as a trail town. I'm telling you. It just don't mix. Never has. Wire comes—the trail goes."

"Now look," said Tom Franzen, "those homesteaders did it all together. One day it wasn't there. Next day it was. So they planned it careful. Somebody figured it out. Bill Mellen—there's your man."

"Get him in here," said Balder.

"He's out on the prairie."

"There's your man who's chokin' off the trail. And chokin' off the town. This place is dead without Texas money."

"Is it?" said Dug Neil, so far silent.

"Isn't it?" challenged Franzen.

"How many months have you got Texas money coming through here? June to October. Five months. Then there is nothing until next June. River Bend just sits around and starves seven months out of the year."

"Five flush months make up for seven lean ones," pointed out Franzen.

"Your homesteader," said Dug Neil, "is here the year around. He comes to town once a week. He buys, he builds, and comes back to buy. He brings his women, he brings his kids."

"Not enough of 'em," said Franzen.

"No?" asked Neil. "Think again. Remember the crowd that came off yesterday's train. There'll be a bigger crowd on today's. Just recall how it has been growing the last month." He stopped, looking around at the group. "Yesterday I did something. I made a count of homesteaders. I checked Bill Mellen's records. You don't see these people. They pass through and drop out of sight on Chickman or down in the coulee. But there's five hundred families within twenty miles of River Bend now."

"How many?" said Franzen, openly surprised.

The train was meanwhile ringing its way into River Bend. The talking quit and these men slowly thought through the puzzle that was before them, each man analyzing what the change meant to him in a hard, close, deep-thoughtful way.

Dug Neil got up and went through the store and in a little while he called back to them, "Come here."

The group moved to the galleried walk. Mellen came off the prairie on his gray horse and went to the group, and looked at them and grinned; he galloped on down to the depot and dismounted and was lost in the crowd. Sunlight dropped straight into the town, laying its burning brightness on the dust, and the dust rose and made its rank, glittering haze in the air and through this haze the group watched the homestead crowd come from the cars and grow thick at the head of Willow.

"My God," said Franzen, "it is a land rush."

"Boys," said Balder, "come back in here." He led them to the office. He waited until they were all inside, and closed the door. "Boys, we've got to figure this out."

Franzen said, "One more year and they'll be starved out and dried out—and they'll be gone."

Dug Neil had an answer for that. "Look down the railroad line to Ephrata or to Dryad. Look at Meridian. They were trail towns once. Then bobwire came and now they're settled communities. Farms all around. You're wrong, Tom. There's your answer."

This group sat still again, chewing on Dug Neil's talk. None of them liked the picture he presented, for they were accustomed to old ways and they looked upon change with distrust and some fear. But they were visualizing the streets of River Bend filled with homesteaders and without saloons. They were seeing these homesteaders crowding the walk and moving into their stores.

Dug Neil, though a prophet of the new order, liked it no better than the rest. "I am sorry to see it happen."

"Like business don't you, Dug?" asked Pete Godefroy.

"I liked it as it was," answered Dug Neil slowly. "I liked everything as it was."

"Nothing stands still."

"No," agreed Dug Neil, "nothing does."

"Boys," said Ed Balder, coming from his long speculations, "we've got to make a switch. From now on we cater to the homesteader. We've got to treat him right and give him what he wants. It occurs to me the first thing which will happen is that those trail herds will rip down that fence before sunset comes. We'll have to prevent that."

"What with?" asked Brinton. "We've got no sheriff."

Balder looked at Ford Green. "Ford's got a man. That's what you brought him up here for, isn't it, Ford?"

"Yes," said Ford, which was his first word during the meeting.

"Well," said Balder, "go bring him here."

Green left the room. He went as far as the front door and looked both ways on the street; then he raised his head toward Webber's second floor and made a signal by nodding his head. He stood by Balder's door until Bill came out of the hotel and joined him. The two returned to Balder's rear room.

"Gentlemen," said Green, "this is Bill Bexar."

Balder looked at the other two county commissioners, Neil and Franzen. He said, "All right?" When Dug Neil nodded and Franzen jumped his chin briefly up and down, Balder gave Bexar a glance that had no particular friendliness in it. "Then you're sheriff. The pay is a hundred and twenty-five. Nothing inside this town concerns you. Your job is outside of it. Do not interfere with Mitchell at all—At the moment the homesteaders are stringing fence across the trail just south of town."

Bexar said in his drowsy, silk-smooth voice, "You want that stopped?"

'No," said Balder, "I don't want it stopped. I want you to see that the trail crowd leaves those fences alone."

Bill Bexar studied his orders through a reflective pause. He put a hand slowly across his sweep of tawny mustache and made a few brushing gestures; his eyes ran

194

the room from man to man, collecting information.

Balder said, "What's the matter? Don't you think you can handle the trail boys?"

"Why," said Bexar, cool and unruffled, "I think there's no trouble about that. They know me pretty well." He had a smooth, feline self-absorption; he had a complete confidence. "I guess I'll take the job," he added, and turned on his heels, leaving behind him a faint feeling of scorn for the people who had hired him, and a faint feeling of unease.

Franzen said with a degree of irritation, "You know this man, Ed?"

"Ford," said Balder shortly, "picked him."

"Don't wholly approve of a killer for a sheriff," said Neil. "But I don't know who else could brace the trail crowd out there."

Ford Green got up. He said, "There is one other thing. You'll have to close up Race Street. If you don't the homesteaders will drive to War Bonnet or Dryad with their business."

Having dropped that one suggestion into the meeting, he left the store. He had been forehanded enough to have a suitable man around when one was needed, and so he had won his point in the matter of Bexar, even though he was perfectly aware of the ill-concealed dislike he left behind him. But although it was a tactical triumph, Ford Green was not pleased with himself. This sudden tide of homesteaders had caught him as badly off balance as it had the other townsmen and now as he crossed the street he was really troubled by the havoc it made with his plans. Above all, he could not afford to have Race Street dry up on him by natural cause and effect. His long-nursed plans called for a violent and spectacular purge of Race Street made under his direction—this for the sake of the fame it would give him throughout the state. If other forces prematurely killed the street, his own

195

scheme of things collapsed.

Moving all this patiently back and forth through his mind, he climbed the courthouse stairs and found Bill Bexar waiting in the office. Green closed the door.

"The commissioners appointed you, Bill. They don't like to feel that you're looking at me for advice. You understand? Better to do these things the quiet way. It would be wise not to see me too often in the office."

Bill Bexar rested against the wall, so perfectly balanced as to give Green the impression that, idle as Bexar was, he could spring out from the wall at the merest prompting. He considered Ford Green, and Green's words, with the shrewd eyes of a man who knew the politics of a town inside out. He nodded. "All right, friend. We will get along. What you want—what you after?"

"What?" said Ford.

Bexar made a slight motion of impatience with his hand. "I always like to know which way a man is looking when I'm working for him."

"You're working for Balder and the other two commissioners."

"Sure," said Bill Bexar, shrewd and skeptical. "We understand all that." His eyes showed a cool amusement and perhaps his lips were smiling, though they were hidden behind the waterfall of his mustache. He waited for Ford to reveal himself. "Sure, friend."

"Balder told you to leave Mitchell alone," commented Ford. "You do that, Bill. Leave him alone for now."

"But not for always?"

"He's got no friends left in River Bend. Today or tomorrow Balder will tell him to close Race Street." He looked squarely at Bexar. "I don't think he can do it. I don't think he'll live to do it."

"You ought to know," murmured Bexar.

"Race Street will kill him when he tries. Then the town's wide open and nobody to stop it—except me, hrough you."

"What do I do then, friend?"

"Then I tell you to step in and you close Race Street. That's why I got you up here. You close it and you leave a track of ruin all the way behind you. You close it the tough way. You play hell and riot—so that it makes a sound all across this state. You see?"

Bexar pondered this at length, then said, "And you get the name for cleanin' it up?"

"That's right, Bill. Now we understand each other."

Bexar said, "I just wanted it clear," and moved from the room. At the door he casually added, "Time for a second drink," and went away.

Ford Green lay back in his chair, feet on his desk, and let his mind move cautiously ahead from one near and certain point to another, and in this way his thoughts went ducking and dodging from shelter to shelter until they were far ahead. Homesteaders were still moving along Willow Street and Mitchell came out of Henkle's barbershop and paused to light a cigar and afterward crossed toward the jail office, leaving the range of Green's vision. Green thought, *Everything he does is too regular. He'll get ambushed for it.*

Bill Bexar came into sight on the opposite side of Race and moved along idly. He looked in at the Arcade, and paused by the Bullshead and seemed undecided; and wheeled across the dust and entered Charley Fair's Pride. Ford Green took his feet from his desk, doubt making its keen cut through him. He watched Charley Fair's saloon and was sorry that he had spoken so freely to Bexar, and then as he wondered why he had done so he realized how easily Bexar had drawn him out. Green rose, now speaking aloud to himself: "Shouldn't have shown my hand to him at all." Yet he realized he had reached the time when he could no longer play a wholly secretive game; he who trusted nobody, and had faith in no soul at

197

all, had had to trust Bill Bexar. He tried to shrug his fears aside but they remained.

Bexar entered The Pride, which at this early hour was wholly empty of trade. He moved to the bar and had a drink and made his noon meal from the lunch counter. He gave the huge room a close look, spotting the doors and the back exits, and took a seat at a table and lighted a cigar, his hands afterward seeking a deck of cards for a game of solitaire. He was deep-engrossed in this game when Charley Fair stepped from the back office.

"Hear you're sheriff now."

Bexar continued his private deal, idly saying, "Expected you'd hear that as soon as anybody."

"I hear most things as soon as anybody."

"Sooner perhaps," suggested Bexar. "This side of a town usually does."

"Drink?"

"I've had mine."

Charley Fair looked to the barkeep, who was the only other man in the place. "Jim," he said, "you can go get your meal now. I'll watch things."

Jim Card left The Pride. Charley Fair moved back of the bar. He put his solid arms on it and watched Bill Bexar, twenty feet away. "Came to see me, didn't you?"

"Usually make it a practice to see the men that run a town," said Bexar.

"Well, friend, what can I do for you?"

Bexar gave Charley Fair a knowing and self-possessed glance. "I'm not the one wantin' anything, friend. You are. What do you want?"

Charley Fair thought about this and presently said, "I had you figured right. I want a wide-open town."

"You ain't going to get it," said Bexar. "Bobwire's going up and your trail is closed. Your street's going to be wiped out."

Charley Fair had a dry answer. "I heard all that as soon

198

as you did. But I still want an open town."

"Talk to Mitchell," suggested Bill Bexar.

"I'm talking to you. That's what you came here for."

"Maybe it was," agreed Bexar. He laid down an ace and built on it. Steps clacked along the walk in front of The Pride. A fast rig moved down Race and dust thickened in the bars of sunlight striking through the open doorways. "I like to see where the weight is in a town. A man always finds it if he looks."

Charley Fair drummed the bar with his knuckles. "Right here. Here's the weight."

"I was thinking of this man Green," offered Bexar. His voice threw out its light, indifferent suggestions for Charley Fair to dispose of; his hands methodically stripped the deck.

"What's he got behind him?" said Charley Fair. "He's a smart man but he's alone. He can't count on Balder and he can't count on Mitchell. No, friend. No weight there."

"He's got me," said Bexar.

Charley Fair said, "I'd like to see those fences torn down out yonder."

"I had orders to see they stayed up."

"If the homesteaders fence me out, I'm through here," said Charley Fair. "But those folks can always be scared. I've seen it done before. I want the fences down and I want the town open."

Bexar put aside the cards. He leaned back in the chair and now gave Charley Fair his undivided attention. "We've done enough talkin', friend. I always play my own hand. Always like to be on the right side of a proposition. How bad you want an open town?"

Charley Fair said, "Must be a couple of thousand dollars' gold in that safe this morning."

Bexar got up from the table. He said, "Let it stay there until I call for it," and by those words sold out Balder and Green and all of Willow Street. He moved out of Charley

Fair's, pacing beneath the street galleries—soft and almost feminine, blue-eyed and with a golden mustache covering his mouth.

As soon as Mitchell came into the jail office Ad Morfitt said, "We got a new sheriff."

"I heard so."

Ad hung up his gun and stood awhile in the room, tired from his night's work, yet reluctant to go home. He was a taciturn man, stocky and undistinguished, yet a man who thoroughly knew his business. Throughout most of his life he had carried the star during the dark hours, obscured by the more spectacular men who rode the town by day. He had seen them come and go, he had seen them run under fire, he had seen them make their gallant plays, he had seen them die. Now he looked at Mitchell and prophesied Mitchell's fate out of his long experience.

"One more man to watch, Dan. One more man pointed against you. You see that, of course."

"Sure."

"This new one—this Bexar—he's the kind I never hoped you'd have to meet. But you will meet him. Ford Green's got that figured out, one way or another." He went deeper into his foreboding. "It won't be very long now. You get so you smell these things comin'. I'd say it will break inside of forty-eight hours."

"Where will it break, Ad?"

Ad said, "Up until today I figured it would be Charley Fair bringing Younger to town. Now I ain't sure. This Bexar—" He was disturbed, this man who seldom was. He looked into the future with a gray and wise and gritty concern. "We got too many wires to trip over."

"You mean I have. You're not in this, Ad."

Ad said with extreme brevity, "I never let a day man

down in my life. I have worn the boards of this town thin from walkin', same as you. Don't tell me what to do." He gave Dan Mitchell an irritable stare, as though the very sound of Mitchell's talk had been improper. "I am damned near old enough to be your father. I'll be on the street at eight o'clock tonight. I'll be somewhere out of sight. When I hear a gun—" He went to the doorway and considered the street and now remembered he had to go home. He looked back with a harassed expression. "You've got your troubles and I've got mine." He went down Willow at a dragging step.

Mitchell took his first tour afoot. Out by the stockyards great billows of dust stained the yellow sunlight where herds were crowding into the loading-pens, and from that direction came the quick shrill cry of Texans handling the stock. Farther out on the prairie homestead wagons moved. The southern inbound stage now came across the Spanish River bridge. Wagons stood beyond the end of Willow in the area used by waiting settlers, stretched in a long row, and people walked in the full beat of light and seemed not to notice its power; all these people, he thought, were toughened to the land. They were farm folk migrating from the settled, expensive East to this promise of new homes and new fortunes. They would stick. Coming down Willow, he saw Henry Dreiser near the edge of Brinton's stable and as he arrived abreast with the boy he noticed that Dreiser looked steadily down Bismarck.

He was so fixed in his attention that he never saw Mitchell until the latter came around and faced him directly; then he put his eyes on the marshal and for a little while it seemed to Mitchell that this young man included him in a great and terrible hate of the world. He would not have been surprised if Dreiser had struck out at him, impelled by blind desire to do injury to something. Mitchell's voice went at him, easy and slow:

"You wanted that girl once."

Henry Dreiser sullenly said, "I don't want her now."

"Then what are you standing here for?"

"Maybe she was hungry, maybe she was alone—but she could have gone back home to where her friends were."

"How do you know?" asked Mitchell. "Easy for you to talk and make out how it might have been. She was the one who had to do the starving. You look well-fed to me. Nothing ever happened to you much. You never got far away from a kitchen or a warm fire. Pretty easy to stick to the things you figure are right when nothing comes along to batter hell out of you."

"She could have gone back home," repeated Henry.

"When you're drowning, my boy, you grab for the nearest thing."

Henry pointed. "Maybe she made one mistake. But why does she stay there?"

"Nothing wrong about working in a dance hall. What do you want in a woman? She's got the same heart and the same mind. And she didn't fool you. She told you the truth. If you're not interested, don't stand here blocking the walk."

He went into Brinton's and got the buckskin, taking up his steady circling of the town. In the middle of the afternoon he struck out beyond the river bridge and caught sight of the fence standing across the trail, one thin black line in the sun. It was beyond four o'clock when he returned. Coming into Willow, he saw Henry again, still by Brinton's. He reined up. "I told you to pull out, didn't I?"

Henry Dreiser said, "I can't leave her there."

"Don't go into that alley unless you want her."

"No," said Dreiser, "I don't want her."

"Then let her alone. You've got your life. She's

got hers."

"She can't stay there," said Henry.

"You turned her down. You made your choice in the matter. Don't let me catch you trying out your damned meddling respectability on her. She's straighter than you are. She's got more nerve. She laid it on the line clean and took her chances. There you sit, crying like a kid. You dropped your candy in the dust and you don't want it because somebody told you the dust was bad, but you still wish somebody would pick it up and wash it off and hand it back to you. You're a kid, Henry, and you don't belong here."

He rode on, leaving Henry crouched at the edge of Brinton's. He had roughed up the young man with his tongue; he had tried to break through and change the hard, inflexible things in Dreiser's head. It was five o'clock, with the sun a low flash against the Aspens, and all the color was beginning to run and change along Willow and along Race and the smell of dust got very strong and Bill Bexar rode out of town, heading toward the southern flats.

Race took on life. Charley Fair stood under the gallery, his crippled hand jammed in his front pocket. Tom Leathers walked out of the Arcade and disappeared in Briar. The War Bonnet stage came and let off two people. Ford Green crossed from the courthouse to Webber's, throwing a quick glance behind him; and Chappie Brink, sober and trembling, stood on his uncertain feet at the corner of Ute, watching Green.

The break would come within the time set by Ad Morfitt. There was always a feeling about these things; it got very strong. Along Race the stage was being set slowly and the sense of it began to run in the town, so plain that it had caused Ford Green to cast his backward glance—so strong that it made Leathers stay in town—so strong that it kept Chappie Brink sober.

But, rounding The Drovers' in the last tour before supper, Mitchell could not keep his mind on it. He was thinking of Rita waiting in her room at Big Annie's and of Henry Dreiser who stood at the head of the alley and was obsessed by the hard right-and-wrong distinction in his mind. There was no way of telling him that right and wrong had a thousand shades. As he sat in the saddle and looked down on the town, all this was clear to Mitchell, but he could not make a young man like Dreiser see it. When he got into Willow again he found Dreiser still there. But he was not alone. Leathers faced him and pointed a finger at him. Mitchell came up in time to hear Leathers say:

"You're wrong if you figure she should come crawlin' up this alley to beg mercy from you. She belongs to herself. She did what she had to do and she don't owe you one damned thing. Take it or leave it like that. There ain't any room in this country for a tinhorn sport. You can't get back the chips you lost in this deal. Either you quit and pull out or you buy a new stack and start over."

Henry looked at Leathers—listening but too involved in his own mind to hear much. Leathers swung around and gave Mitchell a queer stare. He shook his head, turning back to the young man.

"I'd like to be in your shoes, Henry. I wouldn't be standin' here. I'd be down there knockin' on her door and mighty glad I knew she wouldn't ever stoop to cheat." He walked away.

Mitchell followed him. Mitchell spoke at his retreating back. "What you doing that for?" he wanted to know.

"Go on," said Leathers, not looking at Mitchell. "Go on and mind your damned business. Leave a man alone."

Mitchell put about and left his horse in Brinton's, remembering the way Leathers had said those words; and crossed to Webber's for his supper. It was around seven then and shadows began to roll blue and fluid through town. Near eight he rose and strolled to the lobby and was lighting a cigar when he heard a horse rush up Race, with a voice calling out.

"Cattle went through our fence! Somebody's killed! Where's the sheriff?" The voice, rising and rising, shouted that question again: "Where's the sheriff?"

Chapter Fourteen: "Turn Out the Lights!"

Around four o'clock Bill Bexar had headed for the homestead fence. He traveled without hurry and when he reached the covered bridge he drew aside to let his horse have a drink and spent a half hour in the shade, later to go leisurely on. Beyond the bridge the plain was dark with Texas herds thrown off the trail to graze and wait their turn at the loading-pens. Five miles from the bridge he came upon the fence stretched across the main course of the trail, with a narrow aperture left for the road itself to pass through.

Two homestead men stood at this aperture and guarded it with their guns. Bexar said, "Evenin' gentlemen," and continued on without disclosing his identity. He took everything in with his idle glance, the homestead wagons standing at intervals along the fence, the tents and stoves set up for temporary living, the group of men now working under the sunlight's full glare on the west end of the fence. They had pooled forces and were making one great enclosure of a half-dozen or so quarter sections. Crews worked at intervals, digging post holes, and wagons moved in from the Aspens with pine posts, and another crew strung wire.

As he passed on he saw, in the south, the long ragged

line of another trail herd moving slowly forward. It was perhaps six miles away and coming head-on for the fence. This was nearing the end of a long, dusty day and the cattle would be smelling the river water ahead of them, and would hit the fence and mill against it and scatter. There was the narrow aperture for them to use, but for two or three thousand thirsty cattle and a dozen weary trail hands it was an aggravation instead of a help.

Bexar curved toward the Aspens, avoiding home-steaders and cattlemen alike. A mile from the gate in the fence he dismounted and comfortably stretched out on the soil to watch the herd move forward, carrying a lone dust-mist with it. The trail boss, riding ahead, had seen the fence and called up a couple men with a wave of his hand and galloped forward with them; at the same time the homesteaders began to collect from the far ends of the fence line and move toward the middle portion. A pair of homesteaders trotted out to meet the oncoming cattlemen. The sun was now behind the Aspens and the land began to shade from one color to another. Bexar lighted a new cigar and shifted position on the earth, closely observing the meeting of the yonder riders. They came face to face, they sat fast while they talked. The trail boss lifted a hand, pointed at the fence and pointed behind him. There was more talk until abruptly the trail boss and his pair of men wheeled about and trotted back to the herd, evidently finding no satisfaction in the parley.

No change of direction was made. The herd plugged on, traveling at a steady, water-anxious gait. The two homesteaders watched this for a full ten minutes and then swung back. All this was in panorama to Bill Bexar, who watched the dark spearhead of cattle move toward the homesteaders who now began to take station along the fence to guard it. Some of them ran toward their wagons, climbed up to heavy wagon horses, and came lumbering back.

When the herd was within three hundred yards of the fence one of the homestead men rode forward again, obviously to warn the trail boss. The trail boss flung out his hand, waving the homesteader away, and at the same time the punchers riding the flanks of the beef began to trot toward the head of the column, where the trouble would be. Bill Bexar was a mile from all this. Guessing what would happen, he stepped to the saddle and waited. It was seven o'clock, with deeper shadows beginning to flow in the sky and the bright points of chuck-wagon fires glinting along the plain. The head of the trail herd struck the fence and stopped, and all these up-loading cattle began to jam and spread against the barbwire, putting pressure on it. Suddenly one of the homesteaders, knowing nothing of the ways of cattle in mass, lifted his gun and fired a shot to the sky.

Bill Bexar lifted his reins in instinctive response. The horse moved around and started away, and then Bexar reined it back in time to see this trail herd, startled by the shot, suddenly lose its shape and break into a lumbering run. The Texans galloped at the edges of the herd to check the stampede and their voices came wild and keen over the distance. *"Hi-hi-hi!"*

It was then too late. These Texas cattle were fast as deer. The column ceased to be a column and the whole plain smoked up as the beef broke and rushed on, blind and frightened; they went through the fence in one surge, kicking it to pieces so that there was no trace of fence left. Homesteaders wheeled and galloped aside, but some of them were caught in the current, lonely bobbing specks against the sea of tossing horns and tails and heaving dun backs. One wagon, surrounded by the straining herd, was a white island in the mass for a while and then disappeared. Rushing on, the herd split into fragments and in the distance, near the river, other herds which had been peacefully grazing caught the smell of fear and began to stir. Before Bexar's amused eyes the desert was suddenly in motion, herd mixed with herd, all racing toward the river.

Part of this stampede veered his way, as he had foreseen. He wheeled the horse and drew away. In the deepening twilight he sauntered idly across the flats, well clear of the trouble. By dark he swung back toward the covered bridge, and passed grazing bands of beef, now spent and peaceful. Punchers ran by him in the shadows, their voices cursing and calling. Bexar tried to lift the bridge from the dark starlight and saw nothing of it; and was at the water's very margin before he noticed there was no bridge. The pressure of frightened cattle had broken it and carried it into the river. Dead cattle lined the banks when he forded across; and other punchers were moving around him, someone saying, "Where's Jodie? You seen Jodie?"

"He was in the middle of this when it busted."

Bexar idled back toward the wink and flash of River Bend's lights. Homestead fires flared near the end of Willow Street and over the distance he heard a woman singing. He came up against the back edge of town, threaded an alley, and stopped in Brinton's compound. Here he settled against the dismantled bed of a wagon to smoke out his cigar and to bide his time.

Bearing his message of disaster, the homesteader rode shouting along Willow as far as Balder's store, and dropped from the saddle and went in, soon followed by Franzen and Dug Neil and Brinton and Ford Green. Mitchell crossed toward Brinton's and got his buckskin and came out of the stable in time to see a small puncher hurl himself into Willow. Dried streaks of sweat netted the dust on his face.

He said, "Doctor around here?"

"In the hotel," Mitchell said, and watched the little man rush at the hotel's porch and throw himself out of the saddle. Mitchell walked the buckskin to the head of Race Street and paused there, looking into the bright crosshatch of its lights. There had been the beginning inflow of the trail crowd, but now the news of the stampede ran the street and riders came from the saloons and departed at once for the prairie. Charley Fair came outside his saloon, bulky and still in the gallery shadows; the women of the dance hall stood in a cluster at the entrance, their dresses a welter of color. Doctor Utten left the hotel with the puncher and crossed to Brinton's at a brisk walk. Dug Neil merged from Balder's store.

"Dan," he called, "come in here a moment, will you?"

Mitchell turned the buckskin against the hotel porch and stepped down. At this moment Sherry Gault came forward from Gatchell's print shop, walking toward Webber's for late supper. Near the entrance she stopped and looked back at Mitchell and what he saw in her then was a perfection and a grace and a warmth that had been growing into his awareness during the long year he had known her. She was the strength and the completeness and the personal glory a man dreamed of but never expected to find. She was the core of every campfire, the voice in the wind, the call that sounded in the deeps of the hills. These were impressions and half thoughts that raced violently through him as he came up to her and lifted his hat and passed on to Balder's. Then he shut her from his mind. He knew what this meeting would be and what his orders would be. Balder would tell him to close up the town. When he received those orders everything would come to its climax on the dust of Race Street.

Balder's room was full of men. The homesteader held up a handkerchief to cover a bruised mouth. He talked through the handkerchief.

"They said to hell with the fence and came on. Somebody fired a gun and that was the end of the fence. It is a wonder half of the men in front of that stock didn't get killed outright. My wagon went over, my wife and two kids with it. If they hadn't of fell under the wagon box they'd of been trampled to death."

"You sure the sheriff wasn't out there this afternoon?"

"No," said the homesteader. But then he pulled the handkerchief away from his mouth. "There was a fellow riding around out there. Fellow with a yellow mustache. Black clothes. Wore two guns. First time I ever saw that."

"Where'd he go?" asked Balder.

"I don't recall. This herd was moving up to us and that was what we watched."

Balder turned on Ford. "There's your man. You'd better find him. If he saw it and did nothing there's something crooked in this."

The homesteader said, "What about us out there?"

Balder answered, "We'll do the best we can," and nothing more was said for a long drag of time. The homesteader showed his dissatisfaction and left the room.

Green sat dry and still until Dug Neil challenged him: "Well, what about it?"

"Something went wrong," admitted Ford Green.

Tom Franzen spoke up. "I watched that fellow this afternoon. He went into Charley Fair's for a drink and he stayed a good twenty minutes. Charley was in there with him." All this seemed to make an answer, for Franzen swung his question on Green like a ball bat: "You working with Charley Fair?"

Green lifted his head and was on the verge of an angry answer; he met the combined attack of all the eyes in the room. These men had a common suspicion and showed it.

211

So he said, "No, Tom," and held back his feeling.

"I see only two things," stated Tom Franzen. "Either you're workin' with him or else he and this Bexar player you for a sucker. Either way you got nothing to be proud of."

"Now," said Brinton, "what do we do?"

"That fracas out there," said Balder, "will settle itself."

Mitchell had said nothing so far. Now he contradicted Balder. "A bad guess. Inside of a couple of hours this town will be swamped to the dashboard. Homesteaders and trail boys, all looking for satisfaction."

"That's your job," said Balder.

"Is it?" asked Mitchell.

He got then the same sort of a survey Ford Green earlier had received from the group. These men had their doubts of him. In the back part of their heads were all the rumors and suspicions of a year's making. They were solid men and good men for the most part, but they had that inevitable kink of reasoning which was that any man paid to police a town necessarily picked up part of the town's dirt on his clothes. Some of them, he knew, had always been against him. Some of them had thought him too lax with Race Street and some of them had thought him too severe. This was the way of it in a town: a marshal rode the middle of the street and pleased nobody if he did his job well. Looking at them carefully, he read their minds and had his humorless amusement.

Balder shot back his question, "Isn't it?"

"Yes," said Mitchell, "it is my job."

"Then," said Balder, openly relieved, "take care of it."

But Mitchell added his casual afterthought: "My job, as long as I keep the job."

"What's that?" asked Dug Neil, and once more the crowd watched him, and he felt unease and faint fear move through the room.

"Ed's been a litle dissatisfied lately," said Mitchell. He's been dabbling with the idea of getting another man. You got another man ready, Ed?"

"No," said Balder, issuing the word reluctantly.

Mitchell looked down at the seated Ford Green. "You ad a man ready. Where is Bexar now?"

"I don't know."

"Maybe back in an alley waiting for me to ride by," aid Mitchell. "That was the original idea, wasn't it?"

Green remained pale and indrawn and cautious. When he looked at Mitchell his great capacity for hatred showed in his eyes and his great desire to destroy showed there too. But he was a clever man and used his cleverness now. "That's a good excuse, if you want to quit. Why don't ou quit?"

"I've been wondering," answered Mitchell, in the same unvarying tone, "why you hire your chores done. What are you afraid of, Ford?"

"Not of you," sighed Green, his voice coming out in a strained, wind-broken whisper. "Why don't you quit? You can step out now when the going is tough. The town aid you well, but you don't have to think of that. Light out for the hills. You have been a hero in time of peace, ust riding down the middle of the street. Don't take any chance on hurting your reputation now. Get a toothache and run for your hide-out. Leave word with Charley Fair before you go. Tell him everything's all right. You've done it before."

"Ford," said Mitchell, idle and even, "you're smart but your belly is yellow."

"Wait and see!" cried Green and got up from his chair. "Wait and see!"

"I'll wait, but not long," said Mitchell. He turned on Ed Balder. "You want Race Street closed. That's what you called me for, wasn't it?"

"That's it," said Balder slowly.

213

"When do you want it closed?"

"The trail's done for. It is time to change."

Mitchell said, "I know all that. Don't waste talk, Ed."

"Why, now," said Balder, "I've got to make you see it. You're thinking this is all for profit. But there's more to a town than that. A town is people trying to get along. The trail and the gamblers have had their turn. Now it is the turn for the homesteaders. Here we sit trying to figure what is best. Sometimes it is a little hard."

For once this big storekeeper, struggling with a tough problem, made his try at self-expression, and in trying rose above his love of authority and his self-esteem. He looked at Mitchell with some anxiety, as though he wanted Mitchell's understanding, and at that moment there was something to be admired about him. "We have had to get along with the good and the bad as best as we could. That's the way with all towns. They grow up the same and they go through the same breaks. Some do it the easy way and for some it goes tough. Going to be tough for us. Close the street, Dan. Close it your own style."

"All right," said Mitchell. He stood in the middle of this group and found reason to smile. It was not a complete smile, for it had some regret and some foreshadowing of disaster in it, and they saw this and kept still. But he asked one more question:

"Have you any idea where these folks on Race Street go from here?"

"Why," said Balder, "they came from somewhere and they'll go somewhere. I do not say we are doing the kind thing. We are doing what we have got to do. There's a lot of crying in this world."

"I wondered if you understood that," said Mitchell and walked from the room.

He stood on the walk a moment, watching the big freighters roll down Willow for the long haul to War Bonnet. Race Street, he noticed, was filling up again and he lanes of light showed the steady dust steam which ose from the churning of horses' feet. The dance-hall nusic caught on and the Arcade barker stood at the edge f the walk, calling out: "Over here, boys! Best whisky, est games—a good run for your money and no omplaints! Come on over! We've got lots of chips on the ables! Take 'em away if you can! Our loss, your gain—no ard feelings! Come on in and hear the cougar howl!"

The townsmen came out of Balder's store and moved way. Mitchell watched Ford Green cut across the dust to he courthouse and pause at the door to look both ways n the street before he entered. Balder and Dug Neil alted beside Mitchell.

Balder said, "I am going into Webber's for a bite to eat. The rest of the night I will be at this doorway with a Spencer carbine. Dug will be on The Drovers' porch. That's just to tell you where we are, if you want a little help."

They went away before he had an opportunity to answer; all he saw was the embarrassed look on Balder's face when the latter turned off, as though this had been better left unsaid. Still Mitchell kept his position, idle and unhurried from knowing that tonight all tings started from him and all things would end with him. Two things he now noted: Chappie Brink moved over Race's dust to the courthouse stairs and sat down. Tom Leathers patrolled up Race, cast an inquiring glance at Mitchell, and retraced his steps down the street, fading into the shadows around Horsfall's stable. The stars were electric-bright in the depthless black of the sky and a small slow wind came from the south.

Ford Green climbed the courthouse stairs and walked down the dark hall to his office. He had left his door open on leaving the office earlier and now confidently walked

straight at it and banged his head hard against the panels.
He stood still with a hand on the knob and was puzzled
that it had swung shut. He opened it and stepped
through, feeling through his coat pocket for a match to
light the lamp. Bill Bexar's voice came from an unseen
corner of the room:

"Better leave it dark, friend. Said you didn't want me
to be seen with you too much."

Green felt a thready pulse of fear. He stopped moving
ahead and he asked, "Where in God's name have you
been?" and then quietly took one quick sidestep and put
his shoulders to the wall.

"Out watching a stampede."

"Bill," said Green, "where do you stand? I'll play the
sucker for nobody."

"Right where I was when you met me, friend."

"Why didn't you stop that fence business?"

Bill Bexar's voice had a ring to it, as though he smiled.
"A little more fire for the pot. You wanted things to be
kind of tough on Mitchell, didn't you? They'll be tougher
tonight, in town. That's what you wanted, wasn't it?"

"Maybe," said Green, and let his mind feel a cautious
path along this suggestion. Nothing more was said for a
good thirty seconds and he heard nothing at all in the
room; and so it shocked him when Bill Bexar's voice
came to him from the hall. Bexar had crossed the room,
passed in front of him, and gone out of the door without
sound.

"I'll be waiting for you to say the word, friend."

"Where?" asked Green.

Amusement once more rustled across Bexar's words.
"By the back of Brinton's stable," he said and faded into
the hall. His steps made their momentary loose echoes on
the stairsteps.

This room held all the strong heat of the day. Still
motionless against the wall, Ford Green slowly sweated
and struggled with his doubts. Presently he crossed to the

216

window and looked down on Race. His glance ran from The Drovers' on up to Willow where he found Mitchell still idle in front of Balder's store. Green centered his attention on the marshal and the venom of jealousy began to change him.

At this same hour the head barman in The Pride came into Charley Fair's back office, closing the door behind him. "Jett Younger's out in the alley."

Fair said, "Alone?"

"Brought couple of his boys in with him."

"Tell him to stay out of sight for a little while."

And at this same time Irma Gatewood came into the dark coach and found Hazelhurst waiting. This was their third meeting and the first time he had arrived earlier than she. The knowledge of his eagerness turned her warm and she stood in the aisle and knew the inexpressible gratitude of being wanted. He had never yet touched her by so much as the tips of his fingers and while she waited for him to speak she hoped he would at last break down the rigid barrier he insisted on placing between them.

"Mrs. Gatewood," he said, "this is wrong for you."

She tried to brush his doubts aside. "Will we never get beyond that?"

"I think we never will."

"Yes," she told him, "we will." She was supremely confident. "There's nothing else we can do. I'm no child, George. I have been a faithful woman. I never flirted, never stepped out of the straight path. I have been as strict in my judgment of what is proper and improper as any wife could be. Yet here I am, and never for a moment in the last four days have I felt it to be wrong. No guilt, no shame. It is as though I have been asleep and this is the awakening."

"You know what the town would say," he answered,

"and what your husband would say."

"We have been married eight years. Isn't that long enough, if—" She stopped the rest of it, being loyal and without malice. She changed the question. "Isn't it possible for people to make mistakes—and to correct them?"

"Yes," he said, "but you are making no correction, Mrs. Gatewood. Not in me. You know what I am. You know what my life has been like."

"Perhaps," she told him in her light, very sure manner, "this is correction for you as well."

"Ah, if I only thought that."

"Don't you?"

"I have looked on the black side of people most of my life," he told her. "I have had my own black side before me always. I know myself for what I am. I will never be any better than I am."

"And how are you bad, George?"

He said, "You see me perhaps as having some gallantry. I dress well and I seem to live a dangerous life, which is perhaps true. You see the outside of George Hazelhurst. You know nothing of the inside. If there was not emptiness inside George Hazelhurst why would he be living the useless, something-for-nothing life of a gambler? I have a good deal of pride. You see that. But it covers nothing worth having. Nothing at all, Mrs. Gatewood."

"Yes," she said, "I do think you're rather gallant. You are protecting me now."

"No," he answered, "I'm protecting myself. If you lived with me a month you'd have the whole cheap and dirty story of George Hazelhurst. I'd rather you never knew it."

She was gently laughing at him. "What do you think of me, George?"

"It would be rather easy," he told her in sober,

reluctant truth, "to take you away. You must know that. There's been nothing in my life like this."

"Then take me away. It is what I want."

He was long silent, he was mustering up whatever will he had and whatever sense of right he had. She knew precisely what went on in him and she stood back and waited, serenely confident of the answer. He let a long sigh out of him. 'You will always regret it. There is no glory in this, even though it seems the answer to everything. I have been running away all my life. Now you'll be."

"Take me away, George."

"Nothing will change your mind?"

"It isn't in my mind at all. It's in my heart. You don't change that."

"I'll meet you with a rig at the end of Willow after dark tomorrow."

"Couldn't it be tonight?"

His voice was really sad. "Heaven can wait a day. I can't leave tonight."

"Tomorrow night then," she said, her voice going strong and pleased through the coach.

He moved by her and was careful not to touch her. She had her impatient regret of that and she admired him the more. His voice continued strange and depressed to her.

"You know," he said, "life can trap a man very neatly. I wanted everything when I was young. I took all the short cuts. Now here is the greatest thing a man can have—the love of a woman. The tragedy is I have nothing left to offer her. You can have no idea of how a man like me feels in a situation like that." He was at the coach steps, and added one more thing: "You must never be hurt. Good night."

Mitchell's cigar had gone out. He lighted a match and

219

cupped it against his face so that for that moment his face was a target in the shadows of Willow Street, seen by half a dozen pairs of observing eyes. From the doorway of Webber's, Sherry Gault saw it and was struck by its composed, half-kind expression. Knowing the town and knowing all that had happened during the day, she realized more clearly than most people what Mitchell now confronted. When he left the west side of Willow and crossed the dust River Bend would break apart; and it astonished her that this man, who so exactly understood what his first forward motion meant, should not have put on that expression she had seen before—that bare and empty and really cruel cast of mouth and eye.

From the courthouse window, Ford Green saw Mitchell's match flare. From their stations on Race, both Chappie Brink and Tom Leathers saw it. From his spot in the darkness of Neil's side alley, Jett Younger observed it, and Bill Bexar, who was now in the dark wall shadows adjoining Webber's—and not where he had told Green he would be—looked on.

Mitchell took in the good strong savor of the cigar. For a moment he wondered about Henry Dreiser, who had disappeared, and for a while his thoughts turned to Rita with a deep, real care and he visualized her pale face and though he didn't know it, he shook his head for her. Remembrance of Dick Lestrade came to him, with its ache for the boy's misunderstanding, and afterward he had his bright vision of Sherry Gault, fair and beautiful, and he recalled how the drunken puncher had reached out to touch her, and he understood that puncher's feelings thoroughly—that disbelief in a dream against the hot and dusty day. Ad Morfitt came up the middle of Race Street, saw him and nodded and went into Ute. Thereafter the outer edges of living faded for Mitchell and he faced Race Street and threw his cigar into the dust, watching its tip spray brightly as it struck.

He walked across Willow toward the Arcade.

A new crowd of Texans rounded The Droves' and came up Race on the run, dim in the steady dust screen. He reached the front of the Arcade and faced the doorway and looked ito the crowd and noted that this night the trail riders carried their guns. A shout from a man in the street drew Mitchell about because of a vague familiarity of voice and he saw the new group of Texans. Cap Ryker sat on his saddle, ruddy and imperious in the flash of saloon lights.

"I told you I'd come back, friend."

Mitchell swung his shoulders around, putting Cap Ryker behind him. Long ago he had decided how this would go and now it was too late to change. He walked into the Arcade and stopped.

"Turn out the lights, boys. The street is closed."

Chapter Fifteen: Ordeal

Still in Webber's doorway, Sherry watched Mitchell go down Race and pause before the Arcade's door, and as he did so her heart seemed to squeeze small so that breathing grew hard for her. She had no control over her mind. Her thoughts ran in a swift fury of activity, so that she was with him every step, so that she was ahead of him to visualize what would happen. Not knowing it, she fought his battles and saw his body turn and move through the town's wild crossfire and she saw him drop and she heard him speak her name from the deep dust of Race Street.

He had turned from the Arcade's door to meet the sudden call of a man in the middle of the street, and then she recognized Cap Ryker, who had fulfilled a threat to return and right his injuries. What puzzled her was Mitchell's indifference to Ryker. Mitchell, saying nothing at all, turned back to the Arcade door and stepped inside.

She crossed to the courthouse, knowing Green had gone to his office. Running up the courthouse stairs she called ahead, "Ford—Ford," and noticed that his room was dark. But he was inside, for his voice came to her: "What is it?"

She stopped at his doorway. "Why don't you burn a light?"

"Never thought of it."

She hated evasion, she hated secrecy, and now she hated his being here under the cover of darkness, once more reverting to his alien habits. She said angrily, "Light the lamp, unless you're hiding from something."

She heard his quick, rough intake of breath. He moved along the room and scratched a match on the wall; he lighted the table lamp and by its glow she viewed the tin wedge of his face, its pointedness, its lean and bloodless caution. What really made her notice this was the change in his eyes. Every feeling he had seemed to drain into them and stand there in green glowing pools. Against that liveliness the rest of his face was parched and dead. He hated her for her words and showed it. Somehow she got the idea he was greatly troubled, that his careful planning had been knocked aside, leaving him momentarily helpless and confused.

"Sherry," he said, "can't you keep your wicked tongue off me?"

"What are you afraid of?"

Not aware that Mitchell had earlier asked the same question, she couldn't know how terrible the question was to him. It hit a bruised spot, making him flash back his outraged cry:

"Nothing—nothing on this earth! What makes people think I'm afraid? Have I ever backed up from anything? No! I've never run from a living soul in my life! I can fight! I showed you that when I tackled Mitchell! Damn this town! If a man is quiet and minds his own business, if he doesn't get down and roll in the mud like Mitchell they think he's afraid!"

"What they think," she said, choosing her words, "is that you are too sly. Nobody knows what is in your head. You have held yourself away from people. That's the penalty you're paying now, Ford. You can't look down on this town like a cat waiting to jump on something and still expect anybody to trust you." Her words carried her on and her logical mind came to something that rather shocked her. "Why, you're really not human."

He struck her with his question: "What are you here for?"

"Where's that sheriff you brought to town—that Bexar?"

"Out on the street."

"Hiding? Hiding and waiting for a shot at Mitchell?"

That unease and desperateness showed in him clearly. "No, of course not," he jerked out. "Sherry, don't talk like that."

"Get him, then," she asked. "Get him up here."

He watched her with a growing slyness. "Why?"

"He's got to help Mitchell tonight."

"That big man need help?" asked Green in a ragged, gritty voice. "That great man, that lion of courage, that master of the town?" He threw all his emotion into his talk; he went on with his jeering tone. "Why should he need help? He's got a gun and he's got his hands. Good hands, too. Maybe you noticed that. He's the lord here. A little man like me wouldn't be of any use to him. Bexar would just be in his way. Oh, no, Sherry. He's all right. He'll just pick the town up and move it away, and get on his buckskin and parade before the admiring spectators."

She had never actually faced this man with an open mind or with an inquiring heart. Everything in the past had been accepted without much thought; they had long known each other and she had seen much of him and had liked him. She had taken him for what he outwardly was and so gradually they had drifted into an engagement. Nothing had been very compelling; no other man had broken through her reserve to challenge her loyalty to Ford Green—no other man until one day she had noticed Mitchell's glance come to her and long remain.

In the beginning it had not mattered. For she had

resented Mitchell out of some obscure reason and had thrown up her guard against him. She had heard stories of him and had believed them; she had known that he took his last half hour each night at Big Annie's and had been repelled by the thought. As his presence had grown stronger with her and his personality increasingly a challenge to her, she had more deliberately resisted him. Never, until a short time ago, had the inevitable comparison between Ford and Dan Mitchell come up.

That had been only a few days before, with the first doubt of Ford coming to her with great shock and the first questioning of her own love of him somehow sickening her. That time she had evaded meeting an answer, too proud to admit that her engagement could be a mistake.

"Sherry," said Ford, "stop looking at me like that."

Now she had to meet her answer because the need of it was so urgent. No woman, she thought, could love a man and look at him as she looked at Ford Green this moment—with an almost cruel insight into what he really was—his evasive and tortuous mind that never liked daylight, his thin-skinned, acidly jealous pride, his pointed and fox-shaped face. And when, in greatest wonder, she asked herself how it was she had not seen all this before, she had her instant answer. Until Mitchell, no other man had come into her imagination to stand beside Ford and make his weaknesses apparent.

"Ford," she said again, "he has got to fight beside Mitchell tonight."

"No," said Ford Green, at last coming to one firm thing. "He'll never lift a gun for Mitchell. Mitchell made his bed. Let him lie in it."

"You hate him greatly," she said. "I think it is the only honest feeling you ever have had."

"No," said Green. "I have two others. I love you— even when you kick me around with your tongue and your eyes as you're doing now—and I mean to get some-

225

where before I die."

"But he stands in your way and therefore you'll let him die?"

"If I've got that power over Mitchell," said Green, "then I'll let him die."

Her thoughts swiftly ran and swiftly changed. Everything came to her, the images of scenes, the recollection of words idly said and forgotten and not remembered until now. She recalled one phrase Mitchell had spoken: "If a man's not everything to you, he's nothing." That phrase had haunted her and reproached her; it had stirred her like fire. Mitchell, she thought, had changed her by those few words, he had wakened her out of sleep, and this scene now was of his doing.

"Ford," she murmured, "I'm through with you."

Troubled and half-mad as he was, he cried instantly, "I'm the same man you knew before!"

"I know," she answered, despising him and yet sorry for him. "But I never really knew you before. You never let me know you. Or perhaps I didn't care."

"No," he told her. "It is Mitchell. He's made the difference. I have seen this coming."

"Have you?" she asked, actually surprised. "How could you? I haven't known it until this moment." But all that turned into nothing, for the big curfew clock struck its sullen notes to remind her of time's passage. "Where's Bexar?"

"I don't know," he said. "You know what I'm doing? I'm waiting here for Friend Mitchell to drop. And then I'll take over Race Street. I said I'd do it and I'll do it."

She wheeled out of the room. Down the hall she heard him say: "I never turned beggar and I won't beg for you. I've got my pride, too, Sherry. You'll see."

She went down the dark stairs two at a time and tripped on the last step and fell on her elbows. She crouched in the dark, crying for the pain but making no sound, and

226

got up and left the courthouse. It had seemed hours since her entrance there, but it could not have been long, for Mitchell now walked toward the Bullshead, leaving the Arcade behind him. All lights in the Arcade had gone out. The crowd in the place had come to the dark walk, making a silent and waiting mass there; and the lusty pulse beat of this street seemed to be dying away. Chappie Brink still sat on the courthouse steps, and she noticed he had a big Navy Colt on his lap. He had been watching Mitchell. Now he looked up at her, and turned his head to cast a glance at Ford Green's window, and spoke:

"Better get off this street."

"Where is Bexar?"

"Don't know—yet." Then he added, "Ask your man. He knows."

She walked slowly across Willow's dust and turned at Webber's doorway, unable to move farther from the center of trouble. Mitchell was at this moment turning into the Bullshead and then she took time to look around her and see other shapes darkly shadowed on Willow, waiting as she was waiting for the sound of gunfire. There was a blur of people near the end of Willow—a half crowd gathered silently there and in a little while, as she watched it, one man detached himself and moved on as far as the courthouse. Webber's lights crossed the street at this point and when he got into the beam of the lights she recognized the young homestead man, Henry Dreiser. He had a carbine in his arm and now he hooked his head around the corner of the courthouse, took a glance at Race Street, and walked back toward the blur at the end of Willow. That, she guessed, would be homesteaders.

Mitchell stepped into the Bullshead and faced a waiting crowd. The word had gone before him, so that all these men knew what he was about. He looked beyond the Texas cowhands to Lou Wells, who ran the Bullshead, and to Lou's barmen against the back wall, and then aside to the gamblers at the tables. These men lived by chance, self-schooled to show the world nothing. They showed him nothing now. The wheel was spinning and they looked on and waited for the number to come up.

"Lou," he said, "close up and turn out your lights."

All the Texans had their guns. This word had gone out, too; the word that the rule was off. Things like this ran with the wind. One puncher, centered in the room, stared at Mitchell with a speculative, devil-bright attention. Afterward he whipped a glance over to the bar to Wells. "You want any help?"

"Don't interfere," called Mitchell. "You've got no chips in this deal."

"I could buy in," said the puncher and laughed a long, great laugh that filled the room.

This puncher had the crowd with him. These men, thick of blood and heavy-salted by their days of abstinence, could be swayed. A word or a motion would capture them, and in the background Lou Wells, knowing this perfectly, waited for the break to come and said nothing.

Mitchell moved deeper into the room, into the distilled smell of whisky and tobacco smoke; he moved straight at the puncher and watched the puncher's eyes widen and show a deep, thoughtful shine. He watched the puncher's mouth grow broad and he saw the little dilation around the nostrils of this man's nose. He came on, not stopping until the puncher took a backward step, and then the puncher's eyes went down and the trouble was over.

Mitchell said, "All right, Lou," and watched Lou Wells slowly drop his chin as a signal to the barkeeps. They went along the walls, killing the lights. Mitchell turned on his heels, the clack of his boots sounding as loud to him as though he were in an empty room.

This night was hot and sweat collected inside his hat

nd rolled back and forth, trapped by the hatband. He
came to Ute and stepped into Ute's dust, with the Cowboy
Palace in front of him. Half across Ute he stopped and
pivoted to face the darkness of Ute as it ran its narrow
way toward Railroad.

"Evening, Bill."

There was the vague point of a cigar standing against
the black, and the point suddenly brightened and a shadow moved out of the alley's dark. Bexar's face was a dim
blur and his voice came at Mitchell with a singsong tone.
"Good eyes, friend. How'd you see me?"

"It is a likely place to stand. Other boys have stood
there before."

"The town's getting dark, friend."

"It will be darker."

"Then," said Bill Bexar, "all alleys will be black when
you pass them."

"Bill," said Mitchell, as smooth and idle as the other
man, "don't interfere."

"Your town, so far," answered Bill Bexar.

Mitchell stepped into the Cowboy Palace. He said,
"Close your doors, Jack," and moved on. He left this
message at the Bartly, crossed Sage and paid his respects
to Gilson's Rest and Hugh Olvany's Oasis. At the foot of
Race he turned about and viewed his work. Except for the
lone lantern swinging in Horsfall's barn, the lights on the
north side of Race were out, and along that walk Texas
men stood idle, watching this town die and waiting for the
crack of a gun. Noise began to rise in The Pride and some
chair or table smashed the floor and a voice lifted its
lunging yell: *"Yaaaiii!"*

Ad Morfitt came out of Sage's south alley and stopped,
sweeping the street with a careful glance; he saw Mitchell
and came down the street at once. He said, "Watch The
Pride. Don't go in the front end. Keep clear of Ute.
Something's goin' on there." He moved on, diving into

the space between Horsfall's barn and the Oasis. As Mitchell started up the south walk of Race Street he heard shots break close together somewhere in Bismarck Alley.

Having seen Mitchell start into the Arcade, Tom Leathers crossed Race to the south side and took post at the mouth of Briar, thereby constituting himself a flank guard for Mitchell. He was only a matter of fifty feet from the courthouse steps where Chappie Brink sat and in a little while Chappie Brink came over to him.

"Hell with you, Leathers. This is my corner. Go pick yourself another spot."

Leathers grinned. "If you aim to fire that cannon you better hold it with both hands. Thirty years of drinkin' is lovely to contemplate but bad on the aim."

"Go pick yourself another spot," repeated Chappie Brink irritably. Then he added, "Watch the big fellow, Tom. It is gettin' awful bad."

Leathers slid down Briar to Bismarck Alley and took stand in the pit of black. He faced the solid side of Brinton's stable, with Brinton's compound to his left and with Big Annie's house still farther to the left. Light came through the drawn shade of Big Annie's front room but this was only a pallid spot of color shedding no glow on the alley. He tarried awhile to keen the night for sound and substance and, being dissatisfied, turned up Bismarck to Willow and discovered a group of men huddled beyond Brinton's. He went that way at once.

"What the hell you standing here for?"

A man's voice moved back at him: "Go about your business. We'll take care of ours."

"Ah," said Tom Leathers, really pleased at the prospect of a quarrel, "you're speakin' to the wrong customer." He hauled out a match and flamed it against his thumbnail. He had his view of the collected men and found them to be homesteaders, with Henry Dreiser foremost. The light went out, to be followed by Leathers's smooth advice: "I admire your intentions, which are full of mayhem, arson, and general hell. But you don't know much about this kind of a game. Race Street is crowded with experts in the matter of trouble. Better go home and milk your cows."

"Never mind," said one of the homesteaders.

"It was just advice," murmured Leathers. "I guess you're bound to have your fun. But leave the marshal alone or I'll invigorate the bunch of you." He went back onto Bismarck and reached Big Annie's. Next to Big Annie's was an open lot and across the alley from the open lot stood the rear of The Pride. From The Pride he heard the rising rumble of talk. He remained in this blackness and debated with himself as to the best course to pursue, and caught the smell of a horse somewhere near. He made a slow pivot, seeking to orient this smell. Brinton's was a hundred yards above him and therefore its odors would be diluted by the distance. Swinging gradually, he thought he had a clear compass bearing on the horse. It seemed to be to the left of Big Annie's, in the adjoining empty lot.

This was the sort of guessing game he loved. He moved by Big Annie's and reached the front of the empty lot and crouched on his hands, making out nothing with his eyes. But the horse smell was strong enough here and presently he heard the slow shift of weight in the lot and the jingle of a bridle chain.

He backed away from the lot and crawled along the front of Big Annie's house. He put his shoulder against the house, now possessed by the keen joy of a predator come upon a hot scent. He listened but was no longer able to pick up a sound from the lot because of the rising racket in The Pride. He studied this thing in his mind, he put thumb and forefinger against his nose and gently pinched it, and turned to Big Annie's door. He slipped into the house and found Big Annie standing in the middle of her living-room.

She had a worried question ready for him. "What's happening on Race? Where's Dan?"

Leathers pointed to the window at the side of the room. "Count thirty, slow. Then raise that blind."

He backed out, closing the door gently. He crawled along the wall's edge to the open lot. In this position the edge of the wall blanked his right arm, which was his gun arm, and so he stepped farther into the lot and lifted his .44 from its holster. He had reached twenty-five in his own silent counting when Big Annie's blind went up and a full beam of yellow light struck across the back lot to illuminate a horse standing in the lot's middle and to identify the figure of Jett Younger by the horse.

"Well," said Leathers, easy as summer's wind, "you're alone and in bad company."

Younger sprang away from the horse. He put up a hand to ward off the window light. He said in a powerful voice, "Who's that?" He tried to catch sight of Leathers, who still stood in the darkness. He repeated the question: "Who's that?" Then he ducked low and went under the horse's belly, putting himself behind it, and backed slowly out of the light.

Leathers said, as though it were wholly a matter of indifference, "Always like to give a fellow an even break," and walked straight on into the lot. He moved sidewise. When he reached the beam of light he called, "Here I come, Jett," and ran hard forward.

Jett was still back-tracking, and faded now into the darkness. Jett saw Leathers; he grunted Leathers's name.

Leathers brought up his gun and found his target dissolving. He rushed on into the black, with the sudden full riot of battle coming out of The Pride behind him. He weaved aside. He said, "Where you at now?" and jumped aside again. Suddenly another shade in Big Annie's house—a shade on the second floor—flew up and the back end of the lot came into view. He saw Jett clearly. Jett was waiting for a shot, as he was. Firing, he saw Jet's gun make its flash, but Jett's bullet went toward the sky and Jett's feet, catching wire, snagged and threw him. He was on his knees when he fired again. Tom Leathers put a shot straight into that weaving figure and saw the bullet beat Jett down. When he ran forward and bent over, curious but without pity, he saw Jett's lips move and quit moving.

A girl in Big Annie's looked from the second-story window and screamed. The back door of The Pride came open, letting out the full blast of a fight going on in there; and at the same time men ran down Bismarck Alley and a voice yelled at them: "Come one—come on!"

Leathers came from the lot into the alley. He yelled, "Annie—open your door!" He stood in the middle of the alley, hearing the homesteaders pound forward. Big Annie's door swung and light rushed through and Leathers, standing in the fan-shaped glow, watched the homesteaders move up and halt. Henry Dreiser was in front and Henry pointed at Tom Leathers's gun and said:

"What you propose to do with that?"

"Why," said Leathers, and looked at Henry with his thin, sharp grin, "it is a voice cryin' in the wilderness, son. In the wilderness of sin."

"Put it down," said Henry Dreiser. "Put it down or we'll knock you out."

"From a sodbuster," said Tom Leathers in profound astonishment. "From the meek of the earth."

"It may be," said Henry Dreiser, "but it is our earth as well as the cowman's. Put down the gun."

"Boys," said Tom Leathers, "I'd judge you wanted a little fun. There's a man out on Race in some difficulty—

233

a friend of mine by name of Mitchell, the marshal of this town. I expect he'll be coming into The Pride pretty soon, and maybe the Texas crowd won't like that. They don't like him much." He kept smiling but he was sharp and quick and he was dangerous. "Just follow me," he said, and moved to the rear of The Pride. One door stood open, out of which some unknown man had recently fled. Leathers came against the doorway and looked through it and through a rear room. Beyond the rear room was a bright view of The Pride's saloon hall in which Texas men moved and made their wreckage. Glass smashed and the big bar went over with a long, slow roar. Above all this racket cried one strong voice.

"Bust it up—bust it up to kindlin'! Where's that marshal? Why don't he come in here and stop us! Bust it up. Then we'll go drag that fellow out of his hole! Jupe, drag down the back bar! Smash that roulette machine! Bust it up!"

"For a minute," murmured Leathers to the homesteaders behind him, "we'll stand and watch. Couldn't do it better myself!"

He surveyed the homesteaders, seeing their dark faces move and their stirred eyes shine; the wrecking of The Pride pleased them, it was something they approved. What made him marvel was that men such as these, men of families, men whose lives had been slow and peaceful, should suddenly turn quietly savage. Maybe it was something in the air, a scent that reached down deep and woke the latent hell in every soul. Back of them, in Big Annie's open doorway, he saw Rita looking on and then Henry Dreiser turned about and walked through the crowd to her.

"Lila," said Henry Dreiser, "go back in the house."

"My name is Rita. I told you that."

"I wish you wouldn't remind me of it any more. Get back in the house before trouble starts."

"Trouble," she breathed. "You think I worry about trouble?"

"You want to get hurt?"

To Tom Leathers, who had watched her many a night, she usually made a small, helpless presence against a world too big for her. Yet now she looked at Henry Dreiser in a way that made the big homestead man seem immature. "Henry," she said, "don't talk about things you know nothing of. What do you know of trouble or hurt?"

He said, "I'm coming back here and I'm going to tear this dirty house down."

"I guess you could," she told him indifferently. "It wouldn't take much to do and we couldn't fight back, could we? We learn that the first thing. We just keep out of sight and move on when we're told to. Tear it down, Henry. We'll all be going soon enough."

"Where?" he asked. "Where would you be going?"

"Anywhere. That doesn't matter, does it?"

"I have been thinking," said Henry and seemed to call on righteousness for support. "Maybe I've got a duty to do. I'm going to take you out of this place. Someday maybe we can forget about it."

She watched him with her wise, still eyes and spoke very gently: "That would be very hard for you to do, wouldn't it?"

"Yes," he admitted, "it will be hard. But I guess that's what I've got to do. Everybody's got to bear a burden. Maybe this is ours." He drew his vast breath and made the plunge. "I will take you back, Lila."

"Why," said Leathers, "you fool."

Leathers had drifted through the crowd during this talk. He had not missed a word of it. He had heard every inflection in Henry's voice and he had seen every shade of expression on Rita's face. And he was really outraged by Henry Dreiser's self-conscious martyrdom. "You damn young greenhorn. You ain't takin' her back. She's takin' you back. And if I was her, I wouldn't."

Rita brought up her head. "Why?" she asked Leathers. "Why shouldn't I?"

"He's doin' his duty and he'll let you know that for the next forty years. He'll make you cry."

"I can stand crying—if that were the only thing."

"You don't have to cry. There's nothin' to cry for." He had put Henry Dreiser aside. He watched Rita and he was tremendously sober. "I made you smile, the other night. That's what you want—a man who can make you smile."

A tone of wonder lifted her voice. "I never knew what you meant when you looked at me, so sharp. I thought it was something else, Tom."

The noise in The Pride grew greater and that one bully voice kept calling for destruction. Bismarck Alley's dust spiraled and smoked in the beam of light passing out of Annie's door and Leathers saw Rita through its gold-stained haze. She held his attention, she read his face with her great, searching eyes and presently she straightened before him, in a way presenting herself to him, and he saw her woman's sureness come out of its dark place of hiding.

She turned to Henry Dreiser and spoke with a woman's kind regret: "It's too bad, Henry. I hope you find a girl you won't ever have to worry about."

Leathers laughed openly at the crowd. He said, "Maybe you can smile," and watched her smile for him. "You see," he said, "that's the way it always ought to be." He moved back through the homesteaders to The Pride's rear door, still laughing for the great goodness he felt, and he said to the homesteaders, "Now here's our raw meat," and entered The Pride.

He crossed a rear room and reached the main hall. The homesteaders came with him and the Texans, seeing this new intrusion, moved forward. Leathers grinned and he let out his wolf howl and made for the nearest Texan with pure joy in his heart. The Texan seized a bottle from the floor and brought it overhead in a sweeping motion. Leathers hit him full on, grappled for the bottle and got it. He seized the puncher around the waist and butted him on the chin. He stepped away and caught the puncher on the face with a roundhouse swing and sent the man down.

The homesteaders had joined the battle, slugging forward with their meaty arms. Leathers surveyed his scene and emitted a long yell, "*Aaiii!*" A Texan moved at him and Leathers said, "Right with you, brother," and advanced to battle.

Chapter Sixteen: And So Ends

Charley Fair had stood at the end of the bar and watched Cap Ryker enter The Pride with his trail crew. He walked across the floor, knowing trouble was at hand, and said in his affable voice, "On the house, Cap. Glad to see you back."

Cap Ryker was a giant whose anger had been long nursed. He put the flat of his hand against Charley Fair and shoved him aside and he waved his crew forward. "Bust it up—bust it up!"

Charley Fair turned about and nodded at his barmen. They moved out from the bar, catching up short billy sticks as they came. Charley Fair said, "Pass me one of those." He took his stand with them. He had but one good hand but he swung his billy like an overhand scythe, backed against the bar and giving no ground.

The barmen made a little line in the room, against which Cap Ryker's men moved. Somebody got behind Charley Fair and caught him around the throat. Slowly strangling, he beat backward with his billy, and had it wrenched from his hand and then the billy exploded like dynamite on his skull and the world roared and he went down beneath shifting feet.

He never was quite out. He rolled with the tide,

bringing his hands around his head for protection until his mind cleared. A Texan kicked him in the ribs and pushed him on his back, and sharp boot heels ground into his belly and scraped across his face. He was alive again, full of pain and knowing his ribs were broken, but he was a stubborn, savage man and, deep buried in the growing fight, he seized a pair of legs and brought a Texan down and crawled on him and got a forearm over the Texan's throat and put all his weight on the forearm and held it there until the Texan quit fighting. He was struck on the head again and dragged clear of the Texan. A bottle hit him so hard that it broke, its ragged edge leaving a deep, bloody track across his face.

Again stunned, he crawled forward. He got against the capsized bar and crawled over it. A Texan, knocked out by a billy's blow, fell on top of him. He worked his way from beneath the man, cleared the crowd and stood erect to survey the ruin around him—the back-bar mirror that shattered on the floor, the splintered chairs and tables, the broken roulette wheel, the colored windowpanes knocked to pieces. The fight bitterly continued. He had hired his housemen with care and now he saw that they were tough enough to make a stand. He grabbed the edge of his office doorway for support and clapped a hand to the steady drip of blood on his cheek. This saloon was his life and its destruction dredged up all of his powerful anger and he lowered his head and was on the point of charging the trail bunch again when the homesteaders, led by Tom Leathers, came through. Realizing the further destruction at hand, Charley Fair left The Pride by the side door. He left it too soon to catch the scene in front of the saloon.

At the first intrusion of Cap Ryker and his Texans, Hazelhurst calmly said to the players at his table, "Game's closed," and paid off. He sat by the table for a moment, still and cold while destruction whirled a closer circle around him. The bar fell and chairs began to sail through the room. Hazelhurst at last left his table, taking his time about it, and moved toward a corner. Being fastidious, he proposed to have no part in the rough-house fight, but being very proud he would not run away. He collided with several men on his way to the corner, now in a bitter frame of mind. When he got to the wall he put his back to it and took a watchful stand, a figure of unmoved, nerveless reserve. He saw the homesteaders come in with Leathers and he watched Charley Fair drop and roll on the floor. None of this stirred him. Actually one part of his mind went away from the saloon, so that in this fury he thought of Irma Gatewood and felt the warmth she offered him and darkly saw the unpleasant ending which would come to her if she ran away with him. In his own mind he was one cut above a scoundrel; behind the man's pale, proud gravity that self-knowledge lay, to scorch and burn when he saw how impossible salvation was for him. There was no hell so deep as the hell a man made for himself.

He watched Charley Fair go through the side door and to him it was somehow a release of his own obligation to stay. He turned from the corner toward the nearest front door—and was blocked by a Texan.

"I remember you," said the Texan. "You shot Billy Blades."

"Move aside, friend," Hazelhurst said. "I'm going out."

"Try it," said the Texan.

Hazelhurst looked at the Texan, long and incuriously. "It would be nice if a man knew what lay beyond, wouldn't it? Is it a sleep with never a waking? Is it the literal hell we fear? Or is it a better world where a man makes his fresh start? I would like to think that. Sinners would make the best citizens of a better world. They know so much of the fruits of sin. Step aside, please. I'm

240

going out that door."

"You can try," said the Texan.

"Why yes," said Hazelhurst, "I can try. A man runs away but he always comes right back to the thing he ran from. And here I am. I wish I could tell one person that. Maybe—" He said no more. He shrugged his shoulders, conveying every futile and useless and bitter feeling in him by that single gesture, and reached into his pocket for the small gun he carried.

The Texan at once drew and fired. Hazelhurst stepped back; the slamming bullet pushed him back. He put his shoulders against the wall and he stared at the Texan, with neither malice nor regret, and fell dead to the floor.

Charley Fair meanwhile walked down the side of his saloon to Race and met Mitchell by The Dream dance hall. He faced Mitchell. He looked at Mitchell with his hard, straight stare. He said, "That's my place being busted to hell. You're the marshal here. Why don't you stop it? That's my place."

"The town's closed," said Mitchell. "It is closed until Gabriel's trumpet sounds again. Your place is no good to you."

"My God," said Charley Fair, "there's a ten-thousand dollar riot in there and you stand idle! What are you for?"

"You're the man who wanted an open town," said Mitchell. "There's your open town. What are you crying about, Charley? Many a man has gone into your place and lost his shirt. Now you're losing your shirt. What are you crying about? The world's coming to an end for half of this town. You're no better than the rest."

"We will see," said Charley Fair and moved over the dust to Race's north walk. For a moment Mitchell watched him tramp along the dark fronts of Gibson's and the Cowboy Palace. After that he lost interest. The fight in The Pride began to spill out to the street and other

241

Texans scattered along Race now began to drift and run forward and the quick war cry of the trail lifted and passed along.

"Hey—Circle Bar!"

"Johnny—Johnny Jones!"

"Circle Bar—hey, Circle Bar!"

They crossed Race like a Confederate skirmish line and piled up in front of The Pride. They broke from that pile-up and ran down Race at the other saloons still lighted. Mitchell saw Ad Morfitt by the edge of the Arcade, aloof and waiting for the night to grow worse. So far there had been no gunfire on Race. Mitchell went into The Dream and found this place drained except for a few girls and a few last-ditch dancers. He said, "Close out," and heard the music fade. This was the way a street died, in last ragged notes and the crash of poker tables and the sharp, pleased howling of men racing through the dust. This was the night he had known would come. He turned out.

The doors of The Dream were set back from the walk, so that there was a small bay between them and the street; and now, as the lights in the dance hall began to fade, this bay grew dark. He had crossed it and was on the street when a pair of Texans ran in at him in full cry. They clipped him on the shulders and threw him back into the bay. He flung up his hands, turning inside and letting himself slam against a wall. These two were hard-breathing in the dark and one of them yelled, "Johnny Jones—oh, Johnny Jones!"

They came at him again, reaching for him with their hands. "The big fellow himself," one of them rasped. "The old man of the mountain!" Mitchell took a beating on the face before he got away from the wall. He saw them as shadows and bowed his shoulders and plugged ahead. He caught one of them in the chest and drove that one back. The other man was behind him, his fingers grasping

242

at Mitchell's coat. Mitchell made a rapid turn and tore into him. He was cold, he was quiet and quick. Kindness went away and left him willing to destroy, anxious to destroy. He had this man against the wall and for a moment he was free of attack from the rear. He broke the man's grip on him. He seized one arm and ducked and whirled, twisting the arm over his head so that the man, tortured by the strain, suddenly screamed and went out into the walk with a long, tumbling motion.

The other Texan launched a sudden, savage attack and punished him in the back of the neck. Mitchell swung. He circled in the bay, cool enough to hear feet rushing toward The Dream, called by the Texan's scream. He kept maneuvering, he ducked and closed in and rough-housed this puncher against the wall and smashed him in the belly. He had his head low. Now he brought it in close and lifted it with the full power of his shoulders, catching the puncher in the chin. That was all for this man; he went down.

But the crowd whirled into the bay and trapped him. Mitchell reached for his gun. He said, "Watch out—back up." He laid the barrel over the head of the nearest man. He dropped that man and slashed out before him, catching faces with the barrel's length. He said, "Back up, God damn you. I'm through fooling. Back up!"

He thought he said it in an easy voice. But it was a malign cry in the black. He had turned careless as he always did in the heart of a fight. He had forgotten everything and wildness closed in on him so that he crashed straight into the crowd, using the barrel of the gun. He crashed into it and stepped away and watched the ranks break and shift. He bucked ahead again, but now the Texans gave before him and he was out in the street, with the lights of Naab's shooting-gallery shining on him. He had lost his hat and his shirt was down around his hips and his hair lay low on his forehead. Fury smoked out of him; his mouth was long and pulled back from his teeth. He pointed the gun at the crowd and said, "Get out of town!"

There was a little rider, turned mad by the fight, standing stiffly in front of him, a little man with one hand swinging back and forth against the butt of his gun, provocative and suggesting, with yellow-burning light in his eyes.

Mitchell yelled, "Look out behind you, friend," and when the man turned his head, Mitchell dropped him with a sweep of the gun butt. This was the cruelty he never knew he had, and it broke the heart of the crowd. It turned these surrounding men still, until he raged at them again with his talk. "Get out of town! You want to die in this place?"

He watched them shift. He moved out into the middle of the street. Ad Morfitt, who witnessed all this with an old man's tactical eye, suddenly came down Race and stopped by the Cowboy Palace to cover Mitchell's rear. Mitchell had forgotten there were other trail men drifting behind him, or he didn't care. Ad Morfitt saw this and moved to the edge of the dust. He said nothing, not wanting to break Mitchell's attention, but he raised his arm and stabbed a finger at the trail men and stopped them still with that gesture. He kept his moody eyes on them like the poised muzzles of a shotgun.

In front of The Pride one man yelled again, "Hey Circle Bar!" Texans spilled from the saloon and a gun's explosion jarred all the boards of the street's flimsy buildings. The Texans milled into the street and Tom Leathers ran out and the homesteaders knifed through all the various doors of the place. Tom Leathers lifted a long shout: *"Hail,"* and stopped, bitterly smiling.

Looking at him, Mitchell saw that his face was scarred and that his black hair was soaked with blood. This was all he saw for at that moment a shape moved into the edge of his vision and he turned and now watched Bill Bexar come from Ute and enter Race, his boots boiling up the agitated dust and his body swinging easy and soft. He had his shoulders bent forward. He had waited back, he had bided his time—and now he prowled and looked for a kill, and would spot his target and let go in one terrible moment, greedy and merciless and hungry for fame.

"Bexar," called Mitchell.

Bexar, still walking down the street, steadily stared at Mitchell, head thrown half around. In the middle of Race he seemed to tire of this strained attitude and swung his head to the front and put his eyes on the crowd by The Pride. But he took only two short steps and whirled like a cat and clapped his palms against his holsters with force enough to make a strong echo in the night. Mitchell saw his legs twist, his elbows crook, his body bend. Somewhere, far away, he heard Sherry Gault's voice calling. He had his own gun hanging in his hand, a thing Bexar must have observed and considered and discounted, being so thoroughly certain of his own skill. Mitchell saw nothing but Bexar. He saw no other thing or person or shape on the street and he made his snap shot and heard both Bexar's guns pour their broad hollow marks at him and felt the wind of a bullet's passage beside his face. Bexar's mouth came wide open and his hat flew off and he bowed his yellow head at Mitchell and fell to the ground.

Nothing followed the heat of firing. The town was squeezed still, the crowd without voice. Mitchell turned to the hitchracks by Naab's shooting gallery and took the first horse in hand. He climbed to the saddle and moved to the street's middle. From this position he looked down on them, sure and solid before them. He was the center of this town, he was its voice and its law. He was exposed, he was a fair target for them—but because he was a fair target he had them in his hand. This was his secret. He had them because he gave them a full chance at him, and knowing it, they would not take it.

"All right," he said, "the fun is over. Just chalk up Race Street as a place that you used to stop at on the trail but a place that's dead. It died tonight. And maybe a lot of things died tonight."

He saw them shift. They were going toward their horses, they were moving out, kicking up Race Street's dust for the last time. Ad Morfitt remained by Naab's watching them carefully and not sure yet that trouble was over, watching them with an old man's pessimism. Tom Leathers was under the gallery of The Pride and Leathers grinned with an easy, spent deviltry. What Mitchell remembered then was the sound of Sherry's voice calling to him and he turned the horse full about and saw her standing in Webber's doorway, and everything he felt about her was a shock that passed through him and left its tunneled emptiness behind. He raised his hat at her and he smiled, giving her his salute as he had done before, wishing to be remembered this way and knowing he would never ride the street again. This night he was done. So he smiled, and replaced the hat; and at that moment he heard a cry and a scream and a shot, and a bullet tore its way through his right arm, high up.

Men's voices yelled full-out around him. Men ran back for the shelter of the walks. His horse reared high and came down and danced in the dust. He looked straight ahead, seeing nothing. He looked beside him into Ute's mouth and saw nothing. He swung the horse and struck in his spurs, knowing nothing better than to charge the unseen marksman who seemed to be somewhere on Willow. He saw Chappie Brink rise from the courthouse steps and lift his gun at a target on Willow, and then a second shot from that same hidden gun poured its white heat into Mitchell's chest and the sap went out of him and

246

he fell into Race's dust.

He heard, afterward, the repeated racket of gunfire and
a voice calling: "Green!" He braced himself on his hands
and just before the crowd closed around him he saw
Chappie Brink fire repeatedly at the target somewhere on
Willow and then run forward to that spot. It was his voice
that yelled: "Green! I got him—I got him!"

Mitchell slipped back to the dust. Leathers ran out and
stopped down. Leathers said, "For the love of God—Dan!
Where you hit!" Ad Morfitt tore savagely through the
crowd. He said, "Pack him into The Pride." He saw Ad's
face indistinctly. The sand ran out. There was no pain
and no feeling except a lack of feeling creeping along his
chest and this, he thought in the remote center of his
head, was not a bad way to have it be; it didn't matter
much.

Mrs. Gatewood was in the house alone. There had been
talk of trouble tonight and Gatewood, from some hidden
and quiet prompting of citizenship, had gone over to
Willow to see Balder. Now and then she heard the
backlash of violence break over the store buildings and
run in diminishing waves on Antelope. She listened to
the report of a gun and she heard men running along the
walk in front of the house. A little later Will came in. He
was graver than usual and he seemed stirred from
something he had seen.

She said, "Is there trouble?"

"Yes."

"Not Mitchell?"

He looked at her with an intensity not common to him,
as though really searching her mind. "No," he said, "not
Mitchell. Mitchell is on the street. But The Pride is being
knocked to pieces by the Texans."

247

She said calmly, "Why doesn't someone help Mitchell?"

"Some of the men are on Willow, if he needs help. It takes a good deal of courage to step into Race right now."

"I suppose," she agreed. She was in a chair. She sat still, folding her hands together. She put pressure into her hands and she watched Gatewood until he moved behind her. He went on to the far side of the room and stood with his back to her.

"Always some amount of tragedy," he said in his particular, level voice. "George Hazelhurst was shot and killed in The Pride a moment ago."

He had turned from the wall as he spoke and his eyes were on her. She felt them. She sat motionless in the chair with her head lowered, squeezing her hands together to keep from crying and in one wild, crazed moment she had the thought that she was crushing her heart between her hands. She had no knowledge of breathing. The room faded and she was alone.

She heard herself say at last, "You're sure he's dead, Will?"

"Yes."

She remembered how he had seemed to her as he stood in the sunshine of Race, quite a tall man with the look of a malcontent angel cast from heaven, fastidious and cool, with enormous scorn in him, but most of the scorn turned upon himself—and she remembered his voice in the dark car. Once he had lost his indifference; once she had felt the sweep of emotion he had never meant to show.

Will said, "I'm not much of a help to you, am I?"

"I was wondering. You're rather fortunate. You read so much of philosophy that you're prepared for actual trouble. Perhaps people ought to do that. It might be something to lean on." Then she was suddenly aware of what he had said. He had meant something in his quiet way. He had turned again and had his back to her. From this attitude he said:

"It was Hazelhurst, wasn't it?"

"Yes, Will."

"Would you care to tell me how far it had gone?"

"It had gone nowhere. We only sat and talked. But I should tell you—we were to have left town tomorrow night."

He stared at the wall and she felt sorry for him because of the way this flat, unemotional talk would be knocking his world apart. He was far too repressed to show it, but she realized he was descending into his private agonies. She had not really known the quality of his self-control until he spoke to her. He might have been talking about the time of day.

"I had not known it was that bad. As a matter of fact, I thought nothing was really wrong. Perhaps I never looked at you. Man takes a woman largely for granted." He came about. "Was it Hazelhurst, really, or the things he seemed to stand for?"

"What could he stand for, Will?"

Gatewood motioned around the room. "Escape from a dull life."

"Not so much dull, Will, as not being very much wanted. It is a wonderful thing to be wanted."

He lowered his eyes. "Never have said much about that, have I?"

She said, "What do you want me to do? I can leave any time you wish."

He pulled up his head and spoke for himself in a diffident way. "I have one good quality, Irma. I do have some understanding. I don't want you to leave unless you've got to get away. Hazelhurst or no Hazelhurst."

"No," she said and seemed to see the end of her dream. "I had my illusion and it made me very happy. I guess that's all. I didn't think it was wrong but it must have been wrong or else it would have continued."

"Did he encourage you?"

"Oh, never."

Gatewood said, "I must respect him," and drew a vast sigh. "Would you care to walk with me? Or would you rather walk alone?"

She got up. "I've been alone a good deal, Will. It might help if you stayed with me a little."

"It might," he agreed and came to her. He took her arm and he tried to smile at her. They were out on the porch when he said from the bottom of his gentle and serious nature, "People don't change but things do. Perhaps we are not yet too far apart. At least I think we should try." They were on the walk, hearing a shot break out on Race. "I have not told you this," he said, "but I do love you."

Out of her heart, empty and needing substance, she cried, "Why haven't you said that before!"

"I know," he answered. "I know. Let us try, Irma. Let us try to be as we should. It is all we have."

Mitchell swayed gently as though on a swing and light got at his face and he saw the decorated ceiling of The Pride, its bare cupids flying along the wall and the big sunset perpetually blazing in the corner. The sunset was not as bright as it should be.

"Green?" he said. "I'm sorry about that. Is he dead?"

"Yes," said Morfitt, "he's dead. How you feeling? Doc Utten's coming. You feel bad?"

"I had him guessed wrong," said Mitchell. "I thought he'd come at me straight. I thought he would. Must have been a kink in him. Well, there's a lot of dead things around here tonight. Where's Charley Fair?"

"I'd like to know," said Ad Morfitt. "I'd like to know. He put Bexar up to the draw."

"Never trust a man who covers his mouth with a

mustache," said Mitchell and closed his eyes. There was a good deal of talk around him; there was a circle around him and now and then one voice or another slid through the murmuring. He felt hands on him and he heard Utten say, "The third bullet knocked him out."

"Only two," said Mitchell.

"Three," said Morfitt. "The third caught you while you was falling. Utten, don't take so damned long. Don't you know your business? Don't look that way. What you trying to find?"

"A hole," said Utten brusquely. "The end of a hole. Shut up, Morfitt."

Mitchell kept his eyes closed. The swinging had stopped and he seemed to rise and drop back into softness and warmth, and there was a perfume coming to him; and the memory of it made him open his eyes to kill the illusion. But Sherry was with him. She sat on The Pride's rough dusty floor and she had taken his head into her lap, into its curved and yielding warmth, into its comfort and its closeness. She looked down, her eyes turned black as ink. This near to her, he noticed the sweep of her lashes and their length, he saw the faint freckling of her nose and the curvature of her mouth and the small lines of the lip corners which made her, when she chose, look willful and steel-proud. Her breasts were against his head so that he felt the quick beat of her heart.

"A matter of pity, Sherry?"

"No," she said. "There's only one thing I could give you—only one thing you'd ever be satisfied with."

"I had figured it wrong, then," he said. "I had figured I'd lost."

"You said it wasn't anything unless a woman could follow a man into the dust. This is the dust and now I'm in it. Your blood is on me, Dan." She held her voice even, for which he tremendously admired her. She would not cry before him. But her heart was in her words and her

251

heart sounded to him as though it might be breaking. "Why didn't you quit when I asked you? Why wait until—"

He saw Rita standing in the crowd. Rita crying. He saw Tom Leathers turn and wipe her tears away with the point of a finger. "Why," said Mitchell, "how's this?"

"You can see," said Leathers. "You can see how it is."

"You've got luck," commented Mitchell. "Do better than I have done, will you, Tom? Here's Sherry. Look at her sitting in the dirt of this saloon, where she's never been before. I brought her here and she doesn't mind it. But I do." Then he turned his head on Sherry's lap, gently. "No more riding the middle of this street."

"No," said Utten, "not for you, Dan."

"Well," said Mitchell, "what I'd like is to hit for the hills."

"You'll be riding a lot of hills," said Utten.

"Utten," said Ad Morfitt in a drawn, tired voice, "what you talking about? You don't know. You don't—"

Mitchell opened his eyes. He gave Utten a profound glance, reading the doctor's face; and then he nodded a little. Sherry's eyes were blacker and blacker, her lips were the kind of lips a man needed. She was the softness and the endlessness for a man, the fire and the dark, cool deeps. She looked at him, her face unbreakably set, and he knew she held it this way for him. He closed his eyes again, sinking deeper into the surfaces of this girl, catching a faint tag end of what glory could be for a man who wanted something and got it, and never quite had all of it.

Sherry's voice was swift and rising and ringing above him: "Utten!"

"A lot of hills," said Utten in a strange tone. "Not the kind with incense and pearl. Real ones, with rain in them and the smell of pines. It is all right, Sherry. You'll be riding with him, in a couple of weeks. That man survives Race Street."

He felt Sherry's lips come down, hot and firm on him; and everything was there. And, with her face quite close to him, so that nobody else would see this, one tear fell on his cheek. She would never give this much to any other living soul. This, he knew, was her way of telling him he had all from her she could give any man.

MYSTIC REBEL by Ryder Syvertsen

MYSTIC REBEL   (17-104, $3.95)

It was duty that first brought CIA operative Bart Lasker to the mysterious frozen mountains of Tibet. But a deeper obligation made him remain behind, disobeying orders to wage a personal war against the brutal Red Chinese oppressors.

MYSTIC REBEL II   (17-079, $3.95)

Conscience first committed CIA agent Bart Lasker to Tibet's fight for deliverance from the brutal yoke of Red Chinese oppression. But a strange and terrible power bound the unsuspecting American to the mysterious kingdom— freeing the Western avenger from the chains of mortality, transforming him from mere human to the MYSTIC REBEL!

MYSTIC REBEL III   (17-141, $3.95)

At the bidding of the Dalai Lama, the Mystic Rebel must return to his abandoned homeland to defend a newborn child. The infant's life-spark is crucial to the survival of the ancient mountain people—but forces of evil have vowed that the child shall die at birth.

MYSTIC REBEL IV   (17-232, $3.95)

Nothing short of death at the hands of his most dreaded enemies—the Bonpo magicians, worshippers of the Dark One—will keep the legendary warrior from his chosen destiny—a life or death struggle in the labyrinthine depths of the Temple of the Monkey God, where the ultimate fate of a doomed world hangs in the balance!

DOCTOR WHO AND THE TALONS
OF WENG-CHIANG   (17-209, $3.50)
by Terrance Dicks

Doctor Who learns a Chinese magician, the crafty Chang, and his weird midget manikin, Mr. Sin, are mere puppets in the hands of the hideously deformed Greel, posing as the Chinese god, Weng-Chiang. It is Greel who steals the young women; it is Greel who grooms sewer rats to do his bidding — but there is even more, much more. . . . Will Doctor Who solve the Chinese puzzle in time to escape the terrifying talons of Weng-Chiang?

DOCTOR WHO AND THE MASQUE
OF MANDRAGORA   (17-224, $3.50)
by Phillip Hinchcliffe

It is the Italian Renaissance during the corrupt reign of the powerful Medicis. Doctor Who, angry because he was forced to land on Earth by the incredible Mandragora Helix, walks right into a Machiavellian plot. The unscrupulous Count Frederico plans to usurp the rightful rule of his naive nephew. This, with the help of Hieronymous, influential court astrologer and secret cult member. Using Hieronymous and his cult members as a bridgehead, the Mandragora Helix intends to conquer Earth and dominate its people! The question is, will Doctor Who prove a true Renaissance man? Will he be able to drain the Mandragora of its power and foil the Count as well?

Available wherever paperbacks are sold, or order direct from the Publisher. Send cover price plus 50¢ per copy for mailing and handling to Pinnacle Books, Dept.17-293, 475 Park Avenue South, New York, N.Y. 10016. Residents of New York, New Jersey and Pennsylvania must include sales tax. DO NOT SEND CASH.